SUICIDE DIARIES
A NOVEL BY EBONEE MONIQUE

Acknowledgements

"If there's a book you really want to read, but it hasn't been written yet, then you must write it." ~*Toni Morrison*

Suicide Diaries was more therapeutic than anyone could ever know. I am not Lauren Washington, by any means, but I've walked in her shoes and cried her tears. The opener for "Suicide Diaries" popped into my head on May 24, 2007 and on that day I started the journey towards my own healing. I hope you take something away; be it insight into relationships, death, suicide, communication, friendships or moving on when your heart is complacent in pain.

I have to say "Thank You" a million time over (and that still wouldn't be enough) to my Lord and Savior, Jesus Christ. You have loved me when I couldn't even imagine loving myself. Thank you for saving me from self-destruction! You are AWESOME! I have a past, but thanks to God I know I have a future!

Thank you to my parents, Council, Jr. and Anne Rudolph, for always supporting my "out there" thinking and ideas. I love you more than words, hugs, kisses or gifts can say. Thank you for your sacrifices and for giving me the ability to dream. I promise to continue to make you two proud. To my brother, Council "Tee" Rudolph III, thank you for being my biggest cheering section. HigherHustle Clothing ALL day! I'm proud to be your sister/ friend/supporter! Love you! My god-son Octavious: I love you and I'm so proud of you! Continue to "Blend Out" and stand up for what is right! My grandparents- my roots- Council, Sr. and Agnes Rudolph and Howard and Margaret Curle; you all provided me the path to dream & I thank & love you. My entire family: The Smiths, The Curles, The Rudolph's. Y'all know it's too many of y'all to name! I Love you all. All my aunts, uncles and cousins- thank you! Jamie Shannon Curle, you are still inside of me and I will always remember to "Put one down for big cuz". I love you. To my bestie, Nish, you're a superstar & "we're still together!"! Tasha- my sister through it all- Faith- my free-spirit love- and Lynette- my black butterfly- I love you all. Our complex friendships were the spring board for what was to become Lauren and her friends. No matter what kind of drama we get into, we always have each others' backs. A special shout out to my round-the-clock reading team: Mommy, Lynette, Marvin, Kenisha and Kamaria. It's something special to find people who are as passionate about reading your work as you are about writing it! You all made it worth staying up into the wee hours (after begging from the reading team to get something out to them ASAP) on chapters. Thanks for the feedback and eagerness to read my stuff (remembering that I'm an artist and I'm sensitive about my ish!). I love y'all for that. Thanks for not letting me drive you crazy with my stories! Love y'all. Much love to Florida A&M University, Jeanetta, JaNay, SISTUHS, Mr. Miles and WANM 90.5, Ebony Dukes, Candace Smith (my superstar), Afrika Lander, Kellee Thurman, Ileana Ramos, Demetria Jordan, & everyone else who visit my Myspace page and comments on my stories! To my Brovas: "Mr. You Can't Hate" Sean D. and Dreese "Please say the baby", thanks for the encouragement. Let's get it! Spotlight is on us. To everyone in J-school at FAMU- we the best! ☺ To Greater Bethel Baptist Church and Chamberlain High School (c/o 2000), for being apart of the village. Ms. Army Gipson, Ms. Olga Barnes, and Mr. Adams, Ms. Frisco, Mr. E.L. Williams, Ms. Anne Kimbrough and any other teacher that pushed me beyond my limits. I am who I am because of your insistence that I was better than mediocre. All my friends, foes and everyone in between; thank you for inspiring me in some way, shape or form. To folks that talked behind my back, told me I wouldn't be anything and laughed at my dreams, Thank You! If we could just get out of the "Crab in a barrel" syndrome, we would all be cool. Everyone has their time to shine so STOP HATING and just do your own thing! Stop being a modern day "Mad Rapper". Sophie, I love your little bad self! And to my man, best friend and encourager, Marvin. You made it possible for me to trust again. Thank you for loving me beyond my flaws. Thank you for your enthusiasm in my dream. "I'm a movement by myself, but I'm a force when we're together!"

To my guardian writing angel, Ms. Elissa Gabrielle, thank you, thank you, thank you, thank you! You have given me confidence in my talent and helped me see the reality in what I'd only daydreamed about before! I love you, sis, and I look forward to where we're going. To my Peace In The Storm Family, let's get this! It's all about PITS, honey! To the artists, editors, publicists and authors who have contributed to the success of this book. Many thanks to my MySpace friends & supporters! To my mentor, Sheneska Jackson! You were the catapult! I miss you! I still remember tell him to "caress your mind, not the behind!" Tyler Perry, my other motivator in this game. You are an inspiration to us all. Please keep doing your thing! I'll see you soon!

And lastly, to "T", thank you for inspiring my life. There isn't a day that goes by that I don't think about you. This book is dedicated to your memory. I hope your child will know what a wonderful person you were. My heart yearns to talk to you- or just see your face- but, throughout this writing process, you've made your presence very clear to me! Thank you for leaving your footprints on my heart & just like you sang to me one time..."I will always love you..." Rest In Peace, love.

If I forgot to list your name, charge it to my bad, bad mind; not my heart. Love is love and it's not calculated by what's listed here.

Until next time, which will be my 2nd book, titled "Walk a Mile", remember to **"Dream Big & Then Snatch It!"**

This is just the beginning...

Ebonee Monique
www.myspace.com/eboneemonique
www.eboneemonique.com

PRAISE OF SUICIDE DIARIES

"Definitely...A Talent."

~ Karen E. Quinones Miller, ESSENCE Best-Selling Author

"Ebonee Monique delivers an explosive tale filled with heart-wrenching drama, intrigue and real-life issues sure to reach the reader's heart and soul."

~ Elissa Gabrielle, President & CEO, Peace In The Storm Publishing

"A hard-hitting, true-to-life urban drama that will make audiences thirst to learn more about the characters of the story, and about themselves. Ebonee Monique succeeds highly in Suicide Diaries by blending her charming creativity with an amazing literary voice. Suicide Diaries will captivate audiences for years to come."

~ Stacy-Deanne, author of Everlasting and Melody

"Suicide Diaries is a refreshing and relatable read that will provide its readers with a wow factor."

~ Tamika Newhouse, African Americans on the Move Book Club

"Ebonee Monique delivers a poignant and rich portrayal of the torn emotional confusion and whirlwind survivors of suicide's ramifications must endure. With no clear answers, and unlimited "what ifs," Monique accurately captures the indescribable conflict and turmoil in this clever and engaging read."

~ a. Kai, The Discover Kai Poetry Collection

PRELUDE

Have you ever aimlessly searched a crowd of faces? Investigating green, blue and brown eyes for some sort of familiarity? Maybe you've studied the physical attributes and hairstyles of someone, hoping that a make-over could've altered the looks of the person you're searching for. My eyes dart from wide noses, small noses, big hands, little hands, freckles and moles-all while trying to find an ounce of reason to believe that this person could be the one to end my search. But it never ends. For some reason, the heart has a tendency to embrace the truth long after the mind has.

Do you know what it feels like to stand in a room full of people and only be able to run one name, one voice and one face through your mind? It's beyond the point of obsessive and just below pathetic, and yet, the search for closure has no shame. It's like running around a group of people with your zipper down, exposing everything below the belt, and while you want to zip up your pants and cower in a corner out of sight, your hands are frozen, your eyes are set and your mouth can't utter the words that your heart is dying to say: "Help me!" It's like walking in a never ending circle with a blindfold over your eyes, restricting your vision, your heart, restricting your emotions and your soul, restricting your growth. The on-going cycle of finding a sense of peace, while standing in the dark, can be pretty amusing to the unassuming. Close your eyes and imagine the never ending circle you're in and think about what you'd do to get out.

This is my daily routine. Welcome to my world.

Before you start thinking I'm an overly dramatic, obsessed person let me take you to a time when I was far from the person I slowly became.

Lauren Washington

CHAPTER 1

Dear Diary-

I wish I could say that today was out of the ordinary, but it wasn't. I woke up and found Pop asleep with the remote in one hand and a beer in the other. I swear he works too hard and for no reason at all. I've told him over and over that I make enough money to take care of him, and he still works day in and day out driving The Marta. As selfish as it sounds it just looks bad to have my father, of all people, driving a city bus while I make the money I do. But it's what he needs to do for himself, I guess. The contractors haven't been by in two days and I think I'm officially through with their services. Everyday I go back and forth about whether it was a good idea to completely redo the house I grew up in. Pop said he didn't want to move out of Bankhead and that the best gift I could give to him was to remodel the house and raise the property value in the neighborhood. Isn't that like my father to think about all of Bankhead instead of himself? I have to say, though, I like knowing that I'm giving back and still staying in the house that has given me so many memories. Kenya asked me the other day if I was considering buying a spot closer to the radio station, but I told her I'm going to stay in Bankhead until I can't anymore! Her exact words were "If it was me I'd be kissing Bankhead goodbye and Buckhead hello!" I love my girl but she doesn't have any idea how much this neighborhood means to me. I can't just up and leave; I can understand Pop not wanting to either. Not only would we be walking away from our beautiful house but we'd be walking away from mom; I just can't do that. I'm going in early to work this afternoon to record some commercials for Lenny. Brendan and I were supposed to meet for breakfast this morning but he said he had a couple of errands to run for the shop. I used to see him every night but lately it's like I barely get a glimpse of him. Hopefully that will change soon. Our anniversary and my birthday are both coming up and I can't say I'm looking forward to the latter. I'll be 27 years old and I'm just realizing I'm not a spring chicken anymore! But the station and a couple of my promoter friends are throwing me a birthday bash so I guess I should be happy about that, right? Someone is banging on the front door so I gotta go!

TTYL!

Lauren Washington

There I stood in my Morris Brown t-shirt, dingy sweat pants and floral house shoes- with my hair standing on top of my head- and my hands on my hips. It always amazes me that the moment a woman decides to let herself relax, be it a facial, pedicure, hairstyle experimentation or the dreaded monthly waxing, someone is bound to show up and catch her looking like Herman the Munster. Today, it seems, was my chance to flaunt my just-rolled-out-of-bed-breath-banging-like-Bruce-lee look.

"Yeah," I said trying to lace my voice with plenty of attitude to let the short white guy in front of me know I meant business.

Glen Towers had been signed to remodel my house and, yet, he'd been absent for two days.

"L-Lauren, hey ma'am," Glen said nervously.

I stood my ground and leaned my head back with a look of confusion on my face.

"Glen, it's been 2 days since y'all came by here and now you show up at 8:00 in the morning ready to work?" I shot back.

Dropping his head, Glen stood back and stuffed his hands in his tight, dirty Levi jeans. He was wearing a plaid button down shirt with a Nike ball-cap that allowed his dirty blond hair to peek out slightly. He looked as though he hadn't taken a bath in days and he reeked of alcohol. From what I discovered, his wife left him 5 years earlier and it seemed as though his life was on the fast track to destruction.

Kenya was amazed that I'd even hired Glen to work on my house.

"I just don't understand why you'd let a drunk, like Glen, work on something so special to you," she said in disbelief.

There were two reasons why I'd agreed to let Glen get the job. Number one: my father.

"He needs it sugar baby," Pop said yawning one evening over dinner. He knew which words would pull at my heart strings. The nickname, Sugar Baby, had been something he and my mother had called me when I was growing up. According to him, kisses from me tasted sweeter than any Sugar Daddy he'd ever eaten, and since I was his baby, he quickly threw the nickname my way.

"Just give him a chance," he said winking his eye at me. While I love my father, I wasn't completely sold off of the "he needs it" spiel, which leads to the second reason why Glen got the job, despite his alcoholism and questionable background.

The number two reason why Glen got the job--simply put--he's the best contractor in all of Atlanta. Drunk or no drunk, no one else in the city can touch Glen's years of experience. That being said, Glen signed on to have my house completed in 9 months. It's now 6 months into the job and I can't see the end being anywhere near.

"I-I understand Lauren and I apologize. I've just been busy on a couple of other jobs, that's all," Glen said not letting his eyes connect with mine.

I rolled my eyes and stepped back, allowing him into the partially completed house.

Ladders, dust, tools and complete disarray were all I could see as we walked into the house and looked around. I fanned my hands around as some of the sawdust flew in my face, agitating me.

"Look, Glen, I'm paying you close to half-a-million dollars to remodel this house. Now, if this is too much for you and your guys to handle we can always..." I started knowing I didn't want to finish the sentence.

I wanted Glen to get his money and, even more importantly, I wanted my house completely revamped. Waving his grimy hands in the air Glen cut me off with a sheepish grin.

"I promise Lauren. Trust me. We'll have this completed in time," Glen said glancing around the room.

"Okay," I said crossing my arms across my chest. I didn't want to be the bitch, but this *was* a lot of money I *was* investing in this house and it had to be tight.

I strolled into the kitchen and mixed up some eggs, bacon and grits for Pop and I, and quickly devoured my portion. I glanced around the room as the workers piled in the door and began hammering and sawing throughout the house; I was content. *Maybe a stern talking to was all Glen needed*, I thought as I headed to my room to shower and change.

I quickly jumped in and out of the shower, threw on my House of Dereon t-shirt, jeans and designer flip-flops and stood in front of the mirror contemplating how to do my wild hair.

My jet black tresses, which hit the middle of my back, were a gift and curse. On one hand it came in handy by making any hairstyle I could ever fathom a possibility without a weave. But, on the flip side, when it got hot in Atlanta I wanted to parade around like Sinead O'Connor with nothing but my scalp to catch the cool breeze.

As I stared at myself in the mirror, while letting the curling iron heat up, I smirked.

"I look just like mom," I whispered as I turned my head and checked out the side profile.

My mom's name was Kori Bordeaux-Washington and she was, from what I could remember, the best mother ever. She worked as an officer for the Atlanta Police Department. Pop tells me she was a tough woman too. When she was pregnant with me she worked a desk job, for safety reasons, but 2 months after my birth she was back on the streets of Atlanta tracking down criminals. I can remember bits and pieces of her life, working all of the time; but I can't remember missing her while she was away at work. Now, as the pages on the calendars turn and my face and body matures, I seem to miss her.

Even though she died when I was nine, I still wake up to the sound of her voice.

I wasn't like the rest of the girls in the neighborhood who had their mothers by their sides. I didn't have anyone's clothes to play dress up in, I didn't have anyone to help me get ready for my high school prom or tell me about menstrual cycles and I didn't have anyone to talk to me about men; but I think I made it out okay. For as long as I can remember, even before mom died, Pop made sure he had a firm grasp on my life.

As I curled the ends of my thick hair, I made sure to smooth my edges down. My hair had always been thick, yet manageable and long; just like moms. Because of my mothers' Creole background--my grandmother was African-American, French, Spanish and Native American--my hair is naturally thicker, longer and slightly wavier than all of my other friends. Regardless of how many times I try to assure them that I'm not bi-racial, they still try to pin the label on me.

My butter pecan skin glistened from my moisturizer and while I normally wouldn't bother with make-up, I was feeling good that day and opted for a little mascara, eye shadow and lip gloss.

I smoothed my shirt, which stopped just above my belly button and checked myself out in the floor length mirror in the bathroom before gathering my things to leave.

I kissed Pop on the head before I jetted out of the house and into my brand new silver VW. I'd opted not to get a Mercedes or Range Rover, like everyone told me I should have, because I wanted to stay as grounded as possible. What's the use of staying in the 'hood' if I'm not putting my money to good use? So, with that said, my home remodeling project started and I quickly forgot about the heated luxurious leather seats that my dream Range Rover had. I turned the volume up with one hand as I searched my junky purse for my sunglasses.

It was a beautiful day outside. The sun was beaming down without too much heat, the breeze was blowing effortlessly, making the trees sway from side to side, and little kids were out playing in the streets with their bicycles and jump ropes.

"Hey Mystique!" They yelled out to me, referring to my on-air name. I waved back with a huge smile on my face; it felt good to be recognized because it hadn't always been that way.

During my college years I'd taken an internship at V104 in Atlanta and within 2 years I got a weekend spot hosting a slow jam show. At first I was confused about what I'd call myself; even considered "LW" "Lauren Wash" and "L Boogie" but Brendan told me he liked the name, Mystique. He said it reminded him of me because of the mysterious side of me. And just like that, Mystique was born.

Making the jump over, from the well known V104 to the newly revamped 104.5 "The Buzz," was a transition but I dealt with it and quickly I became the most listened to DJ in all of Atlanta during the 7pm-11pm slot. I was amazed at how much money could be made in radio. In a huge market, like Atlanta, the sky is literally the limit. But I got into radio as a way to deal with my mother's death, not to make money. It gave me an opportunity to shut off Lauren Washington's problems and act as Mystique, the woman of confidence, beauty and fearlessness.

As I drove down the crowded interstate I glanced over and saw a woman staring at me. In a split second she was motioning for me to roll down my window.

"Are you Mystique from 104.5?" The 30 something year old woman said as she shoved her glasses on top of her head to get a better glimpse at me.

Smiling widely, I nodded my head. "Yes, I am." I felt kind of guilty about liking the attention. The woman began clapping her hands and screeching.

"My daughter just loves you," the woman said as the car behind her began honking. We were in bumper to bumper traffic, and now wasn't the time for socializing.

"Tell her to call the station," I yelled. "I'll get her a Buzz gift pack!"

I praised the car gods as my lane began moving, leaving the ecstatic mother of one of my fans in the dust. It wasn't that I didn't want to mingle, but the day was so beautiful I wanted to take it all in with no interruptions.

It was a rarity for me to be up so early in the morning, especially knowing the monster traffic that lay ahead of me. Every time I thought the traffic gods were shining a light on me I ended up with my hands on top of my head, a fistful of hair, curse words spewing from my mouth and a poor excuse for a driver in front of me. But this was Atlanta and as much as I gripe about it on and off air, I love it here.

As soon as I exited I exhaled, knowing the worst was behind me. I barreled into the parking lot of the radio station and sighed heavily as I saw the car of Lenny Shaw, the Program Director for 104.5 "The Buzz," in my assigned parking spot.

"Dammit, Lenny," I said as I slammed my car door and headed towards the glass building bypassing a teenager who looked like he was trying to hustle his way in.

"Lady, they ain't letting no one in," the brown skinned, cute kid said.

"Oh really?" I said putting a hand on my hip.

"Yeah; they told me it'd be another hour or two before I could even drop my single off," he said smacking his teeth as he looked up at the tall building.

I tried my best not to smile as I reached for my badge and swiped it across the electronic entry way.

"Thanks honey," I said turning to find his mouth wide open. "But I'm good."

I loved when people second guessed me. When I started my job at 104.5, people told me I wouldn't last longer than a month; here I was five years and millions of dollars later. The person I'd replaced when I started had been an aging white man who was a bigot. He had bigot fans, bigot co-hosts and a bigot Program Director. The only thing that remained was the bigot Program Director, Lenny; I could deal with that. After the station switched formats from Talk Radio to Urban R&B/Hip-Hop/Talk, I slid right in and never looked back.

"Y-yooo ma!" The cute kid stuttered as he slung his foot in front of the door and tried his best to keep it open. I looked down at his foot and shot him a look that let him know to quickly move it.

"My bad," the kid said moving backwards. "I'm Dee."

I crossed my arms and listened as he rapidly went through a seemingly scripted introduction.

"I got this rap group and...and...we're called Rhymesters. We've got this new joint that I think you'd like. We're from Atlanta and we work really, really hard; we're just trying to come up," Dee said sparking my curiosity. I was always interested in helping fresh talent out of Atlanta. He looked as though he couldn't have been more than fifteen years old.

"What's the name of the song?" I asked.

"Um...y-y-yeah it's called...i-i-it's called "Rhyme it out" a-a-a-annd it's h-h-hot." Dee said getting so excited he was stuttering over every other word. I smirked as I saw the CD dangling from Dee's skinny fingers. As I grabbed it from him, I looked the simple CD over and shook my head.

"How old are you anyway? Shouldn't you be in school?" I said sounding more like a mother than I'm sure he wanted. Dee crossed his arms and quickly dropped his head.

"I'm 13 and these streets is my school," Dee said sounding confident in his improper reply. I shook my head and wished I could tell him to get his narrow behind in school. It would be the only thing to help him in the future. But I understood his frustrations and desperation for success. While some teenagers in Atlanta depended on their parents' million dollar salaries and big names, people in my 'hood' knew about struggles and hustles from day one. There were no parents with big dollars to help out, or big names to lean on. If you wanted to shine you had to hustle to make it happen; otherwise, you were just someone on the sideline watching it happen.

"The streets aren't always going to be there for you," I said as I turned and started to walk away.

"Do you think you could get Mystique to play it on-air tonight?" Dee asked sincerely. I chuckled with my back to him and spun around with a straight face.

"I *am* Mystique, Dee."

"O-oooh," Dee stuttered as he finally looked me in my eyes as if he'd seen a ghost.

"I'll take a listen to this. Make sure you tune in; maybe it'll get picked for the local spotlight," I said turning to walk away. As the doors closed, I glanced at the disk in my hand, and made a mental note to *actually* give it a listen.

"Lenny, do you know you parked in my spot *again*?" I asked rolling my eyes while passing his junky desk. Lenny Shaw was one of the most well-known men in radio with over 40 years as a disc jockey; 30 years of that as Program Director of the ever growing 104.5, known for his ignorant racial jokes, distinctive voice and hilarious dry humor- - Lenny was one of the few people I could say I disliked.

"I didn't figure you would actually be on time," Lenny said without looking up from his computer. He was an old man with troll like features. Wrinkly skin, huge nose- - complete with massive nose hair; smoker's breath and eyebrows that had taken on a life of their own. I sucked my teeth as I made a joke in my head about Lenny's bald spot.

"That's exactly why your ass is bald," I snickered as I tossed my purse on top of my desk. Lenny and I hadn't always irked each other. When I started working there, we would walk on egg shells. We were working closely, after all, and to make the situation uncomfortable wouldn't be smart. But our clash was inevitable; a joke turned into a smart comment which turned into the silent treatment and finally created the environment we call work.

"Why wouldn't I be on time, Lenny? You asked me to be here at 11:00 and I'm here," I said turning my computer screen on and moving the mouse around a few times.

"Whatever," Lenny said under his breath.

I started my daily routine of searching for entertainment, local and national news to try to incorporate into my show and as I reached across my desk for a highlighter, I knocked over a picture of Brendan and me. I loved that man. Growing up I'd never been one of those girls who was waiting on "Prince Charming" to rescue me but when I found Brendan I all of a sudden felt free.

A slight glance from him would ignite butterflies in my stomach while my heart fluttered with excitement. My best friend Jasmine, who is married with twin girls, told me the butterflies, giggling and PDA would die down but I just couldn't see it happening with us; we were different.

Women ask the question all the time, "When do you know he's *The One*?" I've known that Brendan was *The One* from the moment our hands met. It was a feeling I hadn't yet had--even at the age of 19--when we met. My man, Brendan Deondre Lewis, is everything I could've ever dreamed of. Born in New Jersey; he, his mother, Ms. Pat, and older brother, Terrence, relocated to Atlanta when he was 9. He is a professional, the owner of a very successful barber shop and beauty salon named "Cutterz", a romantic, an intelligent and he can be a roughneck.

When you have a man who has the eyes of Boris Kudjoe, the skin of Morris Chestnut, the body of Shemar Moore and the thug appeal of Jay-Z, what else would you expect me to do? As I stared at the picture of Brendan and I cheesing widely in front of a Ferris wheel, sporting matching jeans sets from Old Navy, I reminisced. Brendan and I have been dating 8 years this coming Friday. I know, I know. My friends say it all the time. "Damn! When are y'all getting married?" It's not that I don't want to be Mrs. Brendan Lewis, it's just I'm not trying to rush Brendan into anything *he's* not ready for. I know he loves me and it's beyond what a ring can say. I also know neither one of us is going anywhere. We started dating a day after I turned 19; he was 21 and still fine as hell. Regardless of the circumstances of how we met, it turned out to be one of the best days of my life. I could remember it like it was yesterday.

To commemorate the 10-year anniversary of my mother's death, the Atlanta Police department named a street after her, not far from our house, in recognition of all her years of service to the department. To show their support it seemed like all of Atlanta came out. The streets of Bankhead were packed and I was having a hard time concentrating on anything in particular. I glanced over my shoulders and saw hundreds of people smiling and waving in my direction. It was the type of attention I didn't want. As they replaced the old street name with Kori Washington Way, my heart sank. I gripped Pops hand as I saw a tear roll down his cheek. We both had done a good job of desensitizing our emotions when it came to mom, but I was no longer a 9 year old little girl; I was the woman of my house and I had learned to pick up where my mother had left off. I glanced into the crowd and saw friends from school, neighbors and even some people I'd never met before and in the blink of an eye Brendan appeared right behind me with a tissue.

"Here you go," he said slowly as he handed me the napkin. I hadn't even realized that I had been crying too.

"Thanks," I said nervously taking the napkin from the handsome stranger.

Nothing else needed to be said between the two of us. As he

stood directly behind me and Pop, I felt a sense of security I hadn't felt since the day I found out my mom died. After the ceremony let out Pop eagerly invited everyone over to the house for a fish fry; just like Mom would've liked. As I strolled down my familiar street, with Jasmine silently walking beside me, I finally spilled the beans.

"Did you see that boy who was behind me while they were changing the street sign, Jas?" I said kicking a rock as kids ran past us. Jasmine Wilkes has been my best friend since pre-k and she knows me better than I do. In comparison to Jasmine I was chopped liver, or so I thought. Jasmine had skin the color of coffee beans with long curly hair, which she always slicked back in a tight bun. Her body, from the time we were children until right before she had her own babies, was banging. Her 36D breasts were attention grabbers while her ass, hips and flat stomach were the envy of every girl on the block. Additionally, she had the face of a supermodel and the mouth of a sailor; guys flocked to her like a magnet.

"You mean Brendan?" Jasmine said looking up from the ground. I could tell something was bothering her that day as well. I shrugged hoping she would continue.

"I guess."

Jasmine smiled and bumped me with her big hips before continuing.

"You like him? He's fine, girl! And he's 21!" she said getting excited as she jumped up and down. "Y'all would be so damn cute together!"

I rolled my eyes in embarrassment. "Shut up Jas, damn." I said pulling her shirt towards my festival of a house. People were dancing, talking, drinking, playing dominoes and laughing loudly as I made my way towards the front door.

It was funny how fried fish, liquor, music and friends brought about good times like nothing else. "Hey Sugar Baby! You and Jasmine come over here and get some fish," Pop said from behind the deep fryer he was working.

"I will," I said as I pushed past a crowd of people and headed towards my bedroom.

Jasmine shut my door behind her and plopped on my bed. I sat at the foot of the bed, leaned back and exhaled.

"What's wrong Lauren?" Jasmine asked me as she flipped the television on and started skimming through channels.

I shook my head knowing damn well what was on my mind.

"I just...I guess today made me realize how much I miss mom," I said not taking my eyes off the television screen.

Jasmine sat silently on the bed for a few minutes before she joined me at the foot of the bed.

Jasmine tried her best to comfort me.

"It's okay girl," she said wrapping her arms around my shoulders and pulling me into her.

I laid my head on Jasmine's shoulder and thought about my mom.

"She would've just turned 40, Jas," I said sounding defeated.

Jasmine listened in closely and soon we were both crying rivers of tears.

If there was anyone in the world who could've understood the pain of losing a parent, it was Jasmine.

Her father, Marcos, had been gunned down when we were 7, on the very street that my mother had died on and had, in turn, been re-named after her. It was sadness that had initially bonded us and love that kept us friends.

Jasmine was my support system and while Pop tried his best to be there for me I knew he was hurting too much from his own void.

A knock at my door startled both of us as we separated from our hug.

"Yeah," Jasmine said wiping her tears.

"Jazzy, it's me," a deep voice said through the wooden door.

Before I had a chance to get up from the floor Jasmine had swung the door open and was embracing her high school sweetheart, now her husband, Lance.

Lance and Jasmine were destined for each other. He was the soft-spoken, romantic one and she was the loud, spontaneous one. In each way they balanced each other out.

"Are you okay?" Lance said looking over at me as Jasmine clutched his side.

I liked Lance and despite the fact that my best friend was now spending all of her time with him, I knew he was a good guy.

"I'm okay, Lance," I said sitting on the bed with my legs crossed.

The three of us sat in that room and watched episode after episode of Def Comedy Jam. It was just the therapy Jasmine and I needed.

Jasmine sat cradled in Lance's lap as he flipped open his

mobile phone.

"Hey, man," he said as he played with Jasmine's hair.

"Okay, yeah. We're upstairs in Lauren's room," he said before hanging the phone up and returning his attention on the television.

Jasmine and I must've looked as if Lance were crazy, because he slowly turned to us and shrugged.

"What? It's my homeboy; he came with me and I kind of did leave him downstairs," Lance said matter-of-factly.

"He better not be a thief or a thug, Lance," I said stretching my legs and heading to the restroom.

Jasmine and Lance laughed but I was serious. There were very few people I trusted in this world, besides Jasmine and Pop, and I hoped Lance knew that, although I was quiet, I would kick his ass if anything of mine was missing on the count of his "homeboy".

When I got back in the room there sat Brendan looking more handsome than I'd remembered from the ceremony.

"Hey," he said standing up and walking towards me to shake my hand.

The butterflies had returned. I've been waiting on them to leave since then.

"Jazzy, I've got to get my mom from work so we need to be out," Lance said winking his eye to Brendan who dropped his head.

"Brendan you'll be straight, right?" Lance asked.

Brendan nodded his head awkwardly.

I watched as Jasmine gathered her things and followed closely behind Lance stopping only to hug me.

"Girl, I told you he's fine," she said to me in a giggly school girl voice.

I watched as Jasmine and Lance exited and I was left with Brendan, the consolation prize.

"I-I'm Brendan," he said leaning against one of my walls.

I nodded my head, trying to figure out if I wanted this man in my face.

"Lauren," I said smiling.

The two of us stayed silent for over 15 minutes as Def Comedy Jam continued airing.

"Do you want to sit down?" I asked finally.

"Thought you'd never ask," he said laughing and exposing his deep dimples while he walked towards my bed.

As the credits began to roll for Def Comedy Jam, Brendan reached over and grabbed my hand.

"I'm sorry about your mom. I-I saw that they were having a memorial service for her; I remember it being in the news when I was younger. I had to come out and pay my respects," he said as my heart jumped into my throat.

I could barely move let alone speak as Brendan continued.

"You are so beautiful," he repeated as he looked deep into my eyes.

"Thank you," I finally said as I cleared my throat.

Brendan and I sat on the bed and ran our mouths for almost 2 hours as we talked about the things we wanted out of life, things we liked/disliked and everything in between.

"So you're a barber at Tight Cutz?" I asked listening closely. Everything that came out of Brendan's mouth was interesting to me.

"Well, for now. I mean, one day I'm going to own my own barber shop and it'll be the biggest thing Atlanta has ever seen," he said speaking convincingly. I'd never been around someone, other than car salesmen, who could sell their dreams so well. But I believed every single, solitary word that came out of Brendan's mouth and I hoped that I would be there to see his dreams come true.

I looked out of the window and saw Pop still deep frying fish.

"Your dad is a good man, Lauren," Brendan said joining me at the window and placing his hand on my waist. I can remember his touch as if it were yesterday.

I could feel myself beginning to throb in places I never had before. My body was responding to his contact in an unknown way. The hairs on my neck lifted slowly as my hands clammed up.

I wanted to know what it felt like to make love to this man; our connection was that instantaneous.

"Do they know what happened to your mom or who did it?" Brendan said, destroying my mood.

I shook my head. This had always been a sensitive spot with me but, for some reason, I felt liberated in sharing my story with Brendan.

"One night while mom was working late, she stopped a stolen car and they opened fire on her. They shot her ten times and no one saw anything. Then, to make matters worse, they ran her body over with their car," I said quickly. I didn't want to hear the words coming out of my mouth and I didn't want to visualize my mother in her coffin.

"I know just about as much as the public does. As much as I appreciate the APD doing what they've done to keep my mom's name alive, I feel like they haven't done shit to find who k...killed her."

It was the first time I'd said the word killed since my mother's death.

My mother had been killed.

As I opened my mouth to say more, tears came pouring from my eyes with no control from me. I had tried too long to surpress the overwhelming feeling of lonliness that had been inside of me for years. I wanted to snap my fingers and make my curiosity, pain and tears go away, but as I was finding out now- as I sat trying to contain the spill over of tears and emotion- snapping fingers wasn't going to do it. I felt the back of my throat tighten up as I finally allowed the emotions to take over me.

My mother had been killed.

I sat on the ground and covered my face with my hands as they shook ferociously. It wasn't that I didn't know my mother was dead, but to admit to myself that someone else had played a part in her not being there stung me to the core.

"Are you okay?" Brendan asked kneeling to my level.

"Yeah. I'm okay," I lied as I tried wiping the never-ending tears from my eyes. Brendan, however, saw straight through me.

"No you're not. Come here," he said sitting next to me and embracing me in his arms.

He caught one of my tears with his fingers and wiped it off on his Enyce shirt.

"Talk to me," he said.

"For as long as I can remember I've convinced myself that my mom died of Cancer or a stroke or high blood pressure..." I said sighing.

"Knowing that there is someone out there with so much hate in their heart that they'd take away a mother from a child and a wife from a husband, it...it's kind of sickening," I said loudly.

The only other person, besides Brendan, that I spoke freely about my mother's death to had been Jasmine.

"I'm here," Brendan whispered into my ear as he hugged me tightly.

And there began my relationship with the best thing that ever happened to me.

As I stared off into space, Lenny walked up and slightly kicked my desk.

"Do you think I could get you to cut a commercial like we're paying you to do?" he said sarcastically.

Normally I would've snapped his head off but today was a good day and I was reminiscing about my baby.

"Lenny, I'll do the commercial just for *yooou!*" I smiled as I blew him a playful kiss.

I cut the commercial, prepped for my show and then headed out to grab a bite to eat at Wendy's.

"Hey baby," Brendan said loudly into the phone. I could tell he was probably at the shop by the music that was blasting in the background.

I told him it seemed more like a nightclub than it did a barbershop; but it *was* the hottest barber shop and salon in town so what did I know?

"Hey sweetie," I said as I pulled into the drive-thru and placed my order. I paid for my food and headed back to the station while running down my day with Brendan.

"You know what? I was thinking about the first time we met at mom's memorial service," I said while eating my frosty in the parking lot of the station. My show was beginning in 30 minutes but I knew I needed to hear Brendan's voice just like he needed to hear mine.

"Oh yeah?" he said sounding surprised by my memory.

"Ummmhmmmm," I smiled wishing he was there so I could kiss his juicy lips.

"That was a good day, huh?" Brendan asked.

"The *best* day ever!" I squealed.

"Baby, I've got to go. We've got a staff meeting in like 5," Brendan said very abruptly as I heard a woman's voice next to him.

"Okay. I love you," I said wishing I could get closer to him.

Some days it seemed like Brendan was right next to me, feeling the same way I felt and wanting the same things I wanted; other days it felt like I was closer to a stranger than to him. My heart ached at those moments.

"I love you too," Brendan said before hanging up.

I got my headphones, CD case and mini-disks ready for my show and sat at my desk waiting on Patrice Jonesy, the drive-time diva, to finish her show when my phone rang.

"Hey girl!" Jasmine said on the other end.

"Hey boo," I replied smacking my teeth playfully.

Jasmine was still my best friend and still a beauty. She was also a wife, mother and owner of her own publishing company. Home girl was definitely doing things! After having twins just two years earlier, Jasmine's once banging body was just banged out. With over 50 pounds of added weight, she was miserable but hid it well.

"I know you're about to go on-air but I wanted to tell you what Lance heard!" she laughed.

"What girl?" I asked knowing it had something to do with Brendan.

"I heard for your birthday and/or anniversary that Brendan has dropped big bucks on some exclusive diamonds," she said in a hushed tone.

I wanted to jump up and down and scream, but with Patrice in the same room I had to compose myself. I cleared my throat and giggled excessively as I thought about Brendan proposing to me.

"Did you hear me say diamonds girl?" Jasmine asked me again to make sure she'd said the right words.

"I heard you!" I shrieked excitedly as I got in the sound proof studio by myself.

It wouldn't surprise me if Brendan spent too much money on me. I'm used to it.

He drives an Escalade on 22's, dresses in the most expensive clothing and is only seen in the most elite urban crowds. In a nutshell, my man is a mover and shaker in this town.

"I've gotta go, girl. I'll call you tonight," I said as I checked the time and plugged my headphones in tightly.

The countdown began and as my intro played. I took my position in the black swivel chair. As I hit the MIC ON button on the board, I became "Mystique". I was no longer Lauren Washington worrying about my problems at home, with my boyfriend or upcoming celebrations. I was "Mystique", the chick with enough confidence for all of Atlanta; for four straight hours I could kick back, relax and do what I do best. The beat smoothed out and I found my way back into the ears of all ATL-iens for, another day.

"Hey, hey yall it's your girl Mystique..."

CHAPTER 2

Dear Diary-

There's something about summers in Atlanta that are nostalgic. I think back to days when I'd sit on the front porch with Jasmine eating tomatoes with salt and listening to Ghost Town DJ's while the breeze barely made its way towards us. Pop would be at work and we'd feel like we were grown women holding the fort down. Ha! I had a pretty good show last night; nothing out of the norm. I met a cute little boy outside of the station yesterday and he gave me his CD to listen to; it wasn't bad at all. I think I may play it next week or so. Glen is moving slowly but he's getting things squared away. I still can't even walk into the living room without tripping over some piece of equipment. I want all of this to be done with ASAP so I can enjoy it. Tomorrow is my birthday! I'm finally getting excited too. Today Jasmine, Kenya and I are going out to look for dresses for my birthday bash at Compound tomorrow night. I rarely get a night off from work but since it's my birthday and I'm going to be getting ready for the biggest party the "A" has ever seen, I think I deserve it (Don't I sound vain?)! Anyway, my girls have today planned out to the T. We're going out for brunch this morning, shopping for dresses afterwards, manicures & pedicures after that and off for a massage! I'm working tonight so I'll head straight from the massage parlor and after my show is over guess where I'm going? To Kenya's house for a girls only pre-birthday sleepover. Don't I have the best girlfriends ever? So, I'm pretty excited about my day/night. And with all the commotion surrounding my birthday party I can't forget about my anniversary. Brendan says he has something planned for me tomorrow afternoon. Goodness, look at the time! I've got to get ready for my day of beauty!

TTYL!

Lauren Washington

"Did you tell her?" Jasmine asked me as she stuffed her face with a piece of Waffle. Gladys Knight's house of Chicken and Waffles was, without a doubt, our spot. It was where we went to unwind, celebrate and- - simply- - feed our faces with great food. The down home cooking matched with the beautiful sounds, smells and people was the perfect atmosphere for our tight circle. On any given day you could see anyone walk through the restaurants doors. Like the one time we were there and Puff Daddy and Kim Porter came and sat right next to us. My girls were flipping out but since Puff and I were acquainted through the station, I wasn't too fazed. It also didn't surprise me when Puff slid me his number; with the mother of his children sitting right there. Some guys are no good and I'm so glad I have one that can be trusted.

"Tell me what?" Kenya asked slightly annoyed by the fact that she'd been left out of yet another secret. I shrugged as I reached for my orange juice.

"It's not a big deal and we don't even know if it's true," I said returning my glance to Jasmine who sucked her teeth. I had to remind my friend that even though Lance and Brendan had once been tight friends- - who had by now drifted apart- - his information hadn't always been 100% accurate.

"So tell me, then," Kenya snapped as she tossed her jet black hair over her shoulders.

Kenya Green had been my best friend since my freshman year of college; although we were completely different she was the type of friend any woman would die to have. She was a natural protector so she did everything in her power to make sure everyone around her was cared for.

Like Jasmine and I she was naturally pretty, with natural hair that stopped just below her shoulders. Her slanted eyes, full lips, hourglass figure and creative style were what made her stand out from the two of us. While I thought both Jasmine and I were beautiful, it was something about Kenya that made men stop dead in their tracks; although she had an amazing body, that wasn't the reason. She was original, outspoken, beautiful and successful, and home girl knew it.

Working as a stylist for celebrities, Kenya was less established than Jasmine but that didn't mean she was anywhere near broke. My girl raked in big dough styling all the up and coming R&B groups, rappers and even me. She had flair about her when it came to styling. Her tastes meshed perfectly with the trends.

"Lance heard that Brendan was *supposedly* buying me some

big, expensive diamonds for either my birthday or our anniversary," I said making sure to emphasize the word supposedly.

Kenya raised her eyebrows and shook her head while a smile slowly grew on her face. I could tell she was thinking about Lance's information track record, but she hid it well as Jasmine stared over at her.

"That's great Lauren!" she said sort-of nonchalantly as she patted my hand softly.

"Great? Kenya don't you realize that this time tomorrow she could be engaged to the man of her dreams?" Jasmine said looking over towards me and Kenya.

As hardcore as everyone thought Jasmine was, she always got excited when the prospect of one of us getting married and joining the "Black Wives Club" came up. Kenya shrugged her shoulders and giggled to herself.

"What's so damn funny, Kenya?" Jasmine said trying not to snicker. She knew how she got when weddings and marriage talk came up so she could only imagine what Kenya was thinking.

"Bridezilla returns!" Kenya said finally laughing loudly as she shaped her fingers like claws and poked at Jasmine's arm. All of us laughed as we finished our food and had small talk amongst ourselves.

"So, who can you give me dirt on today?" I said nudging Kenya's side as she laughed.

Her eyebrows rose as she wiped her mouth and prepared to share some exciting news with me.

"Oh. One of my clients told me that NFL-er Michael Seldon is supposed to be screwing his teammate, Rob Trent's, wife and said that it's getting pretty hot and heavy," Kenya said matter-of-factly.

I smacked my teeth and crossed my arms.

"That's all you got? Shoot, I could've looked that information up myself on all those gossip blogs! You're supposed to be my insider source and drop some of these secrets to your best friend," I said hoping she had more and better information.

Although I was in the entertainment industry Kenya was able to maneuver her way in and out of discussions with artists, managers, publicists and friends about the celebrities we all loved, without being detected. Then she'd report to me and I'd feature the exclusive news on my show.

"Dag, girl! I didn't even get a chance to get it all out. I was going to say that one of my sources told me that Rob found out about it and went ballistic. I'm talking about breaking head-lights, stalking Michael and even trying to fight him at a club," Kenya said slowly as I ate the information up.

"What?!" Jasmine and I said in unison. My audience worshiped Michael Seldon and they'd devour the information as soon as I reported it.

"Yup. And someone told me she could be pregnant too," Kenya said adding the cherry to the top of the already decadent dessert. I made a mental note to jot the information down as soon as I got close to a piece of paper. To avoid all liabilities, I made sure to turn the news piece into a blind item. Blind items give away all the information and clues but required the listener to make their own guess of who it was.

"See, that's why I say keep your friends close and your enemies closer," Jasmine said disgusted. She and Lance had their share of problems earlier in their seven-year marriage but since the birth of the twins, it seemed to be pretty smooth sailing. Jasmine and Lance were part of the reason Kenya and I were hesitant to become brides. A year into their marriage Jasmine cheated on Lance attempted to leave him but eventually decided to stay and work things out. It seemed that Jasmine was staying out of obligation rather than out of love. Lance had put up with a lot of her crap and she felt required to love him as much as he'd loved her in the hard times. Their relationship was a strange one to folks looking from the outside. They operated as a loving family with beautiful twin girls and a tight bond but I knew that when they were home, away from the eyes of friends and family members, it was a totally different story. When I looked into my best friends eyes I could see the unhappiness settling in. I sat in silence as I finished my waffle and listened to Kenya and Jasmine trade stories about celebrities who'd cheated on their spouses. Jasmine seemed oblivious to the fact that she was a reformed cheater. Kenya rolled her eyes and directed her attention back to me.

"Anyway, girl, what are you and Brendan doing for the big eight year anniversary?" she said as she sat back in her chair and exhaled. The butterflies I always felt when Brendan's name was mentioned flew around in my tummy rapidly.

"He says he has a surprise for me tomorrow; he's taking me to lunch."

"Do you think he could pro-...?" Jasmine asked sitting forward.

Kenya rolled her eyes again and giggled at the animation

Jasmine was giving.

"Dag, Jas."

"What?" she asked

I watched my two best friends playfully bicker about whether or not Brendan was going to propose. It would all be perfect if he did but I decided not to get my hopes up. After we'd paid for our food and left we headed straight to my favorite designer's boutique, Nicole Miller. It's a fabulous upscale store that I frequent as much as possible.

"Hey Lauren!" Adrienne, the manager, said from behind a tall stack of slacks she was carrying.

"Hey there!"

I ran my fingers over an empire-waisted dress. It was black and white and had cute little yellow daisies all over it.

"This is cute, huh?" I said turning to Jasmine who looked as if she were about to pass out after looking over the $350.00 price tag.

"No! Lauren, take a look at these pieces," Kenya said appearing with three dresses in her hands. It always amazed me how long it took me to find one horribly ugly outfit I liked and how quickly it took Kenya to find a banging outfit. I held one of the dresses up to my body and smiled in the nearby mirror. It was gold and strapless; it was definitely a slim-fitting dress that would show any and everything I'd eaten. I was all for trying out new trends and I trusted Kenya, but I wasn't so sure about this one.

"Just trust me," she said shooing me into the dressing room. I slipped into the dress and turned around in the dressing room and eyed my body with satisfaction. The dress seemed to fit perfectly, from the A line bottom which hugged my hips to the strapless top, which cupped my breasts. A darling little bow tied across the chest giving it the perfection I was looking for.

"Let me see!" Jasmine said loudly as I pulled the curtain back and awaited their responses.

Jasmine covered her mouth while Kenya stood back like her job had been done.

"I told you it was hot!" she said holding her finger up and disappearing around the corner. "Let me get something else!"

"That looks amazing on your Lauren!" Adrienne said as she approached Jasmine and I with her hands on her hips.

"Thanks"

"You know this is from Nicole's summer line and we *just* got it in the other day." Adrienne said winking her eye as she returned behind the cash register.

"Lauren this is definitely the one, right?" Jasmine asked as she smoothed down the bottom part of the dress.

I smiled widely at the mirror thinking, what Brendan would say when he saw me dressed up at the party? I couldn't wait to see the look of pleasure and approval on his face.

"Yeah. This is it," I said twirling around.

"Here, these shoes go perfectly with the dress," Kenya said holding up a pair of stilettos that matched the fabric of my dream dress with a splash of teal added in.

Just that quickly I found my look for the party; everything was falling into place.

We spent the rest of our day doing everything we had planned and thankfully it ended earlier than planned and I had a chance to go home and sit with Pop.

"Hey Sugar Baby, how's it hanging?" Pop asked me as I kissed him on his forehead and joined him on the living room couch.

"Everything is everything," I replied as I watched Judge Joe Brown scream at someone on television. "Where's the Glen?" I said glancing around the quiet house.

There was no one hammering, no one sawing and no one working. I was starting to feel my blood boil.

Pop twisted his lips, letting me know I wasn't going to like the answer.

"He, uh...he got sick today and had to leave early," Pop said looking at me out of the corner of his eye.

"Pop, this is nuts. Next week I'm going to start looking for another contractor because I can't keep hoping that Glen's going to get the work done."

"Sugar Baby, let me talk to him one last time and after that it's all your decision," Pop said setting the remote down and looking at me in my eyes. "Pop, there have been one too many opportunities for Glen. I'll draw up a letter for him and let him know he's being released," I said shaking my head.

After exhaling, my father turned back to the television and turned it up just as Judge Joe Brown was just about throwing the gavel at someone.

"It's your decision," he said softly.

I laid my head back on the couch. I checked the time. I had an hour to nap before I had to get up for work.

I closed my eyes and within seconds I was in the deepest

sleep I'd been in, for a while. I didn't want to deal with Pop, Glen or even the pressures of a possible engagement. For that second, in that oversized couch, I wanted to rest.

When I finally opened one of my eyes, I noticed I was in my bedroom stretched out on my bed.

Stretching my hands upward I leaned back against the headboard and yawned. I'd only been asleep about 30 minutes and still had time to spare.

As I started making the transition from getting out of bed to my closet, I jumped when my bedroom door swung open.

"Hey baby," Brendan said smiling his beautifully perfect smile. I hadn't seen my man in two days and now that I did, my hair was standing on top of my head. Perfect, how fitting.

"Hey," I said trying to smooth down the hairs that were out of place.

Brendan stepped back and laughed with his hands across his chest. I eyed him suspiciously before rushing out the door towards the restroom.

"Lauren you act like I've never seen you with your crazy hair and funky breath," Brendan laughed knocking on the bathroom door.

When I emerged from the restroom with my hair pulled into a tight bun and my breath much fresher, I stood in front of Brendan blinking my eyes.

"Now what were you saying about seeing my crazy hair?" I said standing on my tip-toes and wrapping my arms around his neck.

His arms slipped on my waist as he slowly kissed my waiting lips. If this were all I had as a birthday and anniversary present I'd be more than pleased.

"What are you doing here?" I asked as we finished kissing and headed to my bedroom.

"Do I need a reason to stop by your house?" he asked seriously before relaxing his eyebrows.

I ignored his response and leaned back into his chest as I looked up at the ceiling.

"How was work today?" I asked as I stroked his chocolate hands. I love this man. God knows I do.

"It was straight. You know the same old same old. Cut a few heads, supervise the staff." He said shrugging his shoulders as I sat in his lap.

"What about you? What'd you do today?" he asked looking

me over with a grin on his face.

I told him about my dress and even offered to try it on for him.

"Let me see it tomorrow night. I want to see your fine ass all made-up," he smirked as he slightly moved me so he could get up from the bed.

I glanced at the clock. If I wanted to make it for my show I needed to leave in 15 minutes.

"Want me to drive you to work tonight?" Brendan asked walking towards my dresser and clearing his throat.

I shook my head as I reached in my closet for a new shirt to toss on. I knew I would only be on the radio but I was always prepared in case someone stopped me. I didn't want them to walk away saying *"That was Mystique? She looks worse than I thought."*

"I'm spending the night over Kenya's house tonight. It's like a pre-birthday slumber party," I said enthusiastically as I took one shirt off and replaced it with another one.

Brendan scrunched his face in disgust and started laughing.

"Aren't y'all a little old to be having slumber parties?" he said straightening out his white t-shirt and jeans.

I rolled my eyes. Brendan didn't understand the dynamics of my friendships with Kenya and Jasmine. I was an only child so when the chance to have two sisters came along, I jumped at it. There was nothing like snuggling up to my man after a long days work, but having my girls there for me was a different type of comfort, which Brendan didn't grasp.

"Don't hate because you wish I was having a slumber party with you!" I said sauntering over to him. He watched my hips move from side to side and licked his lips.

If we'd had more time we would've been starting our anniversary early; but I had work and he knew it.

"Just don't start anything you can't finish," he said placing his hands on my hips as I kissed his soft lips gently.

I wanted Brendan to give his all to me and I wanted him to know that regardless of anything, I wasn't leaving his side.

"I love you," I said pulling back and staring into his dark brown eyes.

His response came much slower as he looked at my entire face, searching for something to say before closing his eyes.

"I love you too," he said pitifully.

"What's wrong, baby?" I asked confused by his hesitation to

respond to our normal "I love you's"

He shook his head and stepped back from me while taking a deep breath.

"Come on, you need to be leaving. You know the traffic is going to be insane," he said tugging on my hand as we walked down the stairs.

Although I wanted to shake the feeling that he wasn't telling me something, I couldn't. I knew Brendan like the back of my hand and I knew when he was holding back.

Maybe Jasmine had been right; he was planning on proposing and was getting nervous. Maybe the shop was getting hectic or maybe he was having problems with his difficult mother. There were a million and one reasons that Brendan could be distracted, I just hoped he would snap out of it.

I jumped into my car and rolled the window down as I watched him stroll to his truck.

"I love you baby," I said as I pulled up beside him.

He dropped his head and chuckled.

"Girl, get on out of here; call me in the morning so I can tell you where we're going for lunch."

I blew him a kiss and headed off towards the building that transformed me into a person with no real problems.

"Wake your ass up!" Jasmine screamed as I cracked one eye open and stared at her and Kenya holding a huge cake in their hands.

I'd only been sleep for about 15 minutes and they'd decided it was time to officially celebrate my birthday. I was all for a celebration, but why did it have to be so damned late?

"Oh my goodness," I said rolling over on my back.

My girls gathered around me and finally sat the cake, with a picture of me on it, in front of my lap.

"Happy Birthday, diva!" Kenya screamed as she pulled a gigantic gift bag from behind her tiny frame. Jasmine's eyes lit up as she pulled out her smaller bag. After they butchered the "Happy Birthday" song, they sat in front of me quietly.

"Aren't you going to open your presents?" Jasmine said politely as she scooted her bag in front of Kenya's.

"You are such a brat, Jas," Kenya laughed pulling her bag towards her.

I would've been lying if I said I wasn't ecstatic about getting presents from my girls. Both of them had incredible taste and always seemed to hook me up.

"Okay. Jas yours goes first, I guess," I said reaching inside the black and red bag; as I fished around in the tissue paper I pulled out a narrow white envelope. I tore it open and as my eyes adjusted to the certificate like paper, Jasmine blurted it out.

"It's a trip for two to Jamaica!" she screamed at the top of her lungs.

"Jazzy. Oh my...why'd you...for me?" I said almost out of breath.

Normally Jasmine got me a gift certificate for one of my favorite boutiques and called it a day; this was far more extravagant than any of us expected.

"This must've cost a fortune, Jas. I can't let you spend this kind of money on me and..." I said as I stared putting the information back into the envelope.

"This is from me, Lance and the girls. It's been a great year for the publishing company and I've got the money to spend on those I love," she said grinning as she nudged me. .

I wrapped my arms around my childhood best friend and tried not to cry. Jasmine loved me, and even if she hadn't purchased the elaborate vacation, I knew it.

"Thank you, sis,"

Kenya stood back with her hands on her hips and a devilish grin on her face.

"Open mine, Lauren," she said pushing the monstrous bag in front of me. I could only imagine what it could be; with Kenya there was no telling. The teal and silver metallic bag was the biggest gift bag I'd ever seen in my life.

I took a deep breath, stuck my hand in and felt around.

I squealed as I held up the Baby doll dress I'd been eyeing the day before in Nicole Miller's boutique.

"Oh my gosh! Kenya!" I said as I pulled the dress out and held it up to my chest.

As I fished around in the bag a little more I found two more dresses, three pairs of jeans, three pairs of shorts, some cute shirts and a fabulous pair of Louboutin heels at the bottom. I was completely floored.

"Where did you...how did you?" I stuttered as I eyed the beautiful items.

Even though Jasmine had surprised me with her gift, I knew Kenya's was just as, if not more, expensive.

"I've just been picking pieces up since last year. Every time

I saw something that reminded me of you, I bought it. It's been a good year for me too," she winked as we embraced.

"You guys don't know how much this means to me," I said as I wiped my eyes.

My girls had really outdone themselves this time.

"Let's eat some of this cake," Jasmine said hungrily while she walked to the kitchen for forks and plates. I yawned as I stuffed everything back in their bags. I couldn't wait to tell Brendan everything the girls had gotten me. I knew he'd be thrilled about the trip to Jamaica. We sat and laughed and talked about the usual: men, fashion, celebrities and love.

"Will you be disappointed if he doesn't ask you to marry him today?" Kenya said licking some icing off of her hand. I shrugged my shoulders and tried to think of the best answer possible.

"I want to marry that man, y'all. But I don't want him to feel pressured into anything. I don't want us to rush into something just for the sake of getting married. Right now, we're good; lord knows marriage has lost its value nowadays anyway. People get married but rarely do they want to *stay* married," I said looking over at Kenya.

Jasmine sat quietly listening to me probably feeling like I was talking directly to her. I could see the wheels moving in her head as she thought of something to say.

"Has he gotten better at opening up to you?" Jasmine asked curiously without looking me in my eyes. She knew I didn't tell anyone, not even Kenya, about Brendan not opening up to me. It was something I shared exclusively with her and now she was breaking our code of silence and spilling the beans. I paused to collect myself without getting angry and saw Kenya listening in closely.

"I know there are things in Brendan's past that I don't understand and probably some things I never will. I have to respect the fact that if he tells me he doesn't want to talk about it he doesn't want to talk about it," I said snapping at Jasmine.

Kenya noticed the friction and sat back against a wall watching. It was very rare that Jasmine and I fought but when we did the fireworks came out.

"I'm just saying you've been with this man for almost 8 years now and you still don't know about his past?" Jasmine said throwing the attitude back at me. "Sounds suspect to me," she added rolling her eyes.

I threw my hands in the air as I stood up and walked into the kitchen. Passing by Jasmine I sucked my teeth and muttered.

"At least I want to be with my man and I *know* he wants to be with me."

Jasmine jumped up with her fists balled and stared at me with plenty of fury in her face. I knew I'd crossed the line but so had she and I wasn't backing down.

"Lauren if you think you're so much better than me then why don't you write a book telling me how easy marriage is, huh? Who are you, Ms. Perfect?" she said getting closer and closer to my face.

I'd been in plenty of fights during my life and Jasmine Wilkes didn't scare me in the least. I knew her scare tactics, I knew how she intimidated people and, most of all, I knew she'd never hit me.

"Jasmine what you need to do is back up off of me and calm the hell down," I said nonchalantly.

I wanted to scream: *"Step back or it's on!"*

"No. I want you to tell me who the hell you think you are to say I don't want my husband or he doesn't want me. I *want* him; so know that, aiight? And trust that he loves me. You worry about your boyfriend of eight years and why he has yet to know that you're *the one*; how about that?" Jasmine screamed as I shoved her shoulder.

Kenya jumped up between the two of us and blocked any fists from being thrown.

"Lauren, sit down over there," she said pointing to her black futon.

"And Jas sit down over here," Kenya said taking her to a kitchen barstool across the room.

Jasmine snatched her arm away from Kenya and rolled her eyes.

"I'm out of here," she said grabbing her purse and bolting out of the door with tears streaming down her face. I lay my head back on the futon and as Kenya chased after Jasmine I closed my eyes.

My birthday was already starting off on the wrong foot and a knot in my stomach told me it wasn't about to get any better.

When I got home that morning Pop had actually cooked me a decent breakfast and the kitchen had delicious smells that filled my nostrils and made my stomach smile.

"Happy Birthday, Sugar Baby!" Pop sang as he held a

cupcake in his hand and covered the burning candle. I blew out my candle and eyed my breakfast closely before diving into it. I slowly picked over Pop's eggs and bacon and pondered telling him what was going on between Jasmine and I. Before I could bring it up, Pop had pulled out a jewelry box and sat it in front of me.

"Happy Birthday," he said wiping his mouth with a paper towel.

I stared at the box for what seemed like an eternity before I took it to open it. I gasped when I saw the familiar piece of jewelry that had been restored. The genuine turquoise and silver necklace had been my mother's jewelry. I'd always said that when I "grew up" I wanted one just like it.

"Pop..." I said as I lifted the necklace and held it up to my neckline trying to fasten it. Tears rolled down my cheeks. I thanked him as he wrapped his arms around me.

"It's what your mother would've wanted, Sugar Baby," Pop said fighting back his own tears. After Pop had fastened the necklace we sat at the table holding hands. I gazed into my father's aging face and grinned. Even though his pain, hurt and years of stress had taken a toll on him, he still maintained himself. With his hair in a neatly picked afro and a moustache that covered his upper lip, my father looked nothing at all like me, with the exception of his button nose- - which I'd inherited. I stroked the necklace slowly as thoughts of my mother surrounded my mind. It'd been 18 years since her death and I was nowhere near having closure about the situation. I realized that the police department had done all they could do and while Pop wanted to know the truth I think he was scared of what he'd discover. It was all on me and I felt as if my mother were right beside me rubbing my back telling me to do what I needed to do to live and move on.

"Pop, I know you told me that you don't really know much about mom's mur...death but I think it's time I start looking into it."

Pop listened without speaking. His eyes seemed like they were blinking in slow motion as I continued.

"I've been thinking for sometime about hiring a private detective. You know...someone who can investigate even further than the police have. One of my co-workers is married to the best P.I. in Atlanta and..."

"Lauren, if you are ready to start looking into it that's fine. I'm not going to fight you on it." Pop said as he turned away from me. There was an uncomfortable seriousness in his voice. "Just know that regardless of what you find out, nothing can change the past. But if this is what you need to do for closure, then do it."

I nodded my head quickly and reached over and kissed my father's cheek. For years we'd fought over hiring someone to find out what happened to mom but Pop always objected.

"It's just going to stir up emotions in the both of us that neither of us needs to revisit." He told me when I turned 21 and begged him to let me look into mom's death. I yearned to know who, what, when, where and- most importantly- why someone killed my mother.

"Thank you Pop!" I said relieved that I didn't have to fight him on it. I'd already made my mind up, but it was a relief that he was on my side.

I couldn't stop thinking about the necklace so I caressed it slowly between my fingers. I closed my eyes and remembered Saturday nights when mom and Pop would head out on the town for "date night". It was then that I could *really* see how beautiful my mother was. She'd let her long hair down and put a few curls around her face while barely putting any make-up on. Mom would step into her long flowing dress and heels and quickly spray her collarbone with her favorite perfume, Obsession. As I sat on the bed in my Care Bears t-shirt and shorts, with my pigtails all over my head, while I watched her dress, I'd catch myself giggling. The final accessory would always be the turquoise and silver necklace, which was wrapped around my neck now.

"One day this will be yours," she told me as she turned around and winked her eye at me before joining me on the bed. I stood up and wrapped my arms around her neck.

"You're so pretty mama."

It all seemed like yesterday; and while I had my memories, the only tangible thing I had to prove her existence was her necklace and some photos.

"Sugar Baby," Pop said waving his hands in front of my daydreaming eyes.

"Yeah?" I asked getting slightly annoyed by his pestering.

"I asked you what Brendan was doing for your birthday," Pop said picking up an empty plate and heading over towards the sink before turning back to me. I smiled, forgetting about my drama with Jasmine and my overwhelming feelings about mom and started giggling.

"He's taking me to lunch this afternoon; he's planning to give me my gift." "Sounds...interesting," Pop said turning back to the sink.

"What's that supposed to mean, Pop?" I said glancing at the clock before throwing my hands up.

"You know what? I don't have time to figure it out; we'll talk tonight or something," I said rushing over and kissing Pop's cheek and dashing out of the kitchen towards my bedroom. I giggled as I pulled out the dress Kenya gave me for my birthday. It was perfect for a brunch with my baby, I thought as I turned on the shower and laid out my accessories. I checked myself in the mirror as I tugged on a stray hair on the side of my head. It was clearly another hot day in Atlanta and even at 10:00 AM my hair would frizz up as soon as the humidity hit it. I slicked down my perfectly proportioned bun and turned to the side to catch my profile. I'd smoothed a little bit of bronzer and lotion on my smooth legs and arms while my toes peeked out from the designer sandals. The dress was perfect. It wasn't too tight, yet it was still close enough to my body that it accentuated my shape.

Grabbing my clutch I rushed down the stairs and past Pop who was getting ready for work.

"See you later, Pop," I screamed as I slammed the door behind me.

It was my birthday and despite the excitement with Jasmine earlier that morning, I was already over it and hoped she was too. After reaching my car I looked at the antenna with a grin on my face. Tied with a white ribbon was a red rose with a note attached.

"Meet me at the restaurant where we had our first date. - - Brendan"

I smiled. My baby was full of surprises. Even though I wasn't a huge fan of red roses, any type of romantic gesture from Brendan, was enough to light up my day. As I pulled out of the driveway, I picked up my Blackberry and dialed Jasmine's number. Just like I suspected, she didn't answer. It was like a common routine for Jasmine and I when we argued. We'd yell, she'd run out, I'd call hours later, she'd not answer my calls and eventually one of us would break and call the other and we'd make up. I listened to her message and thought about what I was going to say.

"Jas, it's me. Call me when you get a chance we need to talk about what happened this morning and...just call me." I then tried to call Kenya. I was sure she'd been in touch with Jasmine and would tell me exactly how my best friend was feeling.

"Hey birthday girl!" Kenya squealed excitedly.

I laughed at my friend's animation.

"Hey," I snickered.

I think Kenya knows me entirely too well because before I could even get the question out she was blabbing the information I needed to hear.

"I was just on the phone with Jasmine."

"And..." I said wanting more information.

"And what? You know the child is sensitive and you know the truth stung a little bit I guess," Kenya said sighing before continuing. "But you know you were wrong for trying to call her out."

"And she wasn't wrong for doing the same to me?" I shot back, upset that *my* friend, the one I'd introduced to Jasmine, was now taking her side.

"Wait, wait. I didn't say anything about her not being wrong. I just think the two of you need to talk things out. You both said some things I *know* you didn't mean."

As much as I wanted to object to what she was saying, I knew she was right and she knew I knew she was right.

"I tried calling her but she didn't answer. I left a message," I said letting Kenya know I'd attempted to right my wrong. We continued our small talk and just as the conversation was getting good, I'd reached IHOP.

"I've gotta go, girl. I'm at the restaurant," I said trying to rush my friend off as my eyes locked with Brendan's.

"I still can't believe this boy is taking you to cheap ass IHOP!" Kenya laughed loudly as I wrapped her up.

"Whatever girl!" I said laughing, "I'll talk to you later!"

I flipped down the visor and checked my hair, teeth and make-up. If IHOP hadn't been so near and dear to me in regards to my relationship with Brendan, I might have felt the same way as Kenya. It wasn't at all expensive; it was fattening and most of all it was...IHOP. But it was the spot where we'd solidified our relationship and gone on our first date, and it would always be the best memory of us in our earliest stages.

"Hey baby," I said approaching my man with a huge grin on my face.

He looked damn good. He was wearing loose Red Monkey Jeans with a crisp white t-shirt and his hair was freshly cut. His athletic body seemed as though it was calling my name so I hugged him. I couldn't help holding him for a second longer than normal. I inhaled his Burberry cologne and was instantly ready to take this party back to the house.

"Hey gorgeous," he said as he kissed me on the lips.

"We've got your table ready over here," a flamboyant gay man said as he sashayed towards an open booth. The two of us sat across from each other as Brendan's hands shook uneasily while he gripped the menu.

"Happy birthday baby," Brendan finally said before taking a sip of water. "And Happy Anniversary!" he added.

"Thank you baby!" I smiled "And Happy Anniversary to you too!"

"How was your slumber party last night?" Brendan asked leaning back into the booth and focusing his attention on me. The way his brown eyes pierced my body was unexplainable.

"It was good. Jas and I had a fight," I said rolling my eyes. I didn't feel like reliving the fight or the moment. I wanted to enjoy the time I had with my boyfriend.

"About what?" Brendan said sounding surprised.

I cleared my throat, unsure if I should explain to him that he and Lance had been at the root of our argument.

"It was something stupid, really," I said looking over the menu before switching subjects.

"But she did come through with a bomb ass gift, baby!" I said pulling the envelope from my purse and sitting it in front of him.

"A trip to Jamaica?" Brendan said sounding uninterested.

"Yeah. Can you believe that? We haven't taken a vacation in so long. I think it's about time don't you?" I said talking quickly as thoughts of Brendan, me and the beach danced in my head.

"I probably won't be able to go, though," Brendan said sliding the envelope back to me slowly. My face wrinkled up as the waitress came and took our orders; I returned my fiery glance at Brendan.

"What do you mean you can't go? This thing doesn't expire for another 5 years.

Brendan shrugged his shoulders. "With the business and all I'm lucky that I can even be at breakfast with you," he said looking around the restaurant.

I huffed loudly and sucked my teeth; I didn't want to argue but I could feel my blood boiling.

"Whatever, Brendan. When it's you going to Las Vegas or something with your boys you *make* time, right?" I said with attitude.

"Yeah, but that was before..." Brendan said cutting himself off.

"Before what?" I inquired crossing my arms. Nothing he was saying was making any kind of sense.

"Nothing," he said looking at me deeply in my eyes. Something in my soul told me to hug him, kiss him and hold him until he felt better; but his barrier wasn't allowing me to do that. I was getting angry about it, too, and all I could hear was Jasmine saying that my man wouldn't open up to me.

"I'd like to say I understand but I don't. I never do," I said as the waitress brought our drinks and scurried away.

"I'm not trying to argue with you today, Lauren. It's your birthday!" Brendan said returning to his usual vibrant, funny, outgoing self. His mega-watt smile made me forget about any harsh feelings I was having. I was back to being putty in his hands.

"Fine but we're going to talk about this later," I said raising an eyebrow as he rubbed my hand gently. We ate, laughed and joked just like old times and for a second I forgot about the gift. Had Jasmine and Lance been right and Brendan was going to propose? He *was* nervous, fidgety and sweating like crazy.

I excused myself from the table and headed to the restroom. Every male in the spot turned and I chuckled as I looked back at Brendan acknowledging their stares with slight jealousy. After I'd done the usual hair and make-up check I walked back towards my seat. I ran right smack dab into a small body.

"E-e-eeeeexuse me," the voice said as he bent down to pick up his baseball cap, which had flown off his head.

"I'm sorry honey," I said reaching forward to make sure the person was okay.

"M-mmmyssssstique?" The stuttering voice inquired.

His face looked familiar. But I meet so many people; I was at a loss.

"Do I know you?" I asked stepping backwards as I watched the adorably cute kid hold his hat behind his back as a gesture of courtesy.

"I met yoo-uuuu the other dddday," he said closing his eyes as he struggled to get the words out. I eyed his features a little closer and finally got it. It was Dee, the young teenager that I'd met outside the radio station.

"Oh! That's right...it's Dee isn't it?" I asked just to make sure.

"Yup. Y-ooouuu got it!" he said smiling widely.

"I listened to your CD and it's actually pretty good. I'm going to talk to the Program Director, Lenny, about having you on.

Sound good?" I said making it all up in my head.

I hadn't meant to invite Dee to the studio but with the kid standing in front of me, I wanted to give him some type of news.

"W-wwwoorrd? That's dope," Dee said pumping his fist in the air excitedly.

I grinned as I peeked around an animated Dee and saw Brendan starting to look anxious. I held up one finger to Brendan and turned my attention back to Dee.

"Yeah. I'll check into it with him and I'll hit you back with his verdict. Your number's on the CD right?" I asked.

"Yeah."

"Okay cool. You take care okay?" I said as I patted his shoulder and proceeded to pass him by.

"Mystique?" he said turning to face me.

I lifted my head up so I could hear his voice clearly.

"I'm going to start going back to school on Monday; I'm registered and all," he said proudly.

I beamed and nodded my head. Maybe my influence was a little stronger than I thought.

"That's wassup! You keep that up and you'll be a hot rapper and a smart business man," I said winking my eye and heading back towards Brendan who was on his cell phone.

"Here's your gift," Brendan said with the phone still glued to his ear. I sat motionless as I waited on him to finish his conversation.

"Yo. Let me call you right back," he said.

I looked over the gift and quietly contemplated what could be behind the wrapping.

My heart wanted it to finally be an engagement ring but I knew otherwise. I knew that Brendan loved me but I also knew we both had issues to comb though before making the ultimate commitment.

"You know I love you, right?" Brendan said as he stumbled over his words.

I nodded my head and finally looked into his eyes. They seemed so lonely and so eager for new light that I was moved to run my fingers across his face. To feel the smoothness of his baby face while taking in the beauty he exuded was breathtaking in itself.

"And I love you too," I said while finally opening the gift.

Brendan looked as if he was about to grab his things and leave as I slowly tore through the metallic wrapping paper slowly.

"I hope you like it," he said sitting straight up in his seat.

As I got through the mounds and mounds of wrapping paper my eyes landed on the most beautiful piece of jewelry I'd ever seen. It was a ring; it was *the* ring and it was *my* ring.

The ring sat cushioned in red velvet and was big...no it was huge. The gold band was 24K while the diamond in the center had to have been about five karats. It wasn't my taste but it was still beautiful.

"It's...it's..." I said lifting the ring out of the box and examining it closely.

Brendan held one finger up to my mouth and shushed me.

"I know I'm not always easy to deal with but I love you and you've been there for me more than anyone else has ever been. I don't know where I'd be if I wasn't with you right now," Brendan said while staring into my eyes, which were filling with tears.

"I've grown into a better man because of you and I thank you, baby," he said.

I got up from the booth and joined him on the other side. I tried to hold back the river of tears waiting to jump from my eyes.

"So this ring is for..." I asked not understanding where the "Will you marry me?", drop on one knee, heartfelt, over-the-top proposal was. I'd waited for years and years to be proposed to and I *knew* Brendan wasn't about to simply toss a box at me, in IHOP, and expect me to propose to my damn self. Brendan cleared his throat loudly and bit his bottom lip.

"It's not an engagement ring but it is a promise ring."

I pulled back from our embrace and dropped my mouth. I hadn't heard the words "promise ring" since I had been in the 7th grade. I didn't understand, either. I'd given Brendan eight years of my life, my virginity, my love, my trust and my heart but still he wasn't ready? As much as I'd tried to convince myself that I didn't care if he didn't propose, I did. I wanted him to want to be my husband as much as I wanted to be his wife. Did he not crave my kisses in the morning the way I craved his? Didn't he yearn for the moments when we'd intertwine our bodies when love making? I did.

"A promise ring?" I said trying to calm myself. In my mind I was cursing Jasmine for getting my hopes up for this marriage proposal foolishness.

"Listen to me. Please don't be mad. I love you, Lauren; no ring or vows can define that."

I nodded my head in agreement as I went back to my side of the table. My ears were listening but my face was hot and my hands were sweaty. I'd actually thought that Brendan was about to make me his wife. They say that love makes you do stupid things while looking even dumber. I listened to my man go on about how he wasn't ready for marriage.

"I've got to get everything straight with the business and my mom and brother need me financially right now," he said exhaling. "It's just the timing..."

He always carried the weight of the world on his shoulders and while I wanted to take some of it from him, he wouldn't let me.

"I understand," I said as my eyes darted around the room.

Brendan could sense I was clamming up and simply pulled out his wallet and slapped $30 on the table.

"You ready?" he asked sounding annoyed.

I played with my food as I shook my head, no. He wasn't getting out of talking to me that easily.

"I've got another surprise for you," he said standing up and leaving me at the table. "Come on."

I knew I should've still been mad but deep down, I couldn't be. I followed behind Brendan and exited the restaurant. As soon as the blistering sun hit my pecan skin, I was ready to find the nearest air conditioner and stick my head in front of it.

"Get in," he said as he unlocked his Escalade truck.

I slid into the leather seats and buckled my seatbelt tightly; ready for wherever Brendan was taking me. The sounds of Jill Scott filled the car and I was soon humming along.

We rode quietly in the car before Brendan turned to me and placed his hand on top of mine.

"You know I love you; why are you tripping over a ring?" he asked as he drove onto the interstate and into traffic. I shrugged. I didn't have an answer. I knew I wanted to be married but I also knew that both parties needed to want it.

"Do you know how long I've wanted to call myself Mrs. Brendan Lewis? And each year it just seems like we're getting further and further from it."

Brendan blew out air and stared straight ahead as he gathered his words.

"I love you. Men propose and get married everyday and *know* they aren't ready to take that step. Shit, look at Jasmine and Lance. All that matters is I love you."

"But it's something *I* want; I'm not trying to pressure you to get it. If you don't want to ever get married..."

"I never said that; stop putting words in my mouth," he shot back angrily.

The thing with Brendan was his attitude flared up at the most inopportune times; today just wasn't the day for me. I folded my arms and sat in silence. Before I knew it, we were pulling up to the Westin Peachtree Plaza Hotel. Although I'd been all around Atlanta, I'd never been to this hotel. Brendan glanced over at me and smiled.

"I know you're still mad, but bear with me."

I tried to keep my "I'm mad, don't talk to me," look as I stared out the window.

"Sir, madam; can I take your bags?" the bellboy said as he came to the car quickly.

"They're in the trunk," Brendan said not looking at me.

"Bags?" I said with a slight smile on my face. "I've got my party tonight."

Brendan ignored me and hopped out of the car and slapped some money into the bellboy's hand.

"I've already got our key, so you can just take them on up to the Governor's suite," he said coming around to my side of the car to help me out. He handed his keys over to the valet and got the ticket.

"Brendan what's going on here you've got to..."

"Hush and just come with me," he said grabbing my hand tightly as we followed behind the bellboy who was gripping two pieces of luggage and a tall garment bag. When we got to the suite, I thought I was going to pass out. It was the most elegant hotel room I'd ever seen in my life. Brendan had reserved the Governor's suite, which overlooked downtown Atlanta. I could see the radio station, The Georgia Dome, CNN and even the Georgia Aquarium from where we were. The room was decorated contemporarily with tan and cream accents throughout. The Westin's world famous bed enveloped my body as I plopped down. Brendan smiled from afar as he fixed us a drink and kicked off his shoes and joined me on the bed.

"You trying to get me drunk?" I asked winking my eye.

Brendan had an effect on me that didn't require any alcohol. I was a permanent drunk when it came to him.

"Not at all," he grinned taking a sip.

It was noon and I was ready for the birthday and anniversary present I'd been waiting on, Brendan and I making love. I was also ready to give him a gift that I was sure he wasn't expecting; but would hopefully be happy about.

"Why'd you bring me here?" I asked.

"I wanted to be alone with you; we needed a change of scenery; so I thought your birthday and our anniversary deserved the best," he chuckled.

My head lay on Brendan's shoulder and I closed my eyes as he rubbed my thigh. His hands went higher and higher and before I knew it I was straddling him fervently. I couldn't kiss him hard enough and my body wouldn't move quickly enough. I wanted all of him right then and there, but he had other plans.

"Go take a bath," he said patting my ass I sat up and pouted.

"But baaaaby..." I whined wanting him inside me.

"Go!" he said sternly; I listened.

As soon as I stepped inside the bathroom my eyes lit up. Rose petals followed my footsteps throughout the marble flooring; as I got closer to their ending I saw that there was already a bath drawn for me with rose petals also floating in the sudsy water.

I gasped and turned to call Brendan but was met with his hands on my waist.

"I told you I love you, girl!"

I wrapped my arms around his neck and pulled him into me. I kissed his soft, juicy, pink lips ferociously as if it were the last time we'd be together.

"Unzip me," I said letting go of him and pointing to the zipper at the back of my dress.

By this time Brendan was fully ready for our duo bath. But first, I thought, I needed to give him his gift. I stepped out of the dress and quickly turned back to face Brendan. I let the dress drop and stood in only my tan bra and matching panties. Brendan got in the warm water and watched my strip show from the tub.

"Damn baby," he managed to say as I saw his hand began playing with himself.

I stepped out of my panties and undid my bra seductively as music from the bathroom radio played in the background. I couldn't even make out the song but all I know was that my baby was getting turned on and it was turning me on. My body slowly gyrated to the beat.

"Come in here," Brendan said. He was so incredibly sexy and manly I didn't know how to keep my hands off him.

"Wait. Before I do, I need to give you your present," I said walking towards the edge of the tub and bending down to kiss him deeply.

I bit my top lip and turned around so my back was facing Brendan's face. It took him a minute but when he finally saw it he jumped out of the tub in disbelief. Water and suds splashed all around us as he scrambled to put his hands on my waist.

"Oh shit. Baby...I love you, you know that right?" he said as he rubbed his hand on top of the tattoo with his initials, BDL, that sat near the middle of my shoulder blade. I'd gotten the simple tattoo a month earlier and somehow had managed to keep it from everyone, including Jasmine and Kenya.

I looked over my shoulder and smiled as I saw Brendan's emotional reaction. He ran his hands over the tattoo over and over, as if to make sure it was really real.

"I can't believe you did this," he said with a smile.

I typically wasn't into tattoos. I hated pain, I was always thinking "what if?" and I'd always been against them; they were much too eternal. But when it came to showing Brendan just how serious I was about us, I was willing to do anything. Maybe this would be the nudge he needed, I thought.

We finally made our way into the tub and gave each other an anniversary present neither of us would ever forget.

After back breaking, frizzy hair making, sheet wetting, unbelievable sex, I was worn out and ready to start thinking about my party. The bash was hours away and getting ready hadn't even crossed my mind.

"Kenya called," I said while scrolling through my missed calls. Surprisingly, Jasmine hadn't called. I looked over at Brendan, who'd just jumped out of the shower. As he went through his bags for a fresh white T-shirt and jeans, I watched. I gripped the covers up to my chest and yawned. Brendan looked over at me and winked.

"Tired?" he asked as he chuckled. "I got that effect on you."

"Whatever." I laughed, knowing he was right.

"By the way what did you get from Kenya and your father for your birthday?" Brendan said making small talk as he dried off.

"Well, Kenya got me a new wardrobe. The dress I wore today, that was all her!" I said excited about all the new clothes I'd received. Brendan nodded his head as he looked at the television and listened to me.

"And Pop...well, he gave me mom's old turquoise necklace."

"Oh really? That's cool; you've wanted one like it for a minute, right?"

"Yeah. I couldn't believe he was actually letting me have *her* necklace. That made it the best birthday ever!"

Brendan laughed and went back into the bathroom and shut the door while I continued talking loud enough for him to hear.

"And guess what? Pop gave me the go ahead to hire a P.I. to look into what really happened with mom's death," I said laying my head against the pillow. "As long as I've been asking him to let me look into it; he just decided that I'm ready, I guess. I think he's scared I'm going to get so consumed in trying to find out the truth that it'll take over my life or something."

Brendan returned to the room silently and looked at me for a second before speaking.

"Are you sure you're ready for this? I mean...it's 18 years since her death; the police have been on this for so long that..."

I stopped him mid-sentence, the same way I'd stopped Kenya and Jasmine when they tried to discourage me from looking into the murder.

"I'm sure. This *is* my mother; if I can't make the move to find out who did this and why, then I feel like I'm doing her a disservice," I sighed. I was tired of everyone trying to put off my attempts.

"I hear you. I'm just saying...what if you don't find *anything* or...worse," he asked as he lotioned his legs and arms. I knew he cared for me and was extremely protective, but he needed to trust my judgment.

"If I find nothing then at least I'll know I looked."

Brendan took a deep breath and turned around with a giddy smile.

"If it'll make you happy, I'm with you on it!" he said as he started tickling my feet.

He jumped up from the bed with lots of energy and began looking around the room for his bag.

"Where are you going?"

"I've got to get back to the shop, baby," he replied as he stepped into his boxers and retreated to the bathroom.

"So are you going to drop me back by IHOP so I can get my car?" I yelled from the bed.

"Nope. I've got everything here for you. I'll have a car pick you up at the hotel for the party tonight," he said coming closer to the bedroom with a sly grin on his face.

"But what about my dress?"

"It's hanging in the closet."

"My shoes?"

"Right here."

"I've got to have my make-up, Brendan."

I appreciated the gesture but he was throwing me out of my element and I wasn't sure I liked it. Brendan's eyes watched my composure change as I double checked what he was telling me and headed to the closet to make sure my dress and shoes were there.

"Don't you trust me?" he finally asked as he adjusted his platinum chain that hung to the middle of his t-shirt. Fully dressed my man was still a sight to see.

"I trust you," I said as I headed back to the bed.

Brendan's phone vibrated. He scurried off into the bathroom. It was the fifth time since we'd been in the hotel and I could only imagine who'd been calling.

"Baby, I've got to go," he said as he bent down and pecked my forehead and then my lips. I didn't want him to pull away; I wanted to continue to lick, suck and devour his lips.

"Don't go," I pleaded.

"You know I don't have a choice. I've got a business to run," he said standing over me with his hand resting on the shoulder where his initials lay tattooed on my body.

I already knew that Kenya, Jasmine and my father would flip about the tattoo but the satisfaction on Brendan's face was more than enough to make me disregard their reactions.

"I know. I just wish you *could* stay. You're going to be there tonight, right?" I said pathetically as I stared up into the eyes that controlled my every move.

"I'll be there," he said patting my head.

Just as he started to grab his things, I jumped up from the bed and blocked the door.

The bed sheet trailed behind me as I gripped it close to my naked body.

"What about my car?" I inquired again.

Brendan placed his hands on my stomach and pushed his tongue into my mouth forcefully. I loved when he took charge that way and showed off the thug side of him.

"I told you I've got everything under control, right? I know you need your car; I know you need your girls," he said pecking my lips one last time and pushing past me so he could open the door.

"What are you talking about?" I said with one hand on my hip.

I could see exactly what he was talking about. Kenya stood silent on the other side of the door with a devilish grin on her face.

"Kenya!" I screamed "What are you doing here?"

Brendan smiled and slipped past the two of us. I looked down at myself and felt around at the top of my head and my messy hair; I knew my best friend knew what had gone on in the hotel room.

"I'll see you tonight, baby," Brendan said rushing down the hallway towards the elevator.

Kenya pulled in her suitcase on wheels, make-up and hair kit and began shouting.

"Your man outdid himself this time! Let me see that ring!" Kenya said dropping her bags and rushing over to me.

"It's not what you th-..."

"Daaaamn! I knew he was balling but this is some Russell Simmons type of jewelry, girl!" Kenya said pulling me down on the bed. I wanted to explain to my friend that this wasn't an engagement ring but instead, a promise towards an engagement. The more I thought about it, the easier the angry emotions came.

"Kenya...chill out. Okay?" I said yanking my hand away and walking into the bathroom to get my clothes off the floor. I threw on some sweats and returned to find Kenya in the mini bar mixing together some concoction.

"Where is Jas?" I asked with both of my hands on my hips. It had been our plan that we'd all get ready for my party together; yet one-third of our crew was missing.

I heard Kenya suck her teeth and saw her shoulders shrug.

"I'm tired of being in the middle of y'all's mess," she said emerging from the mini bar with a glass of dark liquor and ice.

"Want some?" Kenya asked raising the glass.

I shook my head and looked at the clock. It was about 5:00 pm and I had a couple of hours to kill so I decided to make the best of the time I had with Kenya. I looked at my best friend as she watched the news. She was wearing her hair in a huge, curly Diana Ross looking style and looked fabulous enough to pull it off. Her cigarette jeans and vintage Coca-Cola t-shirt and jean vest was an example of her unique style, which I envied.

"Kenya..." I said playing with my promise ring.

"Yeah?" she said slowly tearing her eyes from the screen.

"It's not an engagement ring. It's a promise ring," I said softly.

Kenya's eyes grew large, and upon seeing my reaction,

quickly returned to their normal size.

"Well...that's not too bad, is it?" Kenya said stroking my frizzy mane.

I knew she was just trying to make me feel better and that's what was making me upset. I just wanted her to tell me exactly what she was thinking.

"Kenya be real with me, girl. I don't need you to always agree with me," I said bitterly.

This was one of those moments when I needed Jasmine's outspoken opinion and advice. With Kenya I damn near had to pry things out of her, but when I did get it out, it was out.

"Okay. Look. The two of you have been together eight years and he gives you a promise ring? I mean...what other promises do you need? What is Brendan so scared of?" Kenya asked raising an eyebrow.

I knew one of the things he was nervous about--divorce. He had only been three years old when his mother and father separated, leaving his mother a single parent and struggling. Brendan had told me that he barely knew his father and didn't have the desire to after what he'd done to his mother.

"I'll never understand how a man can just up and *leave* his family," he told me over dinner earlier in our relationship. The anger in his eyes as he stared over my shoulder at nothing in particular haunted me for days. I respected his past but at what point was he going to let go and begin to fully live his life with me?

"I think the thing with his father and the fact that he has problems opening up,"

"I know it's a very good excuse...but life goes on and he either has a choice to move on or remain stagnant. So are you going to give him an ultimatum?" she asked me seriously.

I didn't want to be that person. You know the girlfriend who can't deal, function or live without her man proposing. But the more I waited the more I started feeling like it would never happen.

"I don't know; probably not," I said sighing and lying back on the headboard of the bed.

Kenya shrugged her shoulders and stood up from the bed.

"I'll be back. I think I left my purse in the car," she said leaving the room and letting the door slam.

I took my fingers and ran them over my new necklace and smiled. What would mom have done? She probably would've told me to get over myself and the hold Brendan had on me, and tell him what I really wanted from him. My fingers traced the necklace's familiar shape and quickly left and ended up on my shoulder blade, where the tattoo sat.

The look of approval in Brendan's eyes when I'd showed him the tattoo had been enough for me. Our bond was unbreakable. I knew it was permanent but so was our love and relationship. I took a deep breath and exhaled. As I curled underneath the covers I closed my eyes. I needed the rest. I envisioned Brendan in bed with me and was finally content. At times, it was the only way I could sleep at night. He was my everything. And life as I knew it would soon become all about my everything.

CHAPTER 3

Dear Diary-

Tonight is the night. Can you believe it? It's my birthday and I'm sitting here in the Westin with Kenya getting ready for my birthday party at Compound. Brendan and I had the best time together and I have to admit all of his surprises were really thoughtful and unexpected. I finally showed him my tattoo and I thought he'd never stop saying how much he loved it. I'm not sure what's going on with him, though. It's almost as if he tells me one thing and acts completely different. I know he loves me...I know that much, but it's hard to fully agree that he knows what love really is. Anyway, Kenya is here with me and as much as I appreciate her surprising me and helping me get ready, I miss Jas. I tried calling her again but she's playing around and I can't keep chasing behind her. I'm going to enjoy my day and my party and deal with Jasmine tomorrow; if she chooses not to come, oh well. I've got my Nicole Miller dress, my Louboutin shoes, my bronzer and I think I'm ready to go! I'm going to start looking for another contractor on Monday. That's yet another thing I have to worry about. Oh well, at least I have one night off from the station to rest, relax and enjoy myself. Kenya is getting ready to start on my hair and make-up for the party, and she's starting to get impatient. Ha! Hopefully when I write tomorrow I'll have nothing but good memories to jot down!

TTYL.

Lauren Washington

"I have a hot curling iron and a bad hand; do you really think it's a good idea to keep me waiting?" Kenya joked as I put my diary down and sat in the chair.

I was lucky to have Kenya as a friend; not only because she

was completely loyal but also because she could style me, make me up and then do my hair. In high school, Kenya received her cosmetology license, thinking that's what she'd be doing with her life; but after finding fashion she put hairdressing on the back burner.

"Sorry, girl," I laughed sitting Indian style in the chair.

Kenya ran her fingers through my thick hair and sighed.

"What do you write about in those journals? I swear that you're always writing in that damn diary," Kenya remarked as she reached in her bag for some moisturizer for my hair.

I shrugged. I was public about a lot of things but my diary was for me and me only. My psychiatrist and Pop had gotten me hooked on writing down my feelings, as a way of dealing with mom's death. So for eighteen years I've been a journal loving, diary keeping, secret having fool and I love it that way.

"Just what's on my mind," I said focusing my attention on the television.

Kenya knew when to leave something alone and when to nudge me for more information.

"I see," she said picking up a thick comb. I rarely got my hair done but when I did it was always soothing. Some people considered pedicures, manicures or facials to be the ultimate relaxation time, but not me. For me, there was nothing like sitting relaxed in a chair as my hairdresser pulled, yanked, straighten, fried, dyed and styled my hair; that was *my* soothing outlet.

"What kind of style were you thinking?" Kenya said as she continued combing out the kinks.

I shrugged my shoulders as I always did when I got my hair done by her.

"I saw this really cute hairstyle on Rhianna that I think would look hot on you," Kenya said with a smile on her face. I trusted my girl's taste and knew she wouldn't screw me over.

"Okay, work your magic then," I said as I closed my eyes and prepared for her to do her usual straightening, bumping, curling and spritzing routine.

"You know, you should think about cutting your hair; I bet you could rock a Halle Berry look," she said stopping mid-way.

I raised one eyebrow and turned to look at Kenya's face to see if she was serious. She had to be crazy. Cut my hair? For as long as I could remember my hair was my joy and pride. It hung well below my shoulders, just below the middle of my back. It was just like mom used to wear hers and it exactly what Brendan loved.

So cutting it was definitely out of the question.

"I don't mean like Halle Berry short, I meant just take a little off the top for some bangs and maybe layer it," she said picking up a strand of my hair and then glancing down at me. I must've been looking at her like she was speaking Russian because as soon as the suggestion left her mouth she was already calling the dogs off.

"Okay, okay. You don't want to cut your hair," she laughed while sectioning off a piece of hair.

I smirked and returned to my serene place. The heat on the back of my neck felt so warm and comforting I dozed off into a light sleep.

"Okay, let me clean you off," Kenya said pushing my shoulders after what seemed like the shortest nap of all time. I'd been asleep for close to twenty minutes as Kenya straightened my hair to mimic the Rhianna like hair-do. I checked the clock and saw it was almost 9:30 pm and I realized that people were probably starting to arrive at the club. It hit me then…my birthday party; the one I'd hyped up to all of Atlanta for the past three months was finally here!

Jasmine still wasn't there. I'll be honest, too. I really thought I'd wake up from my cat-nap with Jasmine sitting on the edge of the bed, ready for the party. But I checked my phone. No Jasmine. I checked the room. No Jasmine.

"Has Jas called you?" I asked as I looked at my bone straight hair in the mirror.

Kenya began applying her make-up and shook her head.

"Nope."

I dropped my shoulders. As selfish as it seemed, all I wanted was for Jasmine to get over her petty anger and attitude and at least show up for my birthday party. Kenya glanced over at me and saw my disappointment and tilted her head sympathetically.

"One monkey don't stop no show, girl!" Kenya smiled as she turned up the music in the bathroom. Almost immediately, she was sprinting into the living area and had turned up that radio too.

Beyonce's "Get Me Bodied" blasted from the speakers and soon we were both dancing around like we were video girls.

After Kenya and I had done our Beyonce walks, she finished her make-up and then did mine. We slipped into our dresses then she finished bumping the ends of my hair. I was feeling good and the three shots of Patron had me feeling as though this was *the* night I'd been waiting for.

"I think I'm going to say something to him, girl," I rattled on as Kenya slightly curled under one piece of her hair.

"Who?"

"Brendan. The man of my *dreams*," I laughed to myself.

I wasn't drunk but I could feel myself going to a place that was funny and free. Kenya held the curling iron away from my face and stepped in front of me, with one hand on her hip.

"You're going to say what?"

"I dunno. Maybe *I'll* ask him to marry me," I said.

Kenya's eyes shot open widely and we stared at each other for a minute, trying to figure each other out.

"Lauren...you can't...you can't ask him," she said kneeling down in front of me. I didn't want to hear it. I just wanted to listen to the music, dance and have fun but Kenya was persistent.

"Ever since I met you, you've been talking about the special way you want to be proposed to; let Brendan be the man and do that," she said rubbing my shoulder and standing back up to finish my hair. We sat in silence as the music continued blaring throughout the bathroom. Within moments my hair was finished and I was up and ready to go.

Kenya was wearing an 80s inspired skintight mini dress with a wide belt. Her curly hair was pushed to one side and her make-up was. We both looked like the video girls we had pretended we were earlier.

"You ready?" I asked Kenya as I hung up the phone with the car service downstairs. It was a quarter till 11:00 and I was more than anxious to get to my party and see my baby's reaction to my look.

"Give me two seconds!" Kenya screamed.

I stared at myself in the mirror and smirked. My hair had been flat ironed bone straight, bumped under at the ends and parted right down the middle. It was just what I liked: classy but simple.

"Do you have any lotion?" Kenya asked scrambling towards me with her make-up bag in her hand.

"Check my suitcase," I said shrugging. "And bring some," I yelled as I sat on the bed.

We put lotion on our legs and arms and stood up to leave.

"Hold on get my shoulders," I said forgetting all about my tattoo.

"Your ashy ass shoulders need..." Kenya said stopping when

her eyes met the tattoo with Brendan's initials on it.

"Lauren what the..." she said almost screaming at me.

"Kenya it was an annivers..." I started before she cut me off.

"This is outrageous. Are you serious? You got Brendan's name tattooed on you? Why?" she said sounding more hurt than anything. She rushed to my back and began rubbing the tattoo in an attempt to take it off.

"I want him with me forever," I said knowing I sounded stupid.

Kenya stood silent for what seemed like five minutes before she threw her hands up in the air and rubbed my shoulders with the lotion.

"I just can't fucking believe you," she said angrily.

For the life of me I couldn't remember the last time she'd cursed at me let alone been angry with me. But this wasn't the way I wanted the night to go so I tried my best to fix the situation.

"Kenya, don't be mad. I'm not asking you to agree with it and I'm not asking you to do the same thing. All I'm asking is for you to support me, your best friend." I felt the tears working their way to the surface.

Kenya covered her mouth and sucked her teeth.

"Fine, Lauren. Fine," she said as she brushed past me.

We stood silent waiting for the elevator to come and I looked over at her for a sign that everything was okay. She glanced back at me and shook her head.

"I can't believe you. You said that he can't commit to forever right now so why would you?" Kenya asked as the elevator door opened.

I hadn't thought about it like that but what was done was done and I didn't need her questioning what I did.

"If we're going to argue about this all night let me know now. I don't need this at my party, Kenya," I said gripping my purse to my stomach.

I just wanted to go back to the fun we were having in the bathroom, but it seemed Kenya was nowhere near letting this go.

"This is crazy," she whispered as we got off the elevator and made our way to the Lincoln Town car waiting for us.

I was stressing and my sweaty palms and throbbing head were clearly a result of it.

Kenya looked out the left window as I sat looking straight. V104 was blasting from the stereo so I quickly turned the dial to my station.

Jay-Boski, the station's hip-hop DJ, was taking his first mic break of the night and was sounding crunk as ever.

"...Yall got to check my girl Mystique's birthday party out! It's going down at Compound, and from what I hear, it's already packed wall to wall. My homie Crystal Bright is down there now and she's checking in, letting us know what's really good down there. Crystal?" Jay said as his raspy voice cracked.

I loved Jay for how real and sincere he always was with me. He and Lenny could never see eye to eye, therefore he was never hired for a full-time slot. He simply filled in here and there.

Crystal Bright was an intern that had transitioned into a weekend on-air personality and she seemed pretty ambitious. Some days I could hear her practicing her mic-breaks and I could've sworn she was trying to sound like me. Brendan told me I was being paranoid, but in this business you can't afford *not* to watch your back.

"Yeah, Jay! I'm down here at Compound and let me tell you just how crowded it is out here! If you're not down here then you're nowhere! Everybody's here. I just saw T.I. & Tiny walk in the door and Venus and Serena Williams are kicking it up in V.I.P. and that's just the tip of the iceberg. Everyone is out here to show love for our own Mystique as she celebrates her birthday! Happy birthday baby girl! So get on down here now, if you can! You're your girl Crystal Bright with the all new Buzz 104.5!"

I smiled to myself as I thought about all my friends and colleagues who'd promised me they'd come out and show support. I turned my head to look at Kenya and she was staring at me with a silly grin on her face.

"Girl, they said T.I. was in there!" I said excitedly hoping the tension had vanished. She rolled her eyes and started grinning widely.

"I still don't think what you did was a good idea, but it's your life Lauren and you're going to live it," she said raising one eyebrow.

I understood where Kenya was coming from and I completely felt her need to be protective over me but she was right, this was my life and my decision.

"Look, we're about to get into the hottest club in town for the hottest birthday party and we look fabulous. Let's have a good time and worry about all the other stuff tomorrow," Kenya said finally returning to her giddy self.

As the town car pulled up to the club I checked my Blackberry one last time but still no word from Jasmine. The line into the club was so long I couldn't even tell where it stopped. Music was thumping from the outside speakers as people crowded around the entrance. Lights glared from every direction and as the car slowed down, I finally started getting nervous.

"This is bananas!" Kenya said looking out of the tinted window.

I was in awe of everything that was going on. Was this really all for me? I saw skinny girls with their stomachs showing, big girls with their make-up done flawlessly and men who had, obviously, just left the barbershop with their fresh fades. Before I had a chance to vocalize what I was thinking, the door on my side swung open.

"Mystique!" I heard a girl yell from the line. Soon everyone was staring directly at Kenya and I as we made our way onto the red carpet and into the club. I'd been surprised to see some local media. Kenya and I posed for a couple of pictures. My dress was perfect for the occasion and I'd swear a couple of people whispered, *"Where'd she get that dress?"* That made Kenya's night. The inside of the club looked like something out of a music video and I couldn't take my eyes off all the people who were having a good time. Plenty of people stopped me to take pictures and chat. Some even bought me a drink or two. I felt the love throughout the entire club. As much as I felt the adoration, I also felt a strange churning in my pit that told me that tonight wasn't going to go as smooth as I'd hoped.

Kenya and I locked arms and made our way into the V.I.P. section as the sounds of T.I. blasted from the huge speakers, making everyone in the club get on their feet and dance.

I was thrilled to see all of my celebrity friends in the spot. T.I. and Tiny played it cool in a corner while Venus and Serena danced with a couple of their male friends. I thought I saw Trina, Gabrielle Union and Sanaa Lathan in the club too, but with everything that was going on I couldn't be sure. The champagne, liquor, music and fun were flowing around V.I.P. like no one would believe and after I'd had a chance to settle in; I was finally feeling at ease. I stared out over the crowd of people who were partying and grinned.

Kenya sat down next to me and handed me a drink.

"Thanks," I said as I slowly sipped the drink. Even though I was off work, I was fully aware that I was still on public display and had an image to protect. I wasn't getting drunk but I was definitely going to enjoy myself.

"Have you seen Brendan?" I asked Kenya as I scanned the room.

She shook her head and looked over her shoulder at Lorenzo Black who was looking sexy as ever. Lorenzo was one of the hottest up and coming actors in black Hollywood. With five movies under his belt from the previous year alone, he was said to have raked in millions with even more projects on deck. He was fine, too, but in a boyish kind of way.

He had big brown eyes. His skin was reminiscent of fresh hot chocolate while his neatly kept locs stopped at his shoulders. He was an Atlanta native with deep roots in the community and I had to say I was impressed with what he had to offer. If I wasn't head over heels in love, I might have thought about giving him a second look. But word on the street was that he was also a notorious playboy and had been seen around town with just about every black actress in Hollywood.

"Why don't you just go up to him? He's standing by his self," I said elbowing my friend's side. She shrugged her shoulders before returning a glare.

"Girl, please. I am not thinking about Lorenzo Black," Kenya said trying to play down the sexual fantasies I knew were dancing through her head.

It wasn't that she couldn't pull Lorenzo, but I think she was scared of all the extra attention that came with being a celebrity's girl. That's why she always made sure to date "regular" guys. Kenya was so intent on being the only one to have her man's attention that she figured she'd do better with a banker or teacher than an actor or rapper.

"You want me to introduce you?" I kidded knowing Kenya would object. "I know his peoples."

"Whatever," she said as she sipped drink.

I kept my eye on the entrance in hopes that Jasmine or Brendan would soon come in.

"Do you want another drink?" Kenya yelled over the music as I leaned in to get a better listen.

"Yeah. You could get me a..." I started before I was interrupted.

"Happy Birthday Ms. Mystique!" Lorenzo yelled over the music as he leaned in for a loose hug.

"Thanks honey!" I said as I smiled and stole a quick glimpse of his perfect skin.

Before I could ask him what he was working on, if he was

enjoying the party or who he'd come with, he'd turned his attention towards Kenya.

"Hello there. I saw you from across the room and I just wanted to introduce myself. I'm Lorenzo Black," he said looking at Kenya from her legs all the way to her slanted eyes.

I could've screamed at the irony of the situation but instead, I excused myself as Lorenzo got comfortable on the couch next her. Kenya's eyes seemed to sparkle when she and Lorenzo talked and surprisingly he seemed really in tune to her as well. I mingled with a couple of people at the bar before I turned around and saw Brendan enter the room. Whoever I was talking to was now zoned out. My body was there but my mind and heart were with my man. He looked more handsome than any guy I'd seen in the club. He was wearing a pair of pressed jeans and a crisp button down. He was also sporting a pair of mirror tent sunglasses and had a fresh haircut. *My man is so fine,* I thought as I sat my cup down on the bar and excused myself from the conversation.

Brendan couldn't see me from where I was, but my eyes never left him. Just as I started getting closer to him I noticed a woman very close to his side. She wore a texturized short-do and was really small and a little pudgy. If I didn't know that I was Brendan's girlfriend I would've thought she was. I couldn't tell if her hand was intertwined with his or if my eyes were playing tricks on me. He leaned down to her and she whispered something seductively into his ear; he smiled widely and began laughing. I hadn't seen or heard a laugh like that in such a long time, so I stopped in my tracks. Something wasn't right and I knew it. She was wearing a cheap looking halter-top and a pair of jeans that seemed like they were spray painted on.

I watched as Brendan's arm lightly touched the woman's waist. I felt as if someone were hitting me in the chest with a sledgehammer. Not just a regular sledgehammer, mind you, but a sledge hammer with nails glued on the base. My feet seemed to be cemented into the ground because I couldn't move. It was as if I was being tortured. Brendan wouldn't do this; not at my birthday party. After much effort, I began to march past all my guests and towards my boyfriend. The woman saw me and backed away from Brendan quickly.

"I'll be back," I heard her say as she swiftly left Brendan's side.

I couldn't tell if Brendan was shocked to see me or if there was relief plastered all over his face.

"What's going on?" I asked wanting him to reassure me that I'd been seeing things.

"Hey baby," Brendan said leaning down to kiss me on the cheek. I backed away and blocked his kiss with my hand.

"Brendan who is she?" I said pointing to the woman who was at the bar watching us.

"She's a friend," he said shortly.

Obviously she'd been a friend; I wasn't that stupid. I knew she hadn't magically appeared on his arm and in my party. I wanted to know *who* she was and why they seemed to be all over each other. I crossed my arms and looked at Brendan intensely.

"Lauren, look, she's a friend. I'm still allowed to have friends, right?" he said sarcastically with a bright smile.

My mind was racing a thousand miles a minute. I felt like I couldn't breathe. This couldn't be happening to me. Brendan couldn't be cheating *could he?* I'm not sure if it was the Patron or the drinks I'd had in the club but I was feeling a little brave. How dare Brendan roll up in my party with a "friend" I'd never met, let alone invited to my party?

"I want her out of here. I don't know her and she's not welcome," I said harshly.

Brendan watched me with a look in his eyes that I'd never seen before. He looked like he wanted to hug me but he also looked like he was ready to cry. He knew he hurt me with his nonchalant attitude and disrespectful actions.

"So, what? You just want me to leave too?" he shot back. "I said I want *her* out of here. If you think that means you too then fine, leave!" I shouted angrily.

I'd tried my best to hide how I was feeling but Brendan was making this harder than normal.

"Come here," he said pulling my arm as we made our way into a spacious, empty handicapped bathroom.

I could still hear the music thumping and people talking outside the door but my attention was on Brendan who had, by now, removed his glasses and was kneeling in front of me as I sat on the toilet.

"She's just a friend. You said you trusted me," he said reminding me of our conversation earlier. I put my head in my hands and sighed.

"I'm not crazy; I know what I saw. If I was to walk into a club with a "friend" of mine all on me like that you'd lose it," I said snapping at him.

Brendan exhaled as he tried to calm me down. But the alcohol in me wouldn't let him get away that easily.

"I'm sorry," he said softly.

"You promised that you'd always be real with me and tell me what's going on," I said pulling myself together.

Brendan pulled me up from the toilet and pulled me into his body. I felt at home.

"If you want me to get rid of her I will..." he said in my ear.

I thought about it long and hard. I wanted the situation to be done with. If she was a "friend", as he claimed, I didn't want to cause any further friction between us over her. "Just keep her hands off you and vice versa," I said sighing. Brendan had a hold on me and no matter how many times I told myself we needed to work on things, it never happened.

"Thank you," he said kissing my forehead.

We exited the bathroom and took a seat at a couch close to Kenya and Lorenzo, who were still conversing.

We snuggled on the couch together, forgetting our earlier argument, while people danced around us. I was having the time of my life and was glad my baby was able to be with me.

"So you're not wearing your ring," Brendan said picking up my hand to find that it was bare of his promise ring.

I swallowed a huge lump in my throat and took a deep breath.

"I was going to talk to you about that..." I started as I searched his eyes.

"Talk about what?"

I knew what I wanted to say, but I didn't know how to say it without seeming needy, dependent or nagging; however it was going to go, it needed to happen.

"I didn't wear the ring tonight because I wanted to figure out where we're actually headed."

"Uh huh..." Brendan said slowly as I continued.

"I don't want to be your girlfriend forever. One day I'd like to think I could be your wife," I said while Brendan moved his hand away from my shoulder.

It was clear that his body language was changing; I needed to reel him back in.

"You know I love you and, well, we've been together for eight years and if we're going to do it I want to know so I'm not just hanging on."

I saw Brendan's jaw clinch up as I stared at him for a

response.

"Say something," I said in his ear as the music seemed to get louder.

"What do you want me to say?" he asked looking around the room.

It was as tense as it could be in a room full of people bumping and grinding.

I watched as T.I. and Tiny left V.I.P. and headed out of the club and soon, standing in front of us, was the woman Brendan had come in the club with.

"Brendan, I need to get home," she said softly. I could tell she was intimidated by me and as I rolled my eyes she backed up.

Kenya came behind us and stood beside me.

"Is everything straight?" she asked looking the woman up and down.

This was why I knew she was my ride or die; she always had my back.

"We're cool," Brendan said turning towards the exit with the girl behind him.

He wasn't leaving me and he wasn't leaving with her, I thought.

"Wait a minute!" I yelled at Brendan as I reached for his arm.

"Lauren, we'll talk tomorrow."

"No. Listen to me, Brendan. I love you. I'm not trying to pressure you into anything. I just wanted you to know how I felt," I whispered so only he and I could hear.

The club was just about to close and as people bumped into us, I kept my focus on my boyfriend. Something was happening between us and I couldn't put my finger on it. It was like he was purposely trying to get me upset or push me away.

"I'm not ready to marry you and, you know what? I might not ever be," Brendan said nonchalantly.

I felt my eyes stinging before I felt the tears, and before I knew it I was gasping for air.

You know that moment that people talk about when their life flashes before their eyes in a split second? That's what was happening to me in the club. I saw flashes of Brendan and me together, planning our lives and even making love. Where was all this coming from? Earlier that day he'd said we were so tight that we were already married in his mind. Now this?

"What are you talking about?" I asked trying to catch the

tears as they continued to flow.

"I think we need a break. Can we talk about this tomorrow?" Brendan asked not making eye contact with me.

Kenya put her hand on my back and rubbed it softly.

"A b-break? What's that supposed to do? Why are we breaking?" I said angrily.

Brendan struggled for something to say and finally bit his lip and looked at the ground.

"I just need to clear my head, that's all."

I didn't know what was going on or what Brendan was trying to do, but my heart was aching as I stood still. My legs felt like they were about to give out but somehow my mouth found a way to say "Fine." Brendan leaned in to hug me and I felt his strong, masculine hands wrap around my waist and as he inhaled my scent, I did the same. I pulled back from him and looked over at the mystery woman who was silently watching us. I placed my lips to Brendan's and I slowly swirled my tongue inside his mouth. My hands found their way to his back and as I ran my fingers up and down his body, I felt his bottom lip quiver before he pulled away abruptly.

"I love you," he said to me as Kenya pulled me away.

I couldn't mouth the words but I just kept my eyes on him and the woman as they left.

As we sat in the back of the town car, I let out a loud sob and fell into Kenya's chest.

Aside from the day of my mother's funeral, I'd never cried so hard in my life. Just when my tears started to cease, I would remember the love making, the future and the tattoo and the waterworks started all over again. Had I played myself without even noticing it?

Thoughts of Brendan ran through my mind as I got under the covers with Kenya at the hotel.

How could Brendan and I take a *break*? He was all I knew and all I wanted to know and, yet, he wanted a break from me. And just like the old cliché says, "If I knew then what I know now..." I might have walked away with my sanity right there.

CHAPTER 4

Dear Diary-

Well, I'm sitting here at Kenya's house trying to convince myself that it's time to get up, shower and head into work. I told myself I was going to go in early and tackle a couple of things but I'm moving so slowly. Last night was a mixture of emotions. I had the time of my life at the party but the unexpected definitely happened. Brendan and I are officially on a break. I don't know the clear definitions of a break and I don't even know why we're taking the break, but it's where we are. But I can't front, though; I looked damn good last night. I got up extra early this morning, checked out of the hotel, headed to Kenya's house and jogged. I never exercise until I'm mad about something. I'm trying to tell myself this is temporary and that we'll pull through this but I just don't know. Brendan was acting stranger than I've ever seen. It was almost like he was purposely trying to push me away from him and as easy as that would be I'm not going anywhere. I'm trying not to trip out completely and I figure keeping myself busy is the best way to do that. Kenya gave me the number to her cousin who's a contractor and I think I'll give him a call in a minute to schedule an estimate. And the Jasmine situation? Well, as you can see I've got so many other things to stress about; Jasmine is currently on the back burner. Kenya thought that I might have pressed Brendan too hard but I don't know. He seemed like he was itching to find something...anything to argue about and the promise ring was the easiest way out. Hopefully we'll talk soon and iron this out because I can't imagine my life without him.

Well, I need to get home.
TTYL
Lauren Washington

I was irritated and completely aggravated when I arrived at my house. Not only had the drama from the night before stuck with me, but my car was acting up. I took a shower and cleaned up the kitchen before sitting at the table and pulling out the piece of paper that Kenya had given me with her cousin's number on it. While I fully trusted Kenya, this was a huge job and I needed to make sure her cousin could handle what I needed done.

"May I speak with, um...?" I said looking at the paper, "Trey?"

"This is him."

"Oh, hey. My name's Lauren Washington and your cousin Kenya gave me your number and said that you were a contractor that might be able to help me out with some renovations I'm doing in my house."

Trey paused for a second before chuckling.

"You wouldn't be from Bankhead, would you?" he asked still laughing.

"Yes, but do I know you?" I said shortly. I wasn't in the mood for jokes or even laughing. This was business and he was already working my nerves.

"This is Travon Grables. I went to elementary school with you. My family calls me Trey, though," he said.

I tried to rack my mind about a Travon that I knew in elementary school but I knew I'd never remember him. With mom's death happening while I was in the 3rd grade, everything in my childhood seemed like a constant blur.

"I'm not sure I remember you."

"Well, well, well. I guess some things haven't changed, now have they," Trey joked with me.

"I guess so," I said dryly. I didn't know who this guy thought he was but I wasn't feeling his jokes.

"So how have you been? I haven't seen you since I moved out of Bankhead," Trey asked kindly.

I was sure this guy meant well but his kindness was falling on deaf ears.

"I've been fine. Look do you think you'd be able to come over to give me an estimate and let me know if you can handle the job?" I said cutting the personal talk out.

"Sure. You still in the same house, right?" Trey asked.

"Yeah. I'll be here until 2 PM so if you can come by today that'd be great."

"I'll be there in 20," Trey said.

I hung up more irritated than I was before I'd dialed Trey's number. After I finished cleaning up my room, I kicked my feet up and turned on the television and allowed it to watch me. I wasn't in the mood to do anything and I was just pissed. I was mad at Brendan for changing everything he'd promised, I was angry with the mystery woman for being with my man and I was angry at Trey for making me angrier. Looking at my cell phone, I hesitated before dialing Brendan's number. I didn't know what I was going to say nor did I know what to expect but I decided it was worth the effort to find out.

"Hey this is Brendan, leave a message and I'll hit you back when I can. One!"

I didn't leave a message but I knew that he'd know I called. Before I had a chance to second guess not leaving a message there was a knock at the door and I jumped.

Standing before me was Travon "Trey" Grables, my elementary school crush. Why hadn't I been able to remember him earlier? Trey stood about 6'4 and had silky butterscotch skin, jet black eyes, and a smile that would melt any woman's heart and smooth hair that lay perfectly to his head. He was sporting glasses, a button-down shirt and khaki slacks. He looked good, really, really good. For a split second I felt giddy, like I was back in elementary school running the playground with him. As soon as he spoke my reminiscing was done.

"Skeeter!" Trey said as he reached in and wrapped his strong arms around me. I thought I'd escaped my elementary school nickname, which came from a day on the playground when Trey snuck up behind me on the monkey bars and-literally-scared the piss out of me. From then on Trey and everyone in my class stuck me with the name "Skeeter." Lucky for me Trey was the only one who kept the name up until middle school when he moved away.

"Trey?" I said still surprised that he was Kenya's cousin.

"I swear it's been what? Thirteen years? You've grown up Skeeter!" he said closing the door behind him as I cringed at the nickname he just wouldn't let go.

"Yeah, well, it's been thirteen years like you said."

I'd liked him so much when we were growing up and he never paid me any attention other than calling me "Skeeter" and making fun of me.

"So what are you doing with yourself nowadays, Skeeter?" Trey asked looking around the living room where we stood.

"Look, Skeeter was a long time ago so why don't you just call me Lauren?" I said motioning for him to follow me into the dining room. Ladders, paint and tools lay around aimlessly as Trey let out a whistle.

"So who'd you trust this with because they've messed you up?" he said with his hands on his head.

"Gee thanks," I said with plenty of attitude in my voice.

Trey wasn't paying me any attention as he roamed room-to-room looking at the things Glenn had left either unfinished or damaged. I was kind of embarrassed. I'd been expecting some overweight, old guy and yet I had someone who I used to draw hearts on my folder for. I watched in silence as Trey eyed the workmanship of Glenn, hoping he'd be able to give me a good deal. My eyes followed his body closely and then I remembered Brendan.

"Skeeter…"

"I *said* call me Lauren, Trey," I chimed.

Trey chuckled to himself and found a seat at the dining room table and pointed to a chair next to him.

"So you never told me what you've been up to," Trey said sounding genuinely interested in what I had to say. I cleared my throat and smirked.

"I'm working at 104.5 The Buzz, re-doing the house and just trying to live," I said, breathing a sigh of relief. Trey raised his eyebrows, impressed by what I was telling him.

"I never really listen to the radio; it's too much crap on there," he said exposing his perfect teeth.

"Yeah. I can see why you'd say that. Now about the house…"

"I didn't know you were friends with my little cousin, ain't it a small world? Whoever would've thought I would've ran back into Skeeter?"

I tried to keep my composure as the comedic Trey continued with his personal interrogation.

"Whatever happened to…what was her name? I think it was Jasmine or Gina."

I smiled for a second until I remembered I was feuding with my best friend.

"It's Jasmine and she's still around. She got married, had twins and owns her own publishing company," I said impressed by my best friend's successes.

"Really? Do you remember when the two of you got in trouble for stealing tater tots from the lunchroom?" he asked me as he laughed loudly. I couldn't help but snicker, thinking about the trouble that Jasmine always seemed to get me in.

"I remember that mess," I laughed pushing my hair behind

my ears.

"And do you remember when Mr. Maloney fell during the pep rally..."

"And he lost his toupee?" we both said at the same time as we shared a laugh.

Trey sat back in the chair and nodded his head.

"There's the old Skeet...I mean Lauren."

I needed the laugh and I needed the walk down memory lane with Trey.

"What about you? What have you been up to?" I asked putting my hands underneath my chin in an effort to hide my patience, which was running low.

"Well, you know I moved away right before high school, I got married right after I graduated from high school and started my construction company. I just moved back to Atlanta about six months ago so; let's just say you're lucky to have these hands in your presence," he said laughing.

"Wow. Married, huh?" I quizzed.

"Yeah, you know I had to pick myself up a ball and chain sooner or later. A hot commodity like me can't stay on the market for long," he joked as I shook my head.

For a second I imagined what my life would've been like if I would've been the wife in Trey's life.

"So how's married life?" I asked.

"It *was* good until she decided she didn't want to be married anymore," he laughed softly as he clasped his hands together.

"I should be asking you the same question," he said pointing to the huge promise ring on my finger. I looked down at it and quickly hid my finger.

"I...it's not a...I'm not married," I said mortified that an explanation would have to be given.

"Now I heard that platform shoes are out but I didn't know wearing gigantic, non-commitment rings were in," Trey joked in his normal goofy manner.

"My boyfriend gave it to me but it's not an engagement ring," I said ending the conversation.

Trey had always been a funny guy with plenty to say and joke about; sometimes I liked it and other times it seemed aimed directly at me; especially right after mom's death. I couldn't shake the feeling that he was always picking on me.

"How long have you been with this joker?" Trey inquired.

"Eight years today."

"And he hasn't made you the Mrs. yet?"

I bit my bottom lip and shook my head before changing the subject.

"Trey what am I looking at in terms of costs for fixing up my house?"

"I guess playtime is over, huh, Ms. Washington?" Trey laughed pulling out an estimate sheet.

He started jotting down a couple of numbers and pulled out a calculator.

"Do you want something to drink?" I asked getting up from the table and walking into the kitchen.

"Jack Daniels straight up, if you got it," he laughed without looking up from the table.

I returned to the table, with my grape juice, to find Trey's estimate in front of my chair and Trey gone.

"Trey?" I yelled picking up the paper.

"Here I am," he said reappearing from the dining room area. "Did you have a chance to look it over?"

I glanced down at the paper and just about lost my marbles. His estimate was for one-forth of the amount Glen was charging me.

"So are we in business?" he asked raising an eyebrow.

I was speechless. I knew it would cost more money to correct the problems Glenn and his crew had made, so why was Trey's estimate so low?

"I don't think you added in everything, Trey."

"Let me see that," Trey said wrinkling his eyebrows and grabbing the estimate from me.

I knew he'd overlooked something. How could it be so low? Not that I was fighting the amount but I just wanted to make sure I wasn't getting over on Trey.

"There. That should take care of it," he said marking something on the paper and handing it back to me.

I looked over the paper and started laughing loudly. Trey had written in one stipulation to him working for me.

"Ms. Washington must let me call her Skeeter whenever I please."

"Trey, this cost is...are you sure?" I asked after my laughing fit.

"You're my peoples and, honestly, it'd be my pleasure to renovate this house," he said smiling.

"You don't know how much this means to me."

Trey rubbed his face and looked around the house.

"So when should my guys show up? I was thinking we could start on Monday, if that's good with you," he said picking up a picture of me with my parents.

"Monday sounds good," I said signing the estimate and handing it back to him.

"Alright, well here's my card. You have my numbers. If you need anything or have any questions, call me," he smiled as he opened the door.

I pulled his arm and gave him a big bear hug.

"Thanks! You really saved me months of stress!" I laughed as I hugged him tightly.

Trey seemed to be blushing as he hugged me back.

"I guess this makes dropping my client worthwhile," he said laughing.

"Come again?" I asked standing outside of the door as my hair blew in the afternoon wind.

"It was nothing. I just had a lunch meeting with a client but that can always wait until later. This was much more important," Trey said as he stood in front of his red Ford F-150.

"I appreciate it."

I watched as Trey got in his truck and proceeded to back down the driveway. He slowed down and rolled his window down.

"Next time I want my Jack Daniels, Skeeter!"

I shooed him off and dashed into the house just as my cell phone began to ring.

"Hello?"

"Hey baby, it's Brendan. Can you talk?"

"Yeah. I can talk."

"I want to apologize to you for last night. I was wrong for disrespecting you at your own party; I was even more wrong for flipping out on you," he said quickly as if he was rushing to meet a deadline.

"And I'm sorry for everything too. The party wasn't the time or place to start talking about marriage or our relationship," I said curling up on the couch.

I silently thanked God for bringing Brendan around.

"You know I'd never do anything to hurt you, Lauren," he said sounding like he was getting ready to cry.

"I know, baby, I know," I said wishing I was there to wipe each tear that was probably falling from his eyes.

"It's just...I'm realizing now that there's shit about me that I'm not happy with but you've always looked past those things and loved me unconditionally."

I was surprised to hear Brendan talking like that because he rarely ever did.

"And I always will," I said beginning to cry myself. Maybe this was the breakthrough we needed.

"Promise me that," he said sighing. "Promise me you'll always love me."

"I'll always love you, baby!"

He sounded like he was wiping his nose and catching his breath at the same time.

"So what have you done today?" he asked me as he cleared his throat.

I could have inquired about the mystery woman at the club but I figured it would be better to leave well enough alone.

I ran down my morning, being reunited with Trey and hiring him to finish the house. It felt good to talk to Brendan again. It seemed like we were talking for the first time; my heart finally felt at ease.

"After your shift, I was wondering if you could meet me at my house for dinner," Brendan said softly.

"I'd be delighted!" I said checking my watch.

"I'm going to meet with this private investigator in a half hour so I need to throw some clothes on and do something with my hair," I said sweetly.

Brendan inhaled and started laughing.

"So you're really going through with it this time, huh?" he asked.

"Yeah, can you believe it? After all these years of me swearing I was going to do it, I'm actually pushing forward."

"Well, let me let you go. I'll see you tonight," he said.

We hung up and I stood in my living room feeling renewed. My house was in order and my boyfriend was finally getting back on track. The last piece of stress in my life was my feud with Jasmine and that had to change quickly. As I headed towards my bedroom I dialed Jasmine's number.

"Damn," I said as the voicemail came on.

Jasmine couldn't stay mad at me long. Now the ball was in her court. I was done trying. I jumped into a pair of jeans, a nice grey v-neck shirt and a pair of my black pumps. I slicked my hair back into a ponytail and threw on some lipgloss.

I gathered all the paperwork from the shoebox Pop kept on mom's death and I headed out the door.

As I pulled up to the station I saw that Lenny had once again parked his raggedy car in my spot; but today I wasn't tripping. I didn't care about the stupid parking spot; all I wanted was to get inside and meet with the private investigator.

I stepped out of the elevator and was greeted by the secretary and a couple of the interns.

"Lauren, you've got company in the conference room," Abigail, the secretary, said as she pointed to the room down the hallway. I was running about five minutes behind and I hoped it wouldn't be held against me.

"Hello. I'm Lauren Washington. I'm *so* sorry I'm late," I said extending my hand to the older Hispanic man who sat at the head of the conference table.

"Ralph Martez. Nice to meet you Ms. Washington. I have to say my kids are huge fans," he replied, cracking a smile.

He was a short man, standing about 5'4, with a huge gut that stuck out over his belt. His hair was peppered and I saw that he walked with a slight limp as he headed towards me.

I let out a slight breath of relief.

"Tell them I said thank you so much for listening!" I said taking my seat and gesturing for him to do the same.

"Let's get to work, then," Ralph said putting on a pair of reading glasses.

My smile faded as Ralph combed through the information before him. Articles, police reports, pictures and even Pop's recollection of the night were read over by Ralph slowly.

"I remember this case, it's been what? 20 years?" he asked taking off the glasses and looking at me.

"Eighteen actually. Do you think there's anything you can do?" I asked clasping my hands together.

I was nervous; real nervous and my hands would only give that away unless I controlled them.

"I can definitely do my best. I can't promise I'll find anything but it's definitely worth a shot. Let me look over these documents and start asking some questions and I'll get back with you in, let's say, a week or two?" Ralph asked raising one eyebrow.

"Sounds good."

I showed Ralph the way out then made my way to my desk. For some reason my good mood was slowly trickling down. Thinking about Ralph coming back with information on mom's death was a lot to deal with. But it's what I wanted and regardless of what I was feeling, I had to strap on my grown woman shoes and handle whatever came my way.

"Well, I didn't think we'd see you for another couple of hours," Lenny said sarcastically as he typed away at his computer.

I ignored his comment and sat at my desk and began my research. I was anxious but I wasn't sure what for. It was like I was waiting on the unknown to happen and my soul couldn't sit still until it arrived.

"This is Lauren," I said as my office phone rang.

"Hey girl, it's me," Kenya said in her cheery tone.

"Hey."

"So I heard you and Trey hooked up," she said.

"What do you mean *hooked up*?" I asked getting defensive. I wasn't sure what Trey had told her but I was about to set the record straight.

"I mean he's coming by your house on Monday to start working on the house, right? What'd you think I was talking about?"

I rolled my eyes at my paranoia.

"I don't know girl. I'm tripping. I didn't know you and Trey were cousins; we grew up together," I said cradling the phone with my shoulder as I typed up my entertainment news.

"Yeah, his uncle married my aunt a couple of years ago," Kenya said matter-of-factly.

"Well, thanks for the contact. Have you heard from Jas today?" I asked changing the subject again.

"Yeah. She called and asked how the party went and I told her she needed to call you."

"Hmph," I grunted wishing Jasmine would just put her pride aside and call me.

"She's coming around, though, just give her time."

Before I could respond, Lenny was standing in front of me with his hands on his hips.

"Kenya, I gotta go. I'll call you when I get off," I said looking up at Lenny.

"I don't pay you to stay on the phone chatting it up with your homies," he said rolling his eyes and tossing a newspaper in front of me.

"You don't pay me at all, the station does; and what's this?" I said picking up the paper for a better look.

I covered my mouth with my hand and gasped. I was on the front page of the local section. There I was, in my party dress from the night before, looking like I was in a heated argument with

Brendan and the mysterious woman. The headline said:
"Local DJ ends party with a bang!"

"This isn't exactly the coverage the station was looking for," Lenny said walking back to his chair and plopping down.

I tossed the paper in the garbage and massaged my temples. I knew exactly the message this was sending and I was furious that someone had caught me in a weak moment.

The only thing I could do was to downplay it when I went on-air. I'd play it to my advantage because I am the everyday woman; someone that every listener can relate to.

I finished a couple more documents and grabbed my things in preparation for the show.

As I plugged in my headphones, I felt weird. I forced a smile and took my first mic break:

"What up all my ATL-iens?! It's your girl Mystique...the most talked about DJ in all of Atlanta; don't believe me? Check out your local section of the Atlanta Journal Constitution. Oh they're trying to catch me riding dirty, ya'll!" I said laughing into the microphone.

"We're going to talk about this drama a little later, ya'll, but right now I've got brand new music from my boy Ludacris. Check it out. It's The Buzz 104.5!"

That night I had a good show; I played down the rumors dealing with the paper, I played a couple of new joints, talked about the party and even had a chance to play the single from "The Rhymsters." I premiered it during my "pump it or dump it" portion of the show, and not to my surprise, everyone loved the single and wanted more. I hoped Dee was listening.

I headed out to my car and jumped in. I was finally about to see my man and I couldn't wait for the dinner and make-up sex. I also couldn't wait to see the look of pleasure in his eyes as I undressed, pressed my body against his and purred lightly in his ear. I imagined his hands grabbing my waist and bringing me into him as he'd done so many times before. I giggled to myself as I thought of the things we'd do that night. I got on the interstate and headed towards Brendan's condo, which was in expensive Midtown Atlanta. I loved going to his spot; it was sophisticated, clean and a definite step up from his humble beginnings. Just as I prepared to turn off on his exit, my phone began buzzing.

"Hey b-baby," Brendan stuttered; sounding as if he'd had too much to drink.

"Hey honey, I'm almost there. Do you want me to stop and

get anything?" I asked looking over my shoulder at the cars in the next lane.

"No. B-but we've got a change of plans. I need to go to the shop for something so I'll just meet you at the IHOP where we had our first date," Brendan said.

"Are you sure? I can wait for you at the condo if you need me to," I offered up.

After all the IHOP he was talking about was at least twenty minutes away.

"No, I'll meet you there; I might be running late so just sit tight," he said sternly.

"Okay. I'll just order for you," I said sweetly.

Brendan hesitated before responding.

"Yeah. Do that."

"Okay, I'll see you there."

"I love you, Lauren."

I smiled. It was weird how many butterflies I got after hearing Brendan say those words. A silly grin was plastered on my face as I responded the only way I knew how.

"I love you more," I said.

As I pulled into IHOP I thought I'd spotted Brendan's car but was wrong. I sat in our normal booth and ordered myself the French toast and eggs and ordered Brendan the vegetable omelet. I checked my phone after thirty minutes, and still hadn't heard from him.

"Will the other party be joining you?" the waitress asked as she refilled my coffee.

"Yeah. He's just running a little late," I said smiling.

My emotions went from anxious, to worry, to anger and back to worry. I'd dialed Brendan's number repeatedly. When it hit the one hour mark I paid for the food and headed out the door.

"How the hell are you going to stand me up, Brendan?" I screamed into the voicemail as I drove to my house. "You better have a helluva excuse!"

Pop was sitting in the den watching television and after I spoke to him and told him about Trey being the new contractor, I headed up to my room and got into my pajamas. I wasn't about to wait around for Brendan to call me back and apologize. If he wanted to see me or talk to me, he was going to have to do all the work. I laid my head on the pillow and forced myself to fall asleep. It wasn't a content sleep but it was a sleep I needed. Calm before the storm.

Before I had a chance to write in my journal, Pop woke me up by blasting Al Green. He normally did this on Sundays but today I wasn't in the "Love and Happiness" mood. Besides the fact that Brendan had stood me up and Jasmine and I were still at odds, I had a splitting headache.

"What do you know about this Sugar Baby?" Pop said dancing around the kitchen joyously.

He was dressed in a pair of dark colored shorts with bleach spots all over, a white-turned pink-shirt and a pair of reading glasses. Sundays in our household had always been about breakfast, church and then dinner.

Even in our darkest hours, Pop made sure we both stayed anchored in church. I might not have gone every Sunday but I made sure I was in the back pew of the church at least once a month.

I snapped out of my sour mood and joined my father's crazy dancing when the house phone rang. I wiped away a bit of sweat from my top lip and fell into one of the chairs near the kitchen table.

"Al Green's house of music!" I heard Pop say into the phone playfully. I loved Sundays because it allowed us the chance to relax just like old days.

"Hold on. I can't hear you!" Pop said running to the stereo and turning it down.

I picked up a grape and popped it in my mouth as I watched Pop's face go blank.

"Yes, she's here," he said taking the phone slowly from his face. He covered the mouth of the phone with his hand and whispered something to me.

"It's the police. I don't understand what they're saying," he said passing the cordless phone to me. As soon as he said that, my stomach began to flop. What in the world had I done that warranted a call from the police?

"This is Lauren," I said nervously.

"Ms. Washington, this is detective Matthews with the Atlanta Police Department. I need you to come down to the police station immediately."

"Can you tell me what this is all about?" I asked as sweat built up on my forehead. My hands were shaking and I couldn't make them stop. I searched my mind for the good things police called for, and I kept drawing blanks.

The last time we'd received a call at our house from the

police, it was to tell us that mom had been killed. The flashback was more than I could handle.

"We'd like to tell you about this in person," the officer said.

"Sir, if you don't mind I need to know what you need me at the station for," I said. "Just tell me," I plead.

The officer put me on hold and came back to the phone seconds later.

"Madam, I didn't want to be the one to tell you this, and especially over the phone, but we found a Mr. Brendan Lewis last night outside of his condo," the officer said slowly.

"Found him? What do you mean?" I said wanting him to explain.

"Ms. Washington, he was found dead last night," he said pausing "It looks like it was suicide."

In that moment, it seemed like time stopped and I'd stepped outside of my body. I looked at Pop for some type of help and felt my knees wobbling. I felt the tears filling my eyes while I gripped the phone tighter. I couldn't breathe. My head began to swim and before I knew it, I was screaming into the phone hysterically.

"Let me talk to your fucking boss! It's not right to make up lies like that!" I yelled before Pop came and snatched the phone from me.

He talked to the officer while I stood silently looking off into space. This must've been some kind of mistake. How could Brendan be dead? I'd just spoken to him hours earlier.

I hadn't realized it but my entire body was shaking and Pop was slowly walking towards me. The look on his face said it all.

I grabbed Pop by the shoulders and yanked his body harshly.

"No! No! Pop, No!" I said as I fell to the ground. Pop tumbled with me and we sat there and sobbed.

As hard as I tried, I couldn't see, hear or feel anything as we rode down to the police station. It was a familiar ride for me; it was the same path and speed we'd taken when the police called us to say that mom had died, it was the route I took to work everyday and it was even the path I took to Brendan's house.

Sure Brendan had been stressed at work but nothing could have prepared me for the thought of him committing suicide. He had everything; plenty of money in the bank, a hot business, loving girlfriend and an envied car and home.

My heart sank when the police officer escorted me into the interrogation room. I turned to Pop and begged him to come with me. I knew he wasn't strong enough for it, but I needed him; I didn't have anyone else to turn to.

Officer Matthews sat with me as my puffy, red eyes looked up at him for clarification.

His ashy hands reached across the table as he passed a note that was scribbled out in Brendan's handwriting. All it said was, "I'm sorry. I can't take it. Everyone is better off. It'll all make sense. Call my girl Lauren Washington 770-543-5781 - Brendan Lewis."

I scanned the note over and over and before long I couldn't see anything except my tears. Officer Matthews talked generally about what the next steps would be and as much as I wanted to tell myself that it was true—my heart wouldn't accept the truth.

"I need to see him," I said as I interrupted Officer Matthews's conversation with Pop.

After taking a big gulp, Officer Matthews left the room leaving Pop and I sitting at the black table. I gripped his hand tightly and looked at him for some sort of explanation.

"Ms. Washington, I can't authorize you seeing the crime scene pictures but I can give you this. This was on Mr. Lewis at the time we found him," he said handing me the Rolex watch that Brendan never took off.

I held the metal watch in my hand tightly and stroked the face of it. If what they were saying was true, this watch was all I had left of my boyfriend. Just like my mother, all I had to symbolize his existence was a piece of jewelry.

I screamed loudly into the air as Pop held me tightly. He knew what I'd been trying to challenge was true: Brendan was dead.

My everything was gone and life, as I knew it, would be no more.

CHAPTER 5

Dear Diary-

Brendan is dead. It's taken me seven hours and two "happy" pills to say that. When I got the call, I thought it was some sort of bad joke, but it wasn't. Brendan is dead and he killed himself. How is this happening? Why is this happening? I haven't been able to do anything since I got home. All I can do is close my eyes, but even doing that is scary because all I see is him. I try to take a bath but all I smell is Brendan. I cried until I couldn't cry anymore but my heart is all confused. Why? Why? Why? Why? Why? I'm going over our last conversation in my head and I don't know why I didn't see that something was wrong. I feel like it's my fault in a way. Was Brendan crying out for help and I stupidly ignored him? I was supposed to be the one person he could turn to and I let him down. I called Brendan's mom and she wasn't able to come to the phone. I think I'm numb right now. I can't sleep, I can't think and I definitely can't eat. I haven't been able to even think of calling Jasmine or Kenya because I realize I'll have to vocalize that my boyfriend, the man of my dreams, is dead.

I'm going to lie down now, although I know I won't sleep. My heart feels as if everything has been ripped out and readjusted. How do I go on without him?

TTYL

Lauren Washington

How can I go on without ever hearing his voice in my ear or feel his hands caress my body? How could my mind wrap around the thought that our goodbye would, literally, be the *last* goodbye? I couldn't fathom being away from Brendan for a day, let alone forever. My heart ached; it literally ached. I hurt from the crown of my head to the soles of my feet and I needed Brendan to feel better; I needed him badly. I couldn't convince my eyes or my heart that this was *it*. I mean he was me and I was him, right? What was I supposed to do now? What had all of our years together prepared me for except loneliness? When I went to breathe, all I could feel was the huge lump in my throat that felt hot as fire.

I'd cried so much that my breath felt like it was being snatched from my lungs. I tried to grasp something, anything with my hands to make it feel the pain I was in. I dug my nails deeply into the carpet and wailed as my nails scraped past the carpet and hit the hard board underneath. I couldn't imagine my heart beating any faster, my eyes producing any more tears or my body feeling any frailer. I was spent. My mind wandered to how much I loved and dedicated to Brendan. He took it all away? In that moment, I wanted to kill him. I wanted to revive him only to wrap my hands around his neck and strangle him; but not before I told him how much I hated him. But I didn't hate him and that was the twisted part of it. How could I wrap my mind around the thought of never hearing his voice or never seeing his face? That beautiful face I loved to stare at for hours. How could I explain to my heart that what was my forever had only been a short intermission? As the tears blurred my vision, I realized that my breathing was heavy. I wrapped my arms around my body and rocked slowly to my own rhythm. I shut my eyes, allowing a large group of tears to fall from my eyes. I tried to remember the last time I'd seen Brendan, the last time we'd laughed together, the last time we'd kissed and the last time we'd made love. I replayed each moment pathetically searching for the feeling I'd received when it initially happened. A dull ache in my heart caused me to remember that our last memories would be the final chapter in the story of us. There would be no more butterfly kisses, soft touches, encouraging words or hair-raising entrances, which made my body shiver. I reached out weakly, as a vision of Brendan entered my sight. How could this happen to Brendan, of all people? He was handsome, charismatic, had plenty of money and friends and was envied by plenty. Why was he gone? Why was there a huge lump in my throat that was bobbing up and down every time I thought of "What could have been?". I was feeling a range of emotions but pity topped them all. I thought about God and why he'd chosen *me* to be the person to deal with this situation. Hadn't I already been subjected to enough grief for a lifetime? As I sat on the floor, allowing the reality of the situation to sink in, a rush of loneliness came over me. I knew my support system was larger than most, but yet my heart felt as lonely as the day my mother was buried. How could he do this? How could I not know to stop it? Brendan could easily make me smile, simply by the mention of his name, but being faced with the finality of his departure was more than I could bear. I wasn't given the option of a goodbye and nor was I given the chance at receiving closure. How could my heart and soul let go of what had served as my heart and soul? Where was the fairness in my pain? Where was the sense in it all? The cliché "Everything happens for a reason" rung in my ears as I tore myself from the ground. As much as the cliché made sense in everyone else's circumstance, I couldn't understand the reason in Brendan's suicide. I made my way to the bathroom and stood in front of the mirror motionless. My swollen eyes, the bags underneath them, and my tears stared back at me. I watched myself as the water continued to roll down my cheeks, hitting my shirt. After minutes of crying, I inhaled and tried to pull myself together. Brendan had promised me forever but where was he now? How could he leave me like that? My pain wasn't gone but the anger inside of me was boiling over. I was pissed. My tears were now damp streaks down my cheek and served as a simple reminder of my situation. Before I knew it, I was pulling out all of the reminders of Brendan from drawers, underneath the sink, and even on the counters. He was everywhere and I needed him gone immediately. If he could so easily leave me, I needed his every memory out. I pulled together pictures, soap, cologne and a toothbrush and dumped it all in the trash. I didn't feel better but it felt just like sweet revenge, only duller. As I reached underneath the sink and pulled out his overnight bag, I noticed his personal barber clippers and held them tightly. I stared at them closely, dangling them from my fingers in disgust. I didn't have anything against Brendan's passion for barbering, but I needed his memory gone. The clippers swung effortlessly from my hands as my anger took over me. I'd loved his man- - *LOVED* him and this is what I was left with. I loved him but I hated that I did. Why couldn't I just let go? Why couldn't I just cross him off and be done with it? I wanted this whole suicide "thing" to be done with. I wanted my life back. I stared at the clippers closely and cursed Brendan. As I screamed loudly, I flung the clippers at the mirror in aggravation. Just as the glass shattered, the clippers headed back towards my arm and nicked one of them. I didn't know if my loud cries were from the blood coming from my arm or my dreams going up in smoke. This wasn't a dream, it wasn't a joke and it wasn't something I could afford to not believe. But what was real was the red puddle forming on my arm. My body shook ferociously as I clutched my arm to my chest, causing the blood to smear on my shirt. I slid down the wall and sobbed loudly as I watched some of the blood drip on the tile. a As I cried, I tried to tell myself that my physical pain was preparation for my mental and emotional healing.

When it was all over I cleaned up my mess, tried to explain the broken glass and screams to Pop and headed straight to my room to lay down.

I watched motionless as Martin Lawrence joked about Pam's beady beads. I thought about Brendan as I listened. What was he doing before he'd killed himself? Did he think of me? Had I been the reason? What could I have done to stop him? Why hadn't I driven to his condo despite his objections? The endless thoughts poured in and out of my mind.

The police had informed me that he had been found inside of his Escalade with the note and a .32 revolver, which he'd used to put a bullet through his chest. It was all I could picture when I daydreamed.

Even though I knew he was gone, it didn't stop my hands from dialing his phone number over and over, just to hear his voice. The husky, often overpowering voice filled my ears and gave me a little bit of comfort. In those moments, I could pretend he was still alive and things were back to normal.

I lay in my bed barely moving when I heard a knock at my door.

"Who is it?" I said softly.

"Brendan," I thought I heard the voice say. I jumped up from my bed and ran to the door, tripping over the sheets on the way, and swung it open.

It wasn't Brendan; it was Kenya. My mind was playing tricks on me. I could tell she'd been crying and had heard the news. She embraced me and we both sobbed softly. But even though tears were flowing, I still hadn't come to accept that my boyfriend wasn't coming back.

"How'd you find out?" I asked getting back under the sheets and looking over at Kenya who was keeping her distance from me.

"Your dad called me; I came right over," she said wiping her nose and eyes.

I stared at Kenya and somehow felt like I needed to comfort her. She quietly watched me until I called her over to me.

"How are you holding up?" she asked sniffling.

"I'm not sure, really. I just...I can't believe it."

My head was thumping a little bit and my mouth was dry. All I wanted was for Brendan to walk through my door, like he'd done so many times before, and tell me it had all been one huge joke. A cruel joke--but a joke nonetheless.

I'd punch him in the shoulder and tell him I'd never talk to him again; then he'd take me by the waist and kiss me until I giggled. A heavy feeling came over my chest. I just wanted my life back.

"Do you need anything?" Kenya asked sitting softly on my bed.

I shook my head and kept my eyes on the television. I watched as Gina caressed Martin's big ears tenderly as he said some corny joke about how beautiful she was. I bit my bottom lip as I forced myself to watch someone else doing the things I would've given my life to do with Brendan again.

Here I was sitting in my pajamas, in the middle of the afternoon, with my best friend by my side, mourning the loss of my boyfriend. But regardless, I felt the need to keep going, keep busy.

"I need to go to the station," I said removing the covers and marching over to my closet.

Anything I could do to keep my mind off of Brendan, I was game for. Kenya sat frozen on the bed watching my every move, in shock.

"Honey you need to lay down. I think the station can do without you today," Kenya said finally.

I shook my head and proceeded to scan my closet for clothes suitable for work.

"I need to get there; I've got some things to do," I said over and over as I slipped on a shirt and jeans.

Kenya pulled me by the arm and into a tight hug; I tried my best to break free. I pushed and I pushed Kenya's petite body away from me, but she wouldn't let go.

"Just leave me alone, Kenya!" I wailed loudly as my arms flailed in the air. Kenya was fighting me all the way and we ended up on the ground with tears streaking down both our cheeks.

"Just relax, honey," Kenya said through gasps of air. "Relax."

I was still trying to fight her grasp but my energy was draining and the reality of the situation was coming to the forefront.

"Why, Kenya? Why!" I screamed loudly as I kicked my legs and gripped her arm tightly.

I heard my bedroom door open but it was as if my entire body was cement, and as hard as I tried, I couldn't move. Finally giving up, I continued screaming and crying. Out of nowhere, I felt another set of arms holding me down and caressing my back. Was my mind playing tricks on me again? My tears were preventing me from seeing exactly who it was but before I knew it, I looked up and saw Kenya was standing over me crying into her hands while the other set of hands were wrapped around me rocking my body slowly.

I turned around to see who was holding me and I saw the only face, besides pop, I could've wished for.

"I'm here," Jasmine said while she, too, gasped for air. "I'm here now."

My entire demeanor changed and I was finally weeping, crying and howling the way my soul had been begging me to. I leaned back into Jasmine's hold and I cried out Brendan's name.

"Brendan! Damn, Brendan!" I screamed loudly. "Not my baby, ya'll!"

My girls rallied around me and after minutes of horse voice, dry eyed, body aching crying, I was back in my bed resting comfortably. As my eyes drifted off to sleep, I could hear Kenya and Jasmine talking over me softly.

"Lance told me that some of the guys from the shop are saying Brendan had been stressed lately. But why would he do this?" Jasmine said pausing before she continued. "Why would he do this to her and everyone?"

Kenya and Jasmine left me alone in my room and I sat up on my headboard and prayed for Brendan. I prayed that his mother and brother would be okay and that Brendan was at peace when he'd done what he did. But no matter how tight I closed my eyes and prayed for acceptance, as soon as I opened my eyes I was back to reality.

My heart ached, and I couldn't get it to stop. I knew Brendan had been acting strangely but I had no idea he had been stressed enough to take his own life. Why hadn't I seen what everyone else had been able to see? Had I been that consumed with my own agenda?

"Why didn't you talk to me?" I asked as tears streamed down my face again.

And for the first time in a while, no one was there to distract me from the question I couldn't ignore.

CHAPTER 6

Dear Diary-

I go back to work today. I can't run from my life and the truth forever. My boyfriend killed himself; by now everyone else knows what's going on. A lot of my fans have been sending flowers, notes and presents to the station to help me cope. The funeral is set for this Saturday and I even contemplated not going. But I've got to say goodbye, even if he can't say it back. "I love you Lauren," were his last words to me. I feel miserable, slightly depressed and unsure of my purpose. But I'll push through. Ralph was supposed to meet me at the station today but he called and said he needed more time. I'm glad, too. I'll have to deal with that next week.

Pop thinks I need to take a vacation and get out of town for a week or so but I can't. I've got to keep moving to keep my mind off of the fact that eight years of my life is being buried on Saturday. Eight years of happiness is gone. Eight years of togetherness, love and a future. I still can't figure it out and I don't know if I ever will.

I keep looking at my tattoo in the mirror and I don't know if it was a foreshadowing for the current events or just a fitting way to say goodbye. How long had Brendan thought about killing himself? Why hadn't he talked to me about it? So many questions are running through my mind but I've got to get ready to head out the door for work.

TTYL

Lauren Washington

When I was driving to the station, I got the eeriest feeling in the pit of my stomach. I felt like Brendan was sitting right next to me telling me that everything would be okay.

"It'll all make sense," I said out loud, recalling the note found with his body.

I pulled into the station parking lot. I was surprised; for the first time in years, Lenny wasn't parked in my space. I knew I looked a mess. My hair was in a rough looking ponytail and my shirt and jeans were old and ragged. It was a completely different look than any of my colleagues were used to, but I didn't care. I had no reason to focus so much energy on my looks.

As I walked into the office, everyone stopped what they were doing. Whether it was conversations or work, they paused to watch me like a science experiment gone wrong.

I ignored them all and kept my focus. Lenny stood up when he saw me and bowed his head in respect. I knew it took a lot for him to be nice to me so I accepted it graciously.

I looked on my desk and saw a bundle of roses sitting on top of my keyboard. I picked up the card and read it to myself.

"We're all here for you! Lenny & The Buzz staff" Tears filled my eyes as I reached out and touched Lenny's hand softly.

"Thank you,"

"It's my pleasure," Lenny said softly.

I sat at my desk and gathered my news as usual. People avoided me like the plague, not knowing what to say or how to say it. It was better that way, because all I wanted was to be left alone. Kenya and Jasmine called to check on me during the day. They were the friendly breaks I needed. As the clock ticked down to my airtime, I gathered my papers and headed into the studio. I remembered the last time I had been in the studio; I was thinking my life would be starting anew; boy was I right.

"Hey, hey, y'all. It's your girl Mystique. I've been out of the loop for a minute but I'm back! I'm back! I'm back! Just like Diddy said, can't nobody hold me down!" I said laughing loudly.

I had weighed whether or not I would speak on what had happened. Did they want to know the things I'd been fighting? I knew I was jumping out on a limb but I decided they deserved to know since I included them in everything else.

"I share everything with y'all so we're basically like family; and because we're like family I know I can keep it all the way real with y'all. I had a death in my family; the death of someone extremely close to me. My boyfriend of eight years, Brendan, committed suicide this past weekend." I paused as my producer pulled the instrumental down for the more serious vibe I was giving. I could feel myself starting to cry and as I did I paused to gather my words.

"It's been the hardest thing I've ever had to deal with. So...

just like I can talk about all the good things in my life, know I feel pain just like y'all," I said trying to put my emotions in check.

My producer pointed to the phone line and motioned for me to take the live call.

"Buzz, what up?" I said wiping my face off and preparing myself for the backlash.

"Hey Mystique. My name's Shemika and I just want to say that we're all thinking about you and your boyfriend's family! Keep your head up, girl.".

"Thanks Shemika!" I said as my producer pointed for me to answer another call.

"Buzz, what up?"

"Hey, is this Mystique?" the male voice asked clearly.

"Yeah, this is your girl!" I said plainly.

"Well, you don't know me but I've been listening to you since you started at Buzz. I love your spirit and I've got to say my prayers are with you sister! I commend you for speaking out too!"

I was touched and couldn't believe this many people cared about my life.

"Thanks going out to everyone out there who's reaching out and touching me in prayer and thought. I appreciate it so much, y'all! I've got to say that if anyone out there is feeling depressed, sad or doesn't know what to do, make sure you talk to someone. Anyone," I said before introducing Tupac's "I Ain't Mad at 'Cha".

Strangely enough, this song had been one of Brendan's favorites. After my show was completed I packed up my things and swung by my desk to pick up my purse and cell phone.

"Lauren, we've gotten so many calls from people who want to know more about your story," Lenny said waving a stack of phone messages in his hand.

"I think we're onto something," he said raising an eyebrow.

I smiled politely and put the phone messages on my desk. If I was going to tackle a hurdle it would have to be one day at a time.

Instead of heading over to Kenya or Jasmine's house, I headed straight home. I was surprised to see Trey's truck in the driveway and parked my car right next to his.

"Hey," I said looking at Trey and Pop as they sat at the kitchen table drinking beers.

I'd been crying in the car and the last thing I wanted to do was feel pity from my old crush and my father.

"Hey Sugar Baby," Pop said patting a seat next to him. I put my purse on the back of the chair and sat down.

"Do you want one?" Pop asked lifting up the six-pack of Heinekens in front of him.

Trey looked at me intensely while I barely made eye contact.

"No. I'm actually about to take a shower and go to bed; it's been a long day," I said as I proceeded to stretch my arms and yawn loudly.

I excused myself and made my way up to the bedroom, showered, crawled into bed and sobbed quietly until I was numb. The next couple of days leading up to Brendan's funeral were uneventful. I still hadn't been able to get a clear understanding as to why Brendan ended his life. Lance, who was usually full of answers, knew nothing and no one on the street seemed to have any information. I was stuck and I realized if I was going to find out why Brendan killed himself, I was going to have to do it on my own.

While I dressed for the funeral, I tried to tell myself that everything would be okay. Kenya and Jasmine would be meeting me at my house so we could ride over to Brendan's mother's house and then ride to the funeral together. I had all the support I needed.

I couldn't stop my hands from shaking as I pulled my simple black dress over my body. I'd gained a little weight in the week since Brendan died and I could see it, primarily in my face. My appearance had drastically changed and I really didn't care how I looked.

"Let me do your make-up," Kenya said as she pulled out a small make-up bag. I didn't object, although I didn't see the reason for make-up. I was going to a church to see my boyfriend in a casket. I doubted powder and lipstick would help the situation.

I looked decent, though. My hair was pulled into a bun; my simple black dress stopped right above my knees and my Nine West heels were as plain as they came.

As we stood inside Brendan's mother's house preparing to get in our assigned vehicles, my attention went to the absence of Brendan's older brother, Terrence. Brendan had always told me that when they were younger the two of them were glued at the hip.

"Ms. Pat, is Terrence here?" I said looking around the house. The only difference between Brendan and Terrence was that

Terrence was a certified, straight up and down, nerd; he even used to wear pocket protectors. From what I knew, he moved back to New Jersey after graduating high school and never looked back to Georgia or his family. The closest I'd ever gotten to Terrence was the pictures Brendan showed me.

"Oh, my baby couldn't make it," she said dabbing her eyes. She squeezed my hand tightly and I reached over and hugged her plump body.

Ms. Lewis was a short, round, dark skinned woman with plenty of grey hair to show the years of worry caused by her boys. With the exception of her breasts and her skin tone, Brendan and his brother looked just like their mother. The grin that Brendan and his mother shared was eerily familiar. While the two of us were never at odds, we often battled Brendan's attention. There would be plenty of times he and I would have something planned and she'd call five minutes before we left and demand he spend time with her. The good ole guilt trip of "I'm your mama boy; she's just a *girl*," worked earlier in our relationship; but as we both got older, her guilt trips stopped working. There was very few, if any, mention of Brendan's father Darrin. When we met, Brendan had told me that his parents had gotten married as teenagers, up North, and stayed together for fiive years. Soon after the separation, Ms. Pat and the boys relocated to Atlanta and Darrin popped in and out of their lives until Brendan and Terrence were in their mid-teens. I didn't expect to see Darrin there, but I was curious who he was and what he looked like.

I watched as family members and close friends piled into the tiny house. Kenya and Jasmine stood closely behind me while Pop kept to himself on the front porch. It was a rainy day and as I stood beside the window staring at the black limousines, with black mirrored tint, I quickly diverted my attention to something else. I traced my fingertips over a baby picture of Brendan that lay on a nearby table. Kenya smiled sheepishly while Jasmine shook her head in silence.

"Wasn't he a beautiful baby?" I asked. I picked up the picture and held it tightly.

My friends didn't respond and I wasn't sure if I wanted them to. All I needed was someone to listen to me.

The only thing that had kept my attention off of Brendan's death had been the investigation into my mother's murder. In a way, the investigation had given me a purpose to keep going.

I'd talked to Ralph, the private investigator, the day before the funeral and asked him what he'd found out about mom's death. Surprisingly, he had news. He said he'd learned that a neighborhood homeless man, who we all knew as "Dirty Larry", had apparently been around when mom was murdered and had seen "something". As much as I wanted to be excited about finding closure with one aspect of my life, I couldn't be. I listened to him but I was thinking of Brendan and the funeral preparations. Ralph and I agreed to meet on the Monday after Brendan's funeral so he could give me the full run down on what "Dirty Larry" had seen. I didn't feel like now was the time to update Pop so I kept the little bit of information I'd received to myself.

"You ready to load up?" Jasmine asked tapping me on my shoulder.

"Yeah...I guess," I said sighing.

Jasmine held my hand tightly as I walked towards the car. I could see Ms. Pat was having a breakdown as she ducked into the first car. As I headed towards the same car I felt myself going in the same direction. I'd intentionally stayed away from the wake because I wasn't ready to see my boyfriend, the love of my life and my best friend, cold, stiff and in a casket. In a nutshell, I wasn't ready to say goodbye.

"It's okay to cry," Pop said stroking my back softly as a raindrops hit my forehead and trickled down.

I knew it was okay to cry and I really wanted to. But looking at the black limo in front of me, I started to feel as if I was walking to a slow grave. It was like the grim reaper was in front of me and I was walking towards the inevitable. It was closure that I didn't want.

I'd done well up until that moment. I was able to function, live and try to force a smile on my motionless face. But as I walked towards the death mobile, I felt like I was hearing the news all over again.

"We found him dead."

I felt a tear on my face. My head began to swim. Just as I turned to leave, Pop was there with his arms outstretched.

In that second I felt like I was a motherless nine-year old again with pigtails, a kool-aid and pickle addiction, Cross-Color clothes, and a toothless grin. I fell into his arms and wrapped my arms around his body.

"Pop I don't want to go," I said keeping my head in his shoulder.

Pop tilted my chin up and stared into my eyes for a minute

before speaking.

"Sugar Baby it's your choice but I think you'll regret it if you don't at least say goodbye," Pop said wiping a tear from my cheek with his thumb. I thought about it as I stared at the ground and I knew not attending the funeral wasn't an option. I bit my lip, took a few deep breaths and barreled into the car with the rest of the family. I stared out the window as I heard people talking around me.

"Did you hear about the barber shop?" I heard one older woman, who I thought was Brendan's Aunt Cleo, say softly.

I had no idea what she was talking about and as I turned my head to get more information, Kenya was in my face.

"Let me just touch up your nose and forehead and put on a little lip gloss," she said reaching into her bag with excitement. I know Kenya just wanted to help in the best way she could, and since I wasn't openly talking about my feelings, her bag of magic was the next best therapy she could provide.

Even though I was in a car full of grieving people I felt miserably alone. It was as if I were watching everyone talk in slow motion. Their mouths and gestures were moving so slow that I had to shake my head to make sure I wasn't dreaming. I watched as Jasmine, Pop and Kenya talked amongst themselves. I wasn't staring at anyone in particular but I wanted to be where they were; sad but functional. I couldn't function and I couldn't smile. I looked out the window and kept my eyes on the trees as I thought about what I was about to face. That's when I started thinking, *"What are funerals exactly?"* A forced public method of saying goodbye and healing? But in my eyes, I'd said goodbye to Brendan the moment he'd hung up the phone on the night he took his life. Up until this moment, funerals made sense to me. But as I faced my own public goodbye to the man I loved, I started to see it in a different light. Why did I have to say goodbye openly? So that other people could see me grieve and walk away deciding whether or not I'd mourned "enough" or "too much"? Why did this have to be the expiration date? As we rode the interstate, my eyes stayed fixated on the trees, which blew so beautifully in the wind. It was small things like trees that made me jealous; jealous of not being able to enjoy the things around me. I tried to make sense of everything as best as I could. Every thought led back to the infamous question: *"Why?"*

I thought about the possible answers, but none of them seemed severe enough for Brendan to end his life. None of it seemed so detrimental that suicide seemed the only way to go. I'd taken the trip from Bankhead to New Birth Missionary Baptist Church plenty of times before; but this day, everything was moving sluggishly. All the cars, the talk and the drive were all going slower than ever and I couldn't understand why. I wanted to grab a remote and press Fast Forward so I could skip the funeral, the mourning and the stares, just to get in my bed and sleep. The drive seemed familiar. Brendan and I had driven this route before. Memories of our hilarious drives to New Birth echoed in my mind. I wanted it to stop. I wanted thoughts of his hands in mine and his bright smile to vanish from my memory. Even though I was sad, I was also angry. I heard laughter in the limo and turned to see Brendan's cousins giggling about the "good times" with him. I had plenty of "good times" to add, but I could only think about the selfish act that had caused us to be there. How could they act like he was being honored or telling old war stories? Brendan had killed himself and they were acting like he was being given the key to the city. I shook my head looked outside. Brendan was gone, by his own choice and at his own hands. I wanted to tell them all how Brendan had murdered me when he'd pierced his heart with the bullet. Everything I knew would be buried with him.

I tried to tune out the talk and laughter but I picked up a story from one of his aunts who was as calm as they came about Brendan being a "good kid" and how "perfect" he was. My face felt scorching hot as I tried to hold back how I was truly feeling. The truth of the matter was I wasn't only angry with Brendan, I was angry with myself; angry because I couldn't stop my man from killing himself. I was angry because I didn't even know suicide had been an option in his heart or mind. I was riddled with guilt as I stared into the faces of all of his loved ones. I felt as responsible for killing Brendan as the bullet itself. Did I even deserve a seat in the limousine? My mixed emotions were swirling everywhere as I tried to keep them under control. I'd had the responsibility of taking care of my man and, yet, the funeral would serve as confirmation that I'd failed. I mean, look at my track record, I thought; I had a dead mother and boyfriend. I wasn't exactly the angel of luck or life.

There were hundreds of hundreds of cars parked inside the spacious parking lot of New Birth Missionary Baptist Church. The mega church, which was always packed for Bishop Eddie Long's talked about sermons, was now packed to say farewell to my boyfriend. This was the same church I had secretly planned on walking down the aisle and becoming Mrs. Brendan Lewis in. Today I'd be walking down the aisle saying goodbye to what would never be. I sobbed softly into a tissue as the limo pulled up to the entrance of the church. The cement feeling was back and my body was starting to feel like dead weight. With Pop's help I was standing—though not very well. My legs were shaky, my eyes were red and my hands couldn't stop trembling.

As we all piled into the church vestibule to prepare for our entrance, I scanned the room in awe. Some people were already seated while others were scrambling around to the bathroom; but as soon as the family entered the building everyone took their places, as if on cue for some pre-rehearsed play.

"This turn out is wonderful," Jasmine said in my ear as I barely smiled. It should've been comforting to know that so many people loved my boyfriend, but it wasn't. What would've been comforting would've been Brendan walking through the door with his signature grin plastered on his face.

But when I heard his mother wail as she started making her way down the aisle, I knew the comforting moments I wished for would, in no way, be happening that night.

Ms. Pat had allowed me to sit right next to her and Brendan's grandmother, the same place that a spouse would sit.

With Pop by my side, gripping my hand tightly, and Jasmine and Kenya directly behind me I knew I had nowhere to go but to the dreaded casket. The minister had told us that when we entered the church we would bypass our seats and instead circle in front of Brendan's open casket. After paying our respects we would, then, take our designated seats.

As much as I wanted to remember what I was supposed to do, I couldn't take my eyes off all the people staring back at the long line of family members ushering down the aisle.

My eyes caught a couple of people I knew from Brendan's barbershop and they looked just as ragged as I did. I searched the crowd and smiled sweetly at a couple of them and then I saw *her*. It was the mystery girl that Brendan was with. As we passed her pew, I saw her drop her head and weep into her hands quietly. I kept my focus on her even after we passed her row. I knew I needed to talk to her because maybe, just maybe, she would have some answers.

We approached the casket just as grandma Lewis and Ms. Pat were being escorted to the front row. I turned and looked at Pop, whose eyes were blood shot from crying, and quickly turned back to face what I'd been avoiding...Brendan.

He laid there perfectly as if he were sleeping. He looked good, too. One of the guys from the barbershop had come in to give him his infamous Caesar haircut that brought out his deep waves. His beautiful eyebrows and eyelashes were still in tact and as I ran my fingers over his face I jumped at how cold he was.

I lost it. I heard myself scream but I couldn't control what was coming out of my mouth. My hands delicately ran up and down his chest, trying to find the hole that had taken his life. I shook ferociously as Kenya, Pop and Jasmine tried to manage what was happening.

"Brendan!" I screamed over and over as I clinched my hands on the casket tightly. Other people were behind me, waiting to see him, but I didn't care. This was *my* man and no one in the world knew him better than I did. I deserved my time to say goodbye, my time to grieve and my time to release.

I leaned in and kissed his stiff, cold, hard lips. The same lips, which always warmed my entire body up, and always turned me on were now motionless.

"Oh baby, why?!" I said whispering in his ear "Please don't leave me. Come back!"

I knew he was gone but I had to plead my case; maybe God could make an exception this *one* time and give him back. I wanted to believe that miracles happened. But I knew the truth. No amount of pleading, begging or crying would undo what had been done.

It couldn't have been his "time", I thought, as I traced my finger up and down his clean, manicured nails.

He was dressed in a clean, black and white pin-stripped suit. He'd bought it a year earlier to wear to a black-tie function, but when he had to cancel he kept it hanging in his closet for a "rainy day" as he said. Strangely enough the rainy day would be his funeral.

"Sugar Baby, let's go have a seat," Pop said kindly in my ear as I turned and looked at him like he was crazy. How dare he rush me when I'm trying to say goodbye?

I turned back to look into the casket and studied Brendan's face, body and hands. I had to remember everything about him because I knew how forgetful I was. I wanted to remember those almond eyes, beautiful wide nose, luscious lips, smooth skin and strong manly hands. I couldn't forget him-I just couldn't. With hesitance I stepped away from the casket and turned to face all the mourners who were either staring at me or crying.

As I made my way to my seat, I looked over the crowd and tried to think about how excited Brendan would've been at all the people who had come to see him off.

"Brendan!" I heard a woman scream at the back of the church. I turned, and looked over my shoulder, trying to find her. But with the ever growing number of people in the church it was pointless. Just as I turned my attention back to the front of the church, my eyes connected with Trey's.

He was sitting in the pew across from mine, staring at me with a concerned look on his face. Next to him was a cute little girl who couldn't have been more than five years old. I smiled modestly at him and returned my attention to the pastor and prepared for the service of my life.

Brendan's funeral was filled with tears, memories, laughter and love. I couldn't get over how many people had such beautiful stories to tell about him. During some of the stories I would forget where I was and the occasion, and thought I felt Brendan sitting next to me. But as I stared up at the now closed casket I shivered at the reality. After the casket was carried out and put into the hearse, I stared at my feet while I walked towards the car.

We all jumped into the limo as the rain hit the windshield roughly, and headed to the burial site. It was a long ride to the cemetery and I used it to rest my eyes.

"We're going to have food back at the house for anyone who wants to join," I heard Ms. Pat say softly to the silent cary.

There was no more laughter and joking about Brendan's "good days". We were all just barely looking into one another's eyes, as we started coming to terms with the ultimate ending in the next part of the service: the burial.

I kept my eyes closed, hoping that someone would let me be and not make me go to the cemetery. I hoped that maybe they'd forget I was there and just skip over me. But just as I thought, when the car stopped, I felt hands poking my stomach and shoulder.

"Sugar Baby, it's time to get out." ," Pop said as he cleared his throat.

Kenya and Jasmine were already outside of the limo when I got out and,. Wwe gathered underneath the green tent that was set up for us;, I felt dead. I found it easier to ignore the situation rather than deal with it. I knew I could scream and cry as much as I wanted but none of it would get me the answers I desperately wanted.

I stared off into the distance while friends and family cried quietly. We all realized the cemetery was the end scene to the entire play. There were no more wails, there was no more shouting and there was no fainting. By then, everyone understood that it didn't matter. Brendan was going six feet under and we had no other choice but to deal with it.

I looked over at Ms. Pat who looked more dazed than anything. Her hair was standing on top of her head, her dress had make-up stains on it and her hands shook uncontrollably. But even still, she sat there, like me, waiting for it to be over.

After they lowered the casket into the ground and people started walking away, I picked one of the white roses off of the top of a bundle of flowers and held it tightly in my hand. I played with the silver band which still sat on my left hand, while I contemplated what I needed to say to let go. Jasmine, Kenya and Pop hugged one another while they stood behind me and watched without a sound.

"I wish I knew what to say to you right now but I don't. I don't understand how, after all this time, I could feel like I know nothing about who you were. I love you more than anything in this entire world and nothing anyone can do can change that," I sighed as a puddle of tears formed on my cheeks. "You told me that you'd always be here but what now?" I cried.

I looked up at the sky and stared at a grey cloud forming above. The rain had let up, slightly, but it looked like it would be coming back in no time.

After dropping the rose into the casket I tried to rack my brain of other things to say but all I kept coming up with was the obvious.

"I love you," I said watching the flower gently hit the top of the casket.

I wiped my eyes and looked up at the hill where the limousine was. There was a line of people around the car and they all looked like fans I'd seen before.

"You okay?" Jasmine asked putting her arm around my neck.

I nodded and started the trek towards the vehicle that would return me to the world without Brendan.

Up until the day of the funeral, I was able to act like my boyfriend had just been on a long vacation where he was denied phone and e-mail; but seeing the casket lowered and feeling his cold body let me know it was as real as my pain.

"H-hey...Mmmystique," I heard a young man's voice say softly while I walked towards the limousine.

"*Great,*" I thought "*a fan.*"

Jasmine played her role as bodyguard, telling fans to give me space before I could even turn around and ask for a moment of privacy. It touched me that my fans cared so much about me that they'd come out to show me support, but I needed a moment for Lauren, not Mystique.

"Hey, she's really not in the mood for talking right now," Jasmine said politely. I could tell she wanted to snap on the kid but she kept her cool. I turned around to flash a quick smile and saw a familiar face and eyes staring back at me.

"Oh...mmmmy bad," the kid stuttered as he dropped his shoulders and head.

"Oh no...I know you. It's Dee, right?" I said turning and walking towards him.

It was the kid I'd met at the station.

"Yeah. Yyooou remember mmme?" Dee stuttered as he ran his hands over his rough looking hair. He seemed like he hadn't had a decent haircut in at least three months. Nevertheless he was a cute kid. He was wearing a simple, white button-down shirt with a pair of black church pants.

"Of course I remember. How are things doing with you?" I asked kindly.

"The other cat in the group, Lamont, he's tttrrripin," he said talking quickly.

Before I could tell him to slow down and gather his words, he was closing his eyes and doing it himself.

"Lamont, that's my boy. He went and got himself locked up a couple of days ago," he said rolling his eyes.

I turned around to let Kenya, Jasmine and Pop know everything was cool. I knew this kid was genuinely interested.

"I told you these streets aren't a game," I said nodding in his direction.

"Yeah. I hhheear that," he said trying to laugh.

"So how's school? You got back in, right?" I asked.

"Yeah...I...I'm ggooood!" he replied grinning excitedly. I could tell Dee was thrilled to know that someone, even someone like me, cared what he was doing.

"Well you make sure you remember me when you blow up and when you get that degree in your hands," I said winking at him.

Then it struck me. Had Dee come to the funeral just to show his support for me? If so, the least I could do was thank him.

"Did you come out for me?" I asked raising an eyebrow curiously.

"Not entirely," he said sucking his teeth and looking over his shoulder at a distraught looking older woman who I assumed was his mother.

She looked like she was 30 to 35 years old with a serious overbite, long blonde weave, golden skin and hazel contacts. Her body was flabby and her beer belly couldn't be contained in the tight black and red dress she was sporting. If it wasn't for the red eyes and nose she was sporting I would've thought she was going to the club instead of a funeral.

I returned my stare back at Dee who was crossing his arms.

"My ddddad's funeral was tttoday and since wwwweee missed the fuuunneeeral moms made me ccccooommee to the burial," he said hurrying to get the last of the words out.

I looked around the cemetery for any other funerals that were taking place at the same time; I couldn't see any. But I thought this cemetery was the biggest one in Atlanta. His father's service could've been taking place anywhere.

"Well, I'm really sorry to hear about your loss," I said wanting to escape the rain that was beginning to trickle.

Dee stared at me like he wanted to say more but couldn't.

"Dee, bring your ass on!" his mother yelled loudly as she jogged off towards a beat up old Chevy sitting on some dusty looking rims.

"I'm sorry about your loss too," he said matter-of-factly. "I heard about it when you said it on air."

I nodded my head and reached out to hug him. For some reason I felt the need to hold him, hug him and let him know that everything would get better for him. I knew what it was like to lose a parent at a young age and I hoped that Dee's mother would comfort him the way Pop comforted me.

As I let go I stared into Dee's eyes and a certain sense of familiarity fell over me; one that I hadn't felt before.

"What was your father's name?" I asked quickly.

Dee smirked and started to jog towards the direction of his mother.

"I wouldn't even call that nigga a father," he said running backwards. "He was a daddy."

"But the bastards name was Brendan Llleeeewwwis," he said nonchalantly.

Kenya, Jasmine and Pop all stopped what they were doing and focused their attention on Dee.

"W-what did you say?" I said almost marching towards Dee who, sensing my aggravation and disbelief, stopped in his tracks.

"I said my dad's name was Brendan Lewis, why?" he said with attitude and no stuttering.

I felt my legs getting ready to give out and before I had a chance to extend my arms and break my fall, my body hit the ground with a loud thud. If what Dee was saying was true, the man I thought I knew everything about was slowly starting to become someone I knew *nothing* about.

CHAPTER 7

Dear Diary-

Isn't it strange how you can think you know a person and rudely be proven wrong? Less than five minutes after he was in the ground, I found out that Brendan had been keeping a huge secret from me. He has a 13-year old son named Dee! It's the same kid from the rap group "The Rhymesters". As numb as I was when they put the casket in the ground I think I'm more frozen now that I know Brendan was keeping secrets. Of course this could all be one big misunderstanding and this kid and his mother could be way off. Kenya and Jasmine are in disbelief too. Lance says he heard a rumor about Brendan having a kid but he never saw a kid so he never thought anything else of it. This has definitely solidified my decision to look into Brendan's lifestyle and death. A part of me is exhausted and literally drained. I can't bear to deal with any of this until I have some concrete information. I'm supposed to meet with Ralph but this situation with Dee can't wait any longer. Lance knows where his mother stays and me and Jasmine are going to go over there to get some answers. Nothing at all is making sense but I can only hope that soon it will. Trey is at the door and I'm not sure what for, but I need to go.
TTYL
Lauren Washington

"Hey, I thought maybe you were sleep," Trey said looking like he had been caught in the act of doing something he wasn't supposed to.

I was aggravated. Not necessarily at him but more or less at the situation. I was looking at him and hearing him but my mind wasn't connecting the dots.

"Hello! Earth to Skeeter," Trey said laughing with his hands behind his back.

I snapped out of my daydream of Brendan and focused my attention on Trey.

"I'm sorry, Trey. I've just got a lot on my mind right now," I said opening the door wider so he could come in.

I was wearing a tight vintage t-shirt and a pair of Capri leggings that hugged my body like they were too small for me. I had every intention of going out and exercising that morning, but the closer I got to the door the more nervous I felt about seeing someone I knew. They, of course, would ask how I was and I would have to lie and say "okay" or "I'm coping". I wasn't okay and I wasn't coping. I was sad as hell and starting to get angrier by the day.

"I just wanted to...uh...I wanted to bring you these," he said pulling a bundle of daises from behind his back.

For as long as I could remember, daises have always been my favorite flower. They signified the innocence of my childhood and the carefree days I'd spent doing nothing. It was also the flower we'd placed in mom's hair when she was buried.

"Daisies!" I said trying my best to smile widely.

"How'd you know?" I asked taking the flowers and walking into the kitchen to find a vase.

Trey took a seat at the kitchen

"I've got a good memory, I guess," he smirked.

After I put the flowers in water and had prepared them neatly, I spun around to him and narrowed my eyes.

"Good memory, from what? I've never told you I liked daisies," I said joining him at the table.

I was getting used to Trey's presence in my house and as much as I wanted my own space and time, he was a really good listener. It had only been a week since he started work and I was already seeing improvements in certain areas of the house.

"Think back to Ms.Buzzett's "Flower Power" play we had to put on," he said fidgeting with a piece of paper on the table.

My jaw dropped. Ms. Buzzett, our fourth grade teacher, had the entire class put on a play, called "Flower Power", about the importance of plant life and we all had to dress up as our favorite flower. I remembered it vividly as Pop sewed my white and yellow suit together the night before the play. I stood proudly on stage, the next day, wishing my mom was there to see me shine. Trey's goofy self went as a weed because, as he put it, "even weeds were flowers to someone."

"That was almost twenty years ago, how'd you remember

that?" I asked not knowing if Trey was flirting with me or not.

He chuckled and crossed his arms.

"How could I forget your stick legs and huge feet?" he asked laughing loudly.

I rolled my eyes and sucked my teeth as I got up from the table. If there was any thought in my mind that Trey was flirting it had just flown out of the window, right along with my patience.

"I'm kidding, I'm kidding," he said trying to catch his breath as I stood with my arms folded.

"What did you need, anyway?" I asked cutting his apology in half.

"I was coming by to see if your dad was here, we were supposed to be going to look at some tile for the kitchen," he said sitting back in the chair with a grin still plastered on his face.

"Oh, well, he should be back in about ten minutes; he just went to the corner store for some jerky."

The two of us stood silently in the kitchen not knowing what to say to each other, but soon enough Trey was filling the silence, as he always did.

"I'm so sorry about Brendan..." he said not looking into my eyes.

I had this urge to laugh, because it was the one time Trey had ever been serious with me and, yet, I was biting my lip out of nervousness.

"Thank you. I really appreciate you coming to the funeral," I said hoping the awkward silence would end.

"Who was the pretty little girl with you?" I asked smiling as I thought about the butterscotch colored little girl with braids and beads in her hair.

Trey started smiling at the mention of the little girl and put his hand over his heart.

"That's my baby girl, Shawntae," he sighed with his eyes closed. "That's my world."

I stared at Trey with an envious look. I wanted a child and I wanted the love I'd somehow lost with a bullet and a note.

"That's wonderful."

"Her mother and I are in court for custody. She's living the single life now and Shawntae is the one suffering. So, let's just hope she gets to stay with her dad full-time. She's a perfect little girl."

"And she's beautiful," I managed to say when I returned to the kitchen table with Trey.

"I've got to say she's got all of my looks, thank God!" he joked.

I laughed quietly.

"I don't know if that's a good thing," I said finally getting my one jab in.

Trey grabbed his side in fake pain and winced. "Ow! That hurt, Skeeter!"

I slapped his arm playfully and jumped up from the table, trying to escape the return slap I knew was coming.

Trey reached out and tried his best to get me but was unlucky. We ran throughout the house like kids playing tag. I ran up the stairs with Trey close behind me. Laughter rang throughout my house as I hid behind a wall. After Trey passed by the wall without seeing me, I ran back towards the kitchen.

I thought I had outsmarted him but when I turned to check my back he was standing right behind me with a smirk on his face and his hand in the air ready to slap me back.

I grabbed his hand and tried my best to keep it away from me.

"You can't even slap me!" I teased as he tried to break free.

By this time, unbeknownst to me, we were close enough to kiss; as Trey placed one arm around my waist in an attempt to grab my other arm I got chills. I slowed down and soon my smile disappeared. Trey was still playing but almost immediately, he was staring intensely into my eyes. I wasn't sure how long we were standing in that position, with his hand wrapped around my waist and one of my arms wrapped around the back of his neck, but as much as I was telling my body to break away I couldn't. His hands lightly traced my back and ran delicately down my spine and onto my butt. I didn't know what to do, because as much as I wanted to touch him—I couldn't. I was putty in his arms.

Trey went in for a kiss and I pulled away, just as Jasmine walked into the kitchen with one twin on her hip and the other one holding her hand.

The three of us stared at each other and it was then I knew that what I was doing was wrong. I had, after all, just buried my boyfriend and here I was gallivanting around like I had no cares in the world.

I pushed Trey away and darted past Jasmine and the children towards my bedroom in embarrassment.

"Move," I said not making eye contact with my best friend.

In minutes, Jasmine was at my door with the children in tow

and a look of concern, surprise and anger showed on her face.

"What the hell was that?" she said in a whisper.

I brushed her question off I slipped on a pair of jeans and pulled my hair into a ponytail.

"You do realize you just buried your boyfriend, the love of your life, right?" she said sitting Michelle on the floor and placing Mikayla on my bed.

I loved Jasmine but the last thing I needed was her judgmental words.

"Don't you think I know that, Jas?" I said spinning around with my hands on my hips.

How dare she challenge whether or not I was grieving? The only excuse I could come up with, for my close encounter with Trey, was grief. I was grieving and wanted to be close to someone who could make me feel half the way Brendan did.

Yeah, I told myself, *that was the reason*; it was a damn good one.

"I'm just saying," she said sitting on the bed and dropping her head.

"Are you ready?" I inquired with one eyebrow raised.

Jasmine struggled with her children as I hurried down the steps and past Trey who was waiting with a fretful look.

"Hey, wait..." he said grabbing my arm lightly. I turned to look at him and couldn't connect my eyes with his. I was ashamed that I had even allowed myself to get caught up in emotions from the past. I didn't care about Trey, hell I barely tolerated him, so why hadn't I been able to pull away?

"I'm sorry. I was wrong for that," he said nervously.

I nodded my head and stared out the window as he spoke. It wasn't that I was ignoring him, or even angry with him, I just didn't want to risk staring into his eyes and getting that tingling feeling all over again. Staring out to the street gave me the perfect distraction.

"It's okay, Trey," I said exhaling as soon as Pop opened the front door. I slid my arm out of his grasp and exited after kissing Pop on the cheek.

I turned to look back and Trey was still standing in the same spot, with the same fretful look on his face, staring into my eyes.

I got into my car, laid my head on the steering wheel and waited for Jasmine.

"Thanks for the help," she said sarcastically as she strapped the children into the car seats.

I ignored her smart comment and started the car.

"Not another word about what you saw, okay? It was a mistake and I'd appreciate it if it stayed between us," I said not taking my eyes off of the road.

Jasmine nodded her head and I knew she had my back. I knew too many of her secrets that had gone into my "friend vault."

The "friend vault" stored many of our mistakes, hardships, embarrassments and slip-ups that were only heard by the two of us and were never repeated. I trusted Jasmine with everything I had, so I didn't doubt her when she said it was locked away.

As we pulled up to Dee's house, which was incidentally close to Ms. Pat's house, I cringed. It was a ragged house and when I say ragged, I meant it. You know the house on the block with the mold on the siding, torn screen door, dirty toys in the yard and beat down cars in the driveway? Dee's house was the one that made that house look like a mansion. It was *that* bad.

"Are you sure this is it?" Jasmine asked curiously as she looked back at Michelle and Mikayla.

I checked the directions again and nodded my head.

"Yup. This is it," I said opening my door and signaling for her to do the same.

Each of us grabbed a twin and prepared for our journey. I stepped over dog crap, mud puddles and trash as I made my way to the front door. The house looked like it had been built in the 60s and hadn't been properly cared for. There were trees hovering over the patched roof and dead plants at the entrance. It could've been a cute house if only someone would paint it and keep it clean.

Jasmine knocked on the door as I switched Michelle to my other hip. I played with one of her thick twists. She smiled at me just as Dee opened the door. He looked like he had seen a ghost and quickly stepped outside the torn screen door and closed it behind him.

"Mmmyyystiqqque, wwwwhat yoooouuu ddddddoooiinnng hhhere?" he said as he straightened out his dirty white t-shirt and denim shorts.

Jasmine stared at Dee and I assumed she was looking for a hint of Brendan in him. I could see it, but only in fractions. He stuttered like him when he was nervous, he had his skin tone, his cuteness and his tiny bow-legged stance. It was all there.

"I came over to talk to your mom, is she here?"

Dee stood silent for a second before opening the door and

allowing us in. I could tell he was embarrassed. But I wasn't judging him, I just wanted to know the truth.

"Ma!" he screamed as he cleared newspapers from the dirty living room couch, making room for Jasmine and I to sit. As soon as our butts hit the couch, we sank into it. It was made with that itchy material that 70s outfits were made of and as much as I wanted to scratch, I knew it would've been rude.

"What boy?" Dee's mother said appearing in the living room doorway with a blunt in her hand and wearing a pair of tights and an oversized t-shirt.

Her blonde hair was now pulled back away from her face and I could tell she was a half-way decent looking lady. Her hazel eyes were missing that day, but her bad body was still very much there.

"Ma, this is Mystique...reemmeeemmmbeerr I was tttelling you about hhheer, from 104.5?" Dee said smiling widely.

I saw his mother roll her eyes and then scream at the top of her lungs at Dee.

"What the hell I tell you about that damn stuttering? Get that shit under control!" she said harshly as she settled into the loveseat across from us.

Dee stood against the wall with his head hung and aura of disgust and hate lingering over him.

"Y'all wanted something?" she said focusing her attitude towards Jasmine and I.

Luckily, both of us were used to people like her. You know the people; the ones who hate the world for everything they've never been *given*. The ones who walk around taking what they can from others in order to get by.

"Hey, I'm Lauren and this is my friend Jasmine. I was talking to Dee yesterday and he was telling me about his father who died..." I said swallowing, hoping the lady would stop me and tell me Dee had been lying.

"Yeah, so what?" she said taking a drag from the blunt in between her dirty fingers.

"I'm sorry. What's your name?" Jasmine asked loudly as she challenged the woman with her own attitude.

"Tanya," she said as she blew the smoke from her blunt into our faces. If I wasn't holding Michelle and Jasmine holding Mikayla, I might have gone Bankhead on her; but with Dee staring at me I wanted to keep it professional.

"My boyfriend was Brendan Lewis and..." I started as I let

my hands move freely.

"Oh, so you're the uppity bitch, huh?" Tanya said sitting the blunt down in a nearby ashtray and leaning back into the love seat. "Yeah, I've heard about you."

I cleared my throat and smiled at her comment. For as long as I could recall, I'd been called uppity and bourgeoisie but I knew it only derived from the fact that I was light skinned and kept to myself. Judging a book by its cover made people miss out on the fact that I was born, raised and bred in one of the toughest neighborhoods in Atlanta. Just because I didn't wild out every second of the day didn't mean it wasn't in me.

"Look, Tanya, we're just trying to find out if Brendan is Dee's father," Jasmine said cutting in with her hand in the air. She sat Michelle on my lap and leaned forward a little bit, letting Tanya know she could act crazy too.

"Hell yeah that's his daddy! Look at them damn eyes and lips and tell me that ain't his son!" Both Jasmine and I looked over to Dee and stared at his features. I knew deep inside that . Tthis was Brendan's son. My only question, though, was did he *know* he was a father. Before I could finish asking the question, Tanya was already blowing up at me.

"What do you mean did he know? Was the nigga there when he went up in me raw? Was he in the damn delivery room when I pushed this mutherfucker out?" she said pointing towards Dee who stood back with his arms crossed and head down. He looked like he was in deep thought but I couldn't tell; Tanya kept talking.

"He had been sending us payments up until about five months ago and when I threatened to put his ass on child support that nigga just got ghost on us," she said with a hint of sadness in her voice.

I sighed and tried to hold back the tears I desperately wanted to let out.

"Can we see his birth certificate?" Jasmine asked as she patted my leg softly and continued with the interrogation.

"What the hell are y'all all up in *our* business for?" Tanya shot back with her eyebrows burrowed into her forehead. "Brendan, Ms. Pat, Terrence and everybody in their family knows about me and Dee and they don't even give us the time of day," she said rolling her eyes again and clutching the seat in anger.

Based on what I was seeing, I understood why no one wanted to be around Tanya. She was rude, loud, mean and just plain foul. I tried to catch my breath and keep my composure as I looked around the room for a distraction. My eyes met a picture of Dee as a baby. While Jasmine and Tanya talked amongst themselves, often getting close to a screaming match, I reached over and grabbed the picture. If the baby in the picture wasn't wearing Jordan tennis shoes and a small chunk chain, I would've sworn this was a picture of Brendan. My hands shook while I traced my hands up and down the picture.

"Look, if you won't show us the damn birth certificate then why should we believe this is even Brendan's kid?" Jasmine said forgetting Dee was in the room.

"And who the hell are you supposed to be? Why the hell do I need to prove anything to you and this trick?" she said nodding in my direction.

She and Jasmine stood up from their seats and stood nose to nose; ready to throw down. It took everything in Dee and me to get between the two of them and break it up.

"You don't know me, bitch!" Tanya yelled loudly as a man came rushing from the back of the house with a gun in his hand.

"Whatever, you doing all that talking, shake something!" Jasmine started to reply, just as I shoved her to shut up.

The man stood in the doorway wearing a wife-beater, a pair of boxers and a do-rag. I wasn't as scared of him as I was of the heat in his hands. All I had done was come down to see what the truth was and now I had a gun pointed at me.

"Put that down!" Dee said stepping in front of the ashy, dark skinned man with the confused look on his face. I could tell he had been sleep and our loud conversation probably frightened him.

"What the hell is going on in here?" he said, slowly bringing the gun down and staring at me and then Jasmine and the babies.

Jasmine's leg was tapping a mile a minute as she and Tanya stared at each other as if they were challenging each other to make a move.

"Go back to the room, man-man," Tanya said not taking her eyes off of Jasmine.

As soon as the man left, I threw both of my hands in the air and shut both of them up before they could even get anything out.

"This *is* Brendan's son, Jas; it's true."

"How do you know?" she said looking defeated.

"What do you mean how the hell she know? I just told your stupid ass he was the father." Tanya said plopping onto the couch with a sly grin.

"This *is* Brendan's son," I repeated as I ignored Tanya's comment.

"Look at this baby picture of Dee; it looks exactly like the one Ms. Pat has of Brendan," I said handing the photograph to Jasmine who looked at it with wide eyes.

I inhaled and quickly blew out the air. This was a lot to handle and as much as I wanted to take it all in, my head was swimming and I felt like I'd been hit with a sledgehammer. Saying "Brendan's son" out loud had more of an impact on me than I thought it would.

Before I could turn and tell Jas not to respond she was already in Tanya's face spewing off at the mouth.

"Looks like, you need to do a better job of being a mother; look at this pigsty and look at *you*. Dee would've been better off with his father than this mess," she said backing up as Tanya geared herself up for a reply.

"Brendan could've taken that motherfucker from me a long time ago, but he didn't want to. Hell, I'm still young and I don't need a fucking child holding me down. Ms. Pat was supposed to take Dee years ago but her flaky ass backed out on me. And if you think I'm such a pig then get your sorry ass outta my pigsty," she said sucking her teeth and opening the screen door to let us out.

Dee had already left the room and gone to the back of the house. I wanted to say goodbye to him but the last thing I wanted was for "man-man" to bring his crazy self back out with his gun in hand.

"And let me catch that ass out in the streets, it's over!" she said pointing to Jasmine.

Flicking her off with a polite bird, Jasmine loaded both of her children up in the car and then got in.

"I can't believe you just showed your ass like that. You know Lance is going to go off on you when those babies start talking like that."

My best friend was a *great* mother but her temper often got the best of her and when it did, every mothering trick she'd learned went out the door.

Just as I put my car in reverse, I saw Dee running out of the house flagging me down.

"Mystique...I nneeeed tooo ggggiiivvee yoooouuuu sssooommmething," he said as he pulled out a piece of paper and pen from his pocket and looked at me for my address.

Normally I would've shot Dee down, especially giving out my home address, but this *was* Brendan's son, wasn't it? I took his paper and pen and scribbled my address on it.

After he got my information and I pulled out of the driveway, Jasmine laid her head on the headrest and exhaled.

"Looks like we've opened up Pandora's Box."

They say when you open Pandora's Box, everything bad happens. I was wondering if I could handle anymore.

I've always been told that food is one of the best ways to cure heartache. With that in mind, I headed to the Whole Foods grocery store to pick up some food for dinner. I had invited everyone close to me, maybe as a means of keeping them within arms reach.

Pop didn't want me keeping so busy that I couldn't express my pain, but after I reassured him that I was dealing with things in my own way, he allowed me to have the dinner party.

I was making collard greens, yams, ribs, cornbread, potato salad, macaroni & cheese and a nice, moist red velvet cake to top everything off. Jasmine was bringing her legendary Peach Iced Tea and Kenya was stopping to get fresh rolls. I eventually picked up all the items I needed.

I stood in the baking aisle trying to figure out whether or not the new cocoa powder would be okay in my Red Velvet recipe. I glanced up and my eyes followed a figure that looked exactly like Brendan. It wasn't that he was dressed like him, resembled him or even kind of walked like him. This guy was Brendan, but how? I dropped the powder on the ground and pushed my buggy towards Brendan. I was behind him and everything about him was pointing towards it actually being Brendan. He walked like him, his head was shaped just like him, his skin tone was identical and he was dressed like him. This couldn't have been happening; I thought as I pinched myself, Brendan was alive! I started thinking of things I'd say to him when I snuck up on him and yelled, "Surprise!" I continued to follow him until he turned down the beer aisle and as I opened my mouth to call out his name, he turned to face me. It wasn't Brendan. When I blinked, it was like the man standing before me looked nothing like I thought. He was darker, bigger, and uglier and didn't have any of the qualities of Brendan. I sheepishly bowed my head and pretended I was picking up a bottle of Red Stripe beer and scooted my way out of the aisle to get the rest of my things.

After paying for and loading my bags of groceries in the car,

I sat with my head in my hands. Why was my mind playing such horrible tricks on me? It had convinced me that Brendan was alive and well, and shopping in Whole Foods grocery store. Go figure.

"Get yourself together," I said as I put the car in drive and turned on the radio.

I rode with the radio blasting, while my thoughts were in other places. So much was going on in my life that I hadn't even taken a moment to breathe. I hoped that I would be able to smile without putting on a front. I wanted so badly to pick up the phone and dial Brendan's number but I knew it would only cause me more emotional trauma.

I lugged each one of the bags into the house and began preparing the food for my guests. Normally I would let my collard greens soak overnight in turkey, but with a time crunch I did my best to work things out. Whenever I stress about anything, cooking or radio would always guarantee to get me out of my funk. But my situation with Brendan's death wasn't a funk; even cooking couldn't get my mind off of it. But, as usual, a friendly distraction came to take my mind off things.

"Yum. It smells good in here girl!" Kenya said walking through the kitchen door with a Publix grocery bag in one hand and her Balenciaga purse in the other.

It was true. The aroma in the kitchen was outstanding; after hours of slaving in front of the stove, I was ready to take a break.

"Whew!" I said taking the bag from her hand and sitting it on the kitchen table.

"Busy day?" Kenya asked raising one eyebrow. I'd purposely not invited Kenya to Dee's house because I figured the less people the better. Looking back, I wished she had gone instead of Jasmine.

"Yeah, I guess you can say that," I said massaging my neck with my eyes closed.

"How did everything go at Dee's house?" she asked standing up and taking my neck into her hands and applying pressure. I moaned a little bit before shutting my eyes and allowing Kenya, my multi-talented best friend, to do her thing.

"Stressful is all I can say," I managed to say while she moved her hands up and down my tense neck.

"What happened?"

"You know the usual with Jas. She got there and got in a screaming match with Dee's mother over whether or not Brendan was the father."

"What's new?" Kenya laughed lightly.

"And then Dee's mom's boyfriend came out with a gun in his hand after they were fighting," I said exhaling.

Kenya stopped. I opened my eyes and looked up at her face. "A gun?"

I gestured for Kenya to sit in the chair across from me; when she did I finished my story.

"So here I am trying to get some answers and this lunatic, looking like Bobby Brown on crack, comes out waving this gun," I laughed while Kenya stared at me in shock.

"It's okay, Kenya. We all made it out in one piece but Tanya did promise to rough Jasmine up if she saw her in the streets," I said chuckling.

Kenya chuckled, like I knew she would, and she put one of her hands on the table beside mine and looked into my eyes.

"Is it his son?"

"I think so. I really do," I said biting my lip and staring back at Kenya. By this time I had grown used to saying, "Brendan's son" and it flowed well. It hurt like hell knowing he had been keeping a secret like that from me, but I'd accepted it.

I think Kenya thought I was going to be a big ball of mess, which I was when no one was around, but at that moment I was okay. I was able to pretend, if only for that moment, that Brendan was in the next room and none of this was happening.

"How old is that boy? He looks a little old to be Brendan's son," Kenya said rubbing my hand sympathetically.

I had figured it all out while I stood over the hot stove with greens and potatoes boiling; it came like an epiphany.

Dee was thirteen years old, possibly turning fourteen that year, and Brendan was twenty-nine. That would've made him around the same age as his son was now when Tanya gave birth. Unbelievable but it didn't shock me.

Growing up, it seemed like everyone in our neighborhood was having babies before they could even drive. The first one of my classmates to get pregnant was a girl named Táchira; she was, even in the fifth grade, a fast little girl. She wasn't an especially pretty girl but she could dress her ass off and she knew it. She came to school almost daily with a new outfit and hairdo. She and Trey had been boyfriend and girlfriend during some of fourth and fifth grade and I often wondered what he saw in her. She was curvaceous as hell, had a raspy voice, was rude, had huge breasts and had the boy of my daydreams. In elementary school, the only drama that goes on is "who is going with whom" and Táchira's list of boyfriends read like an elementary celebrity list. On the first day of the sixth grade, I heard the teacher call her name but didn't see the fashionista anywhere in sight. Two weeks later when she finally showed up for class I noticed an eleven-year old Táchira sporting not only the latest duds but also a huge baby bump. She was pregnant. Our teachers tried to ask Táchira and her parents to cover her up but they saw nothing unnatural about the state their daughter was in and refused. I watched in awe one day, during gym, as the other little girls clamored around her and rubbed her stomach like she was the Queen of the pack. She was ahead of all of us, obviously, and Jasmine and I couldn't believe someone our age was about to be a mother. Some of the boys teased Trey, saying he was the father but I'd heard that it was an older boy in the neighborhood named Andy that had knocked Táchira up. Three months after the first day of school Táchira's best friend, Portia, came around telling everyone that Táchira had given birth to a baby girl. As exciting as it was, I still couldn't believe that at eleven years old, Táchira was now a mother. Táchira never did come back to school after having her daughter. Jasmine said she saw her about a year ago working at Pizza Hut in the Airport.

I broke out of my daydream and looked at Kenya who was waiting on an answer.

"Brendan would've gotten Tanya pregnant when they were about thirteen or fourteen. It is possible," I replied.

"How do you feel about it?" she inquired carefully.

"I mean...I feel like...I feel like he was keeping something from me. He obviously didn't want me to know about this son of his and it makes me wonder what else he was hiding," I said as I stood up and went to the stove to stir my pots.

"For thirteen years him and Ms. Pat have been paying her child support and doing what he's had to do as a father," I said shaking my head in disbelief.

"And you know what gets me? How no one knew Brendan had a son. How is that possible?" I asked not wanting any feedback.

I took a deep breath. I sensed a migraine coming on and calmed myself down.

"That's crazy," Kenya said looking off in a daze.

She looked pretty that day with her full, curly afro pulled back effortlessly at the top of her head. I put the tops back on the pots and exhaled. I knew Kenya didn't want to sit and talk, day in and day out about Brendan's death. It seemed to take a lot out of her, especially since she'd never known anyone close to her who had died.

Standing in front of my friend, I grinned. I wasn't sure where I would be, in the wild state of affairs, if she and Jas hadn't been there to provide me company. At times, though, I wished I could just crawl up to my bed and hide underneath the covers while crying. I wanted to feel sorry for myself; I mean, hell, I *had* lost my boyfriend. But they were keeping my spirits high and my distraction level even higher. I thought about what was going to happen after we all returned to our normal routines. It was those times I feared most.

"Don't you look cute?" I said pulling at Kenya's grey ruffled button down shirt.

She was wearing a fabulous pair of skin tight jeans and open toe stilettos. I looked at her and she giggled. She knew exactly why I was looking at her. We were about to have Sunday dinner and here she was looking like she was going to walk the red carpet.

"Shut up!" she said pushing me lightly. "I just wanted to get dressed up, that's all."

"Umm Hmm," I said narrowing my eyes as I studied her behavior.

I knew when she was lying and I knew when she was trying to hide something from me; that day her actions were telling me it was both.

Nervously, Kenya checked her phone and typed a couple of messages to someone before finally looking up at me. I had my hands on my hips, a grin on my face and I wanted answers.

"Fine! Pull it out of me, why don't you!" Kenya squealed excitedly.

I raised an eyebrow and listened in closely.

"Do you mind if I invite Lorenzo over for dinner?"

"Lorenzo who?" I asked, puzzled.

"Lorenzo Black, girl," she said rolling her eyes into the back of her head as she giddily laughed.

"Lorenzo Black?! Why would you be inviting him to dinner?"

"We've been talking every day since the club and he was saying this morning how he wanted some good, old fashioned, home cooked food," she said looking at me sympathetically, hoping for a yes. But I wasn't giving in that easily.

"So what? That's your boyfriend now?" I joked.

Kenya just blushed. I couldn't believe it. The one type of

man she vowed to stay away from had, somehow, turned my girl completely out.

"You've been holding out on me..." I said hitting her with the towel.

"He's a really good guy, Lauren. I *really* like him."

"So now you want to invite that man to my unfinished house to eat up all my food?" Kenya snapped out of her daydream and tilted her head to the side, like she was looking for a little compassion. I had to admit; the mere fact that Lorenzo had Kenya whipped was kind of frightening. Kenya was the one who didn't take much BS, which resulted in a number of guys getting the cold shoulder from her. For the longest time, Jasmine and I were thinking she'd never find someone who met her criteria, which was spoke proper English, dressed as well as she could, held at least a Bachelors degree and wanted kids. Of course, that was the tip of the iceberg; Kenya had other specifics that even I thought were crazy.

"It's fine with me, girl," I said shaking my head.

"Thank you!" she smiled as she jumped up from her seat and embraced me.

"Just be careful with him, you know how those actors are," I said. But Kenya wasn't listening to me; she was already on the phone with Lorenzo giving him directions to my house.

I didn't care about him being in my house, after all I wasn't phased by his fame, but I had been looking forward to relaxing with all my friends and family; he wasn't one of them.

I checked the clock and finished up some things in the kitchen. After giving Kenya instructions on how long to cook the rolls, along with what time dinner would be served, I scurried up the stairs to take a quick shower. Now that I knew someone else would be in the house, other than family and friends, I needed to make sure I looked decent. I knew Lorenzo had heard about Brendan because he was a regular at Brendan's shop. I wanted him to take a look at me and think I was doing okay, even though I wasn't. I wanted to look bold and fearless, but I knew that as soon as the clothes were stripped off I was back to being the shivering cold, scared, nervous and down right gloomy woman.

As I got in the shower I heard Pop downstairs talking to someone, Lorenzo I assumed. I pulled my hair into a ponytail on top of my head and I leaned into the warm shower water. I sighed with contentment as I lathered my body and noticed that extra weight was starting to show.

"Got to start exercising," I said.

The water fell in welcomed drops and trickled down my back and breasts and it felt alarmingly great; like no other shower I'd ever taken. I wanted to stay there and relax; as I closed my eyes I saw Brendan's face again.

"I love you baby!" I heard his voice say.

I jumped and flopped against the wall as I gripped the shower curtain for support.

I knew I looked crazy but as I turned off the water and sat motionless in the bathtub, I broke down again and thought about what Brendan's death was doing to me. I couldn't do anything without seeing his face, I couldn't talk without wanting to hear his voice and I couldn't think without wanting to know why. I crumpled in the tub and cried. It was when I was away from the distractions, the people and the laughter that I allowed myself to show my true feelings. When I couldn't hear anything else but Brendan's voice ringing in my head, telling me "I love you," I didn't fight it; I couldn't. So I just sat there. While I clung to the shower curtain, my naked, damp body laid out in my bathtub waiting for the strength to get up. I replayed memories of my relationship in my head; the good and bad times; and the more I cried the weaker I got.

I'm not sure how long I was lying in there, but when a knock at the door came it took everything in me to say: "Help." I couldn't move. It was like an out of body experience and I was standing over a shell of myself who was trying, extremely hard, not to break down. But the breakdown was inevitable.

My whisper for help wasn't heard and seconds later I heard footsteps leaving. I closed my eyes again and inhaled deeply, trying to get my energy together. If this person was going to hear me I needed to be louder.

"Help!" I managed to shout, though this time it wasn't much louder.

"Lauren, are you in there?" I heard Jasmine ask me from behind the door.

Before I could answer, Jasmine was swinging the door open and staring at my naked body in the tub. Immediately, she could tell something was wrong.

I didn't care about Jas seeing me naked, hell; she'd seen me nude plenty of times before and in more awkward situations. She rushed over to me and the look in her eyes told me she was scared.

"Lauren, what's wrong?!" she screamed loudly as she tugged at my arm, which flopped like a fish out of water.

All I could do to respond to her screams was turn my head to the side and look at her with a silent cry for aid.

"Let's get you up from here," she said finally realizing I wasn't going to be talking or moving on my own.

She lifted my body, and wrapped her arms around my waist. My limbs flailed wildly as she pulled me from the tub and onto the tile in the bathroom. I heard footsteps racing up the stairs and knew everyone had probably heard Jasmine's horrified screams and was trying to see what was wrong.

"Cccclose the door," I said breathing heavily. The last thing I needed was for Pop, Kenya and Lorenzo to run in on me with my ass in the air.

Jasmine did as she was told and as we lay on the floor she wrapped a towel over my body and rocked me slowly. Pop pounded on the door and was growing antsy, even after Jasmine told him I was okay.

After Jasmine shooed everyone from upstairs, I finally stood up and wobbled to my bed. Jasmine dressed me silently, not mentioning the breakdown she'd witnessed; I scurried under the covers comfortably.

"Are you okay?" Jasmine asked finally sitting on the side of my bed. I was sipping on some hot tea and, remarkably, I did feel a lot better; but I was not okay.

"He's *gone*," I sighed as I looked into the dark liquid. I couldn't cry anymore. They say when you're all cried out, you'll know and this much was true for me on that Sunday evening.

"I wish I could say I understand what you're going through, but I don't. But just know that regardless of anything, I'm here for you," Jasmine said rubbing my hand softly.

Jasmine was the closest thing to a mother I'd had since my mother's death. She'd been there when I got my period, and she showed me how to wear a pad and tampon. She was the first person I called when I lost my virginity to Brendan and when we had a pregnancy scare. She was the comforter I needed.

"Close your eyes and rest, I'll clear everyone out of the house," she said standing up.

I sat my tea on the nightstand and turned to Jasmine with my eyes widened.

"No. I slaved over that food for hours; hell, I'm coming down to eat," I said forcing a laugh.

Jasmine raised an eyebrow and cocked her head to the side. "Are you sure, girl? You need to rest," she said.

I nodded my head.

"Let me take a quick fifteen minute power nap and I'll throw something on and be down in a second," I said winking.

I knew Jasmine was worried about me, but I needed to socialize, I needed to laugh and I needed to smile; then, I reasoned, things would start to look up.

I woke up from my fifteen-minute nap and threw on a pretty red and white shirt with a pair of jeans and flip-flops. I felt refreshed as I applied a little bit of eye shadow to my lids. Standing back and checking myself, I knew I looked a mess but told myself I looked cute. My eyes had bags underneath them, my hair was a little frizzy and my face was breaking out around my mouth.

"Damn," I said rubbing one of the pimples that was appearing.

I headed downstairs, slowly, and was met with all the eyes in the house. Pop was the first to speak as he dropped his fork and walked towards me.

"Are you okay?" he whispered in my ear as we hugged. I looked up to him and shook my head before kissing his cheek.

"I'm fine, Pop," I said looking around the living room at the gathering of people who were looking at me with worried looks on their faces as well.

Kenya and Lorenzo were seated on one end of the long Mahogany table, while Jasmine, Lance and the babies were across from them. Pop pulled out my seat next to him and I looked next to my chair at another plate that was full of food but missing a person.

"Remind me to fix the..." I heard Trey said nonchalantly.

He looked fine as usual. My eyes met with his and I was drawn in, but before I knew it Jasmine was clearing her throat, snapping me out of my daydream.

"Sit down, Sugar Baby," Pop said pointing to the chair.

They'd already fixed me a plate and poured me some of Jasmine's iced tea, which I loved. I quietly glanced around the quiet table and smiled. It wasn't like I was psycho or losing my mind; I had simply loved and lost in a huge way.

It seemed as though, right when I sat down everyone grew silent; it was irking me. Trey, however, rubbed my leg and picked up the conversation.

"So, Lorenzo you were telling us about that project you're working on with Tyler Perry..."

Lorenzo smiled, exposing his perfect teeth and started talking about his new movie role. I pretty much kept my eyes on my food, often getting a tingling feeling inside as Trey brushed my arm or my leg accidentally.

"You know the last movie of his I saw was better than I thought it would be," Jasmine said with a mouthful of food.

Kenya and Lorenzo seemed to be really in tune with one another as they both leaned into each other and laughed.

'That's the same thing I was telling him last night," Kenya said poking Lorenzo's side.

"We interviewed him at the station," I said smiling widely, to my normal behavior.

"And he was saying how he's going to start focusing on television and stuff."

From then on everything was good. I was eating, I was socializing and I was distracted.

As people continued their side conversations, Trey looked over to me and grinned.

"What?" I asked turning up my nose.

"I hope it's okay that your dad invited me," he said wiping his mouth.

"No, it's cool. I mean, I wasn't expecting you but it's cool," I said nervously. The Lauren that was sick of Trey and aggravated by him was slowly disappearing. Trey made me nervous, now; an I-know-I-shouldn't-be-feeling-this-way type of nervous. I kept my eyes on Jasmine, who was watching Trey and I like hawks. I excused myself from the table and carried my plate into the kitchen sink. Trey followed me.

I stood over the sink and rinsed off the residue. Trey grabbed me by the waist and slid me out of the way. "Let me get that," he said winking.

I watched him clean the dishes and dry his hands with a paper towel.

"We need to talk," he said low enough for only me to hear. His head was tilted and I had mine hung down.

"I know," I said finally looking into his eyes.

He was so close I could smell the food on his breath; so close I could see exactly how many fillings he had. My mind started racing, as I finally brought my eyes to meet his. Immediately, I stepped back.

"Do you want to go outside?" he asked as he moved his hand closer to mine.

I shook my head and allowed him to hold my hand. Us touching shouldn't be a problem, right? When we got to the front door the doorbell rang, interrupting everything I had been thinking about. A startled Trey jumped and dropped my hand.

Standing in my doorway, shivering, with two backpacks on his back and a look of desperation, was my boyfriend's son, Dee.

Dee, Trey and I stood in our places for what seemed like ten minutes before he finally spoke up. I was pretty sure my face looked screwed up, so Dee made the first move.

"I wanted to bring you this, I'm leaving town," he said handing me an envelope.

"Wait, you're leaving? Where to?" I said bothered by the information.

Dee looked at Trey and then to me and put his head down in shame.

"IIIII cccaaan't live wittth them no more," he said breathing heavily. I could tell he was trying to be tough, but didn't know how to handle his emotions; very much like myself.

Staring into his eyes, I knew I needed to do my best to help this kid out. I watched him as he looked around my house in amazement.

"Tell me what's going on," I said as Dee put his bag down, by the front door and stood frozen.

"IIIII jjjjust gotta go," he said pointing to the envelope in my hand. "But I wanted you toooo hhhaaavvee that."

I'd remembered him handing it to me, but it didn't hit me that it was actually in my hands. I tore the envelope open and stared at the piece of paper. It was Dee's birth certificate, the original at that, with both Tanya and Brendan's signature. My heart sank as I felt my face get hot out of embarrassment. I wasn't angry at Dee, or even Tanya, I was mad at the man who was turning out to be a stranger. I scanned the certificate and learned Dee's real name was, DeAndre Brian Lewis. This *was* Brendan's son.

"Thank you for this," I said holding the paper up before stuffing it back in the envelope and handing it to Dee.

Dee held up his hands and blocked me from giving it back to him.

"You keep that," he said. "I've got a copy."

Pop, Trey, Kenya and Jasmine were crowded around us, staring at Brendan's little boy.

"I've got to go, the bus stops running in a little bit," he said checking the Sponge bob watch on his wrist.

I tugged on his jacket and looked at him deeply for some sort of answer to my earlier question.

"Where are you going?"

"I've got to get out of Atlanta," he said speaking like a grown man. I was impressed by Dee; although he was only thirteen he acted much older.

"What about your mom? You can't just leave her."

"You heard her, Mystique, ssshhhee don't even want me."

I couldn't even challenge what he was saying, his mom had made it perfectly clear that she didn't want him, and would be better off without him, but was she serious?

"All my life I've been hearing how I won't ever be sh... anything...and how I'm nothing and how she hates me; so I'm leaving."

"To go where?" I asked curiously.

"Anywhere is better than here," he replied picking up his bags and slinging it over his shoulder.

"Young man, why don't you come in and have something to eat, we've got plenty for you; maybe you can take some on the road," Pop said graciously.

Dee didn't hesitate. He piled food on top of his plate. I packed him a bag of food to take with him. I didn't know where he was going, but I felt like I needed to stop him. But what was I going to do? Who was I to step in? Yes, he was Brendan's son but was it my responsibility to intervene?

"That boy acts like he hasn't eaten in days," Jasmine said with Kenya close behind her.

"I bet he hasn't," I said putting the top on some Tupperware and putting it in a grocery bag for Dee.

"You saw the way that house looked," I replied to Jasmine.

"So you're really going to send him out there by his self?" Kenya said biting her nail fretfully. "He's just a baby."

She was watching Dee as he ate. All Kenya wanted was for everyone to get along, be happy and content. But this wasn't the Cosby Show, I reminded her, and life doesn't always end perfectly.

"What else am I supposed to do?" I asked not looking at her as I put two Powerade's in his bag.

Jasmine sucked her teeth and rolled her eyes.

"You want her to take that little bad ass into her house or

something, Kenya?"

I spun around and looked at Jasmine with disgust; how dare she say he was a bad ass? She didn't know anything about Dee and what he'd gone through in life. It wasn't like I did, either, but at least I wasn't judging.

"Chill out with that," I said sternly as Kenya blew Jasmine's comment off and went back into the living room to join Lorenzo.

After Dee had finished two plates, he gathered his belongings, said goodbye to everyone, and made his way out the door.

He turned around to hug me and as we embraced I gripped him tightly; I didn't want to let him go. Just like his father, this kid had some kind of hold on me.

I had already lost Brendan, and now that a piece of him was back in my life I didn't know if I was ready to lose that too. Dee definitely couldn't go back to living with his mother, that was a fact, but what was I going to do? Raise a thirteen year old? I could barely wake up on time, how could I be responsible for someone else?

"You make sure you call me when you get to wherever you're going," I said as I let him go and watched him back up.

"I'll do that," Dee said waving at everyone as he walked down the driveway.

I followed him as far as my eyes could see and soon I couldn't spot him anymore.

I closed the front door and stood with my back to it. I felt bad, like I'd done the wrong thing, and in the pit of my stomach I knew my conscience was right. Dee was a bright kid, with a bright future and I needed to step in and be the parent he never had. I had to do this, not only for him, but for Brendan. I was, in essence, righting Brendan's wrongs.

I raced upstairs, grabbed my keys off the nightstand and ran out the door while everyone watched me with their mouths open.

I found Dee sitting on the bus stop with all of his bags surrounding him.

"Hey, get in," I said as Dee's eye lit up with excitement; I watched him as he rushed towards my car and got in.

"You're going to stay with me until we get things straightened out, okay?" I said not leaving him room to answer. "But we've got to get some things straight; we will have order, it *is* my house and you will listen to me."

Dee leaped forward and wrapped his arms around my neck; I felt good.

"I swear I will," he said excitedly. "I'll do whatever you say."

When the two of us walked back into the house, me carrying one bag in my hand and Dee carrying the other two, I could tell by the look on some of their faces that they were astonished at my decision. I showed Dee the guest room and told him to get himself a shower and join us downstairs for a movie.

"Are you sure you want to do this? Are you ready for this?" Jasmine said rushing up to me as Pop and Kenya smiled on in approval.

"I might not be ready but it's what I'm doing," I said

I knew she didn't agree with me taking Dee in and I knew she didn't see my reasoning behind it, but I didn't care. Whatever I needed to do to help Dee out, I was going to do.

CHAPTER 8

Dear Diary-

I don't think I've been up this early since I was an undergrad and had those 7 am classes. Yuck. I had to get up this morning and drive Dee to his school on the other side of town. Being that I sleep in on most mornings (every morning!); I'd forgotten how bad the AM traffic was. We didn't get him to school until close to 9:30. So, let's just say I'm already bad at this parenting thing. I signed Dee in and came back home to catch a couple more hours of sleep. I've asked Trey if he can keep an eye on Dee when he gets home from school, since he'll be working on the house anyway. Pissed wouldn't even be the word to describe how I feel when I glance at the pictures of Brendan and myself that once made me tingle. If I could only talk to him, I would probably scream till I didn't have a voice and then I'd kiss him until my lips hurt. I miss him so much. But I figure the busier I am, the less time I'll have to think about this. I'm supposed to meet with Ralph this morning to discuss some of the things he found out. Lenny made a smart comment about me using the company conference room for personal use so I'll try to do everything here. And then there's the question of Trey. Jasmine gave me an earful last night when everyone left. She kept asking me over and over what I think I'm doing with Trey so soon after Brendan's death. I wish I had an answer for her but I don't. It's not like I'm planning to say "Oh forget Brendan! I hate him!" It's just when I look into Trey's eyes there's something that's slowly pulling me in. Last night Trey asked me out on a date and when I hesitated he told me to think about it. I don't know, though, that does look a little off, right? Every time I look at Trey it's like I feel Brendan right over my shoulder; it feels wrong. Well, I need to get showered and dressed to meet Ralph in a half hour. I'm not sure I'm looking forward to this meeting, though. What did he find out? The suspense is killing me.

TTYL!

Lauren Washington

As I showered, I thought about my journal entry and decided now wasn't the time for me to start getting involved with anyone; if Trey wanted me that badly, as his touches and body language suggested, he'd wait, right? But the question was: how long should he *have* to wait? I was a big ball of confusion and I really didn't know which way I should be going. On one hand I wasn't ready to let go of my relationship with Brendan, even though he was dead; on the other hand I didn't want to live in the past. I had time to decide,I thought, as I stepped out of the shower and ran to my room to get dressed.

"Skeeter! Someone's here for you!" I heard Trey yell from downstairs. I hung my head over the railing.

"Can you stop yelling in my house? Tell Ralph I'll be right down," I said shaking my head as I wrapped the towel tighter around my body. Trey winked his eye and chuckled before heading into the living room where I could see Ralph's feet at the table.

I threw on a pair of jeans and a t-shirt. I pulled my hair back into a loose bun and lotioned my body before darting down the steps.

"I'm *so* sorry, Ralph," I said extending my hand and shaking his graciously.

"Would you like anything to drink?" I asked raising an eyebrow. I needed to be as nice as I possibly could to the man who, possibly, held the answer to my mother's death.

"I'm okay," Ralph smiled.

I took a seat across from him, clasped my hands together and sighed as I prepared myself for the worst. Maybe it was just as simple as a hit and run and the person just got scared and left, I thought. But no, someone had shot my mother.

"First let me say I'm sorry about your boyfriend's su..." he said starting to say.

"Thank you," I said cutting him off. I was here to handle one tragedy and he was throwing me off with the other one.

"Now, about what you found," I continued clearing my throat.

Taking my cue, Ralph opened a folder and placed it in front of me to see. I couldn't make out, what I was seeing but it looked like portions of police reports.

"I don't understand," I said looking up at him perplexed.

"It seems that between November 1988 and July 1989, there were about fifteen domestic abuse police reports filed by your mother," Ralph said as my eyes shot open. *Domestic abuse* reports? I'd never even seen my father yell at my mother, let alone put his hands on her.

"What does this mean?" I asked wanting to cry. This couldn't be a good sign and I knew it.

"Well, when I went in to pull the files for the reports, all of them were gone," Ralph said sucking his teeth. "So, I'll have to dig a little deeper on that one." He moved the stack of papers out of my way and dug in his bag for more folders and papers.

"Domestic abuse? I don't understand."

"Why don't you talk with your father and find out as much as you can about any arguments he and your mother might have had. Nine times out of ten, the reports would've been filed regarding a significant other."

My head starting hurting as I thought about what Pop could've known about these reports and how they tied into mom's death.

"And you think these reports have something to do with her murder?" I inquired as Ralph shifted his lips from left to right.

"They could. I just found it really unusual that *all* of the reports are gone."

I agreed with him, if mom had filed fifteen domestic abuse reports against Pop and they were all missing, what could my father possibly have been hiding? I tried to focus on the rest of the information Ralph was giving me, but I kept thinking back to all the times Pop had begged and pleaded with me not to get a private detective and I wondered, had he been trying to keep me from finding all of this out?

"Now, do you remember I told you I spoke with a local man who said he was there the night your mom was killed?" Ralph said in his thick Hispanic accent.

I nodded and took a deep breath.

"It turns out he saw something but not everything," Ralph said pulling out a piece of paper.

"It seems like he saw your mother and her killer arguing loudly with one another. He said your mother was apologizing profusely and the next thing he knew he heard gun shots."

I covered my face as I tried not to visualize my mother being shot, but it was useless.

"So she knew her killer?" I asked pulling my head up at the realization.

"More than likely," Ralph said as he adjusted his reading glasses. "He didn't report anything because he was high that night and wasn't sure who'd believe him."

I listened closely with a kid-like stare. I wanted to run away and forget about anything I'd ever wondered about mom's death. It all was becoming more than I'd imagined.

"He says it was a late 80s model, brown, tan or black Chevy."

I exhaled loudly. I knew Pop wasn't capable of doing any type of harm to his wife, but my Uncle Rico, my father's brother, did have a dark brown '88 Chevy throughout my childhood. I hoped and prayed that my assumptions were way off; that Pop had a good explanation for all the coincidences.

"I'm going to talk to a couple more people and find out some things and I'll call you when I have something new," he said to me as I stared off into the kitchen.

I thanked him for his help and made my way to the TV room to take a break. I tried to process everything but I was on information overload. Mom knew her killer, she was arguing with the person and she'd even filed some domestic abuse reports. Why hadn't the police been able to uncover *any* of this? My blood was boiling, my mind was racing and tears were slowly trickling down my cheeks when Trey walked in.

"Skeeter do you know where..."Trey started before seeing me.

I was balled up on the couch and wasn't paying attention to anything he was saying. I was a mess. I had done a really good job of keeping myself together when Trey was around, but with him and his workers mulling around my house, I had no choice but to let it out.

"Are you...are you okay, Lauren?" Trey asked.. I glanced up at him and saw the look of concern on his face and I returned my head to my hands and wept silently.

Trey took a seat on the couch and placed an arm around my shoulders and pulled me into a bear hug. I didn't resist, as I cried into his chest.

"It's okay," he said over and over as I thought about mom, Brendan and Pop. Why was I the last to find out everything?

The two of us sat intertwined on the couch in each other's arms. I couldn't let go of him and yet, I couldn't shake the feeling that he was Brendan. He was comforting me the way Brendan always had; he was holding me the way that Brendan did, and he was staring deeply into my eyes the way that Brendan used to.

"I'm sorry," I said finally realizing I was crying on the shoulder of the man I should have been avoiding.

I wiped my eyes and pulled away from him in a hurry. I didn't need Trey getting the wrong idea about our closeness.

"Why are you apologizing? Are you okay?" Trey said allowing me to pull away from him.

He looked like he wanted to say something to comfort me, but as I stood up and continued wiping my face, I saw he was struggling.

"I'm okay," I repeated.

It didn't work and as I straightened my clothes and pushed some pieces of my hair behind my ear, he was still sitting in the same spot staring at me.

"Are you sure you're okay?" he asked again, further agitating me. I couldn't understand why he wasn't getting the hint that I wanted to be left alone. Sure, I looked a mess and I'd just cried in his arms but didn't he realize that I was over it?

"I *said* I was okay, Trey," I replied rolling my eyes and as I crossed my arms across my chest.

He stood up and approached me and, as I saw his hand coming closer to my shoulder, I pulled back.

"What's the matter with you?"

"Nothing."

"Okay, so *nothing* makes you act crazy, then," Trey said laughing at his own joke; I didn't smile.

"Okay, well I guess I'll just get back to my work," Trey said uncomfortably.

His touch turned me on. I had never gone longer than two weeks without sex maybe it was the sweat that was building up on Trey's beautifully sculpted biceps. Either way, I wasn't going to let him know I was horny because of him. I turned around to watch him walk away and caught him staring at me.

"What?" I asked with plenty of attitude in my voice.

"I was just wondering if you had a chance to think about me taking you out; I really think it'd be good for you," Trey said fidgeting with his tool belt.

I sucked my teeth and rolled my neck as I tried, to push Trey away. He was one complication I didn't need.

"It's too soon and it just feels *weird*," I lied knowing that being with Trey gave me a sense of normalcy and calmness. I wasn't supposed to like or lust after someone else so quickly after Brendan's death, was I? My heart still ached to feel his hands around my waist and his breath upon my neck, but here I was yearning for something from Trey.

Trey nodded like he understood and was okay with my decision, but I could tell he was a little disappointed. His shoulders slumped and he exhaled before turning to walk away.

I laid my head on the wall and blew out some air. It was already shaping up to be one of *those* weeks.

When I left for work, Dee had just gotten home and was about to do his homework. Pop was working late. I'd left him a message telling him there were some things that Ralph told me about mom's death that I needed him to clarify. I waited as long as I could before I had to leave for work and still no Pop. He was normally pretty good with getting home everyday at the same time, but today was different and that made me nervous. I wondered if he knew more than he was letting on. After I made sure dinner was ready for Dee and Pop, I made my way to the radio station. My show started in less than an hour and I was in no way prepared for my entertainment news. I rushed in, quickly looked up some news and made my way to the studio with less than five minutes to spare. This was the first time I had ever cut it so close. When my producer, Dave, looked up from his clip board, I could tell the news would make it to Lenny.

"Sorry I'm late," I said plugging my headphones into the board and starting my intro.

I barely skated by. My entertainment news was just enough to get me through but I knew I couldn't afford anymore close calls.

And just as I suspected, Lenny was on the office phone before I had a chance to log off my computer and leave for the night.

"Dave told me about your tardiness. Consider this your first warning. Don't let it happen again," Lenny said.

"Right," I replied hastily. Damn that Dave; he had already sold me out. I checked my watch and yawned; I was tired.

I stopped by McDonald's and picked up a burger and fries and headed home. I thought about my hectic schedule for the upcoming week and was, weirdly happy about the recent chaotic events. Later in the week I was hosting a fashion show for one of the upscale black modeling troupes in Atlanta, and on Friday and Saturday I had club appearances to make. I hoped that Dee could adjust to my fast life and, even more, that I could adjust to having him there.

When I got home Pop was fast asleep on the couch with the television watching him. I kissed his forehead. I watched as he breathed. I knew this man well, almost too well. He had dried almost every tear I'd cried since I was nine until I met Brendan. He was there for every big event in my life and he seemed to feel my pain. But with all the new information surfacing, I needed to find out everything I didn't know about Pop.

I cleaned up the kitchen, put away some dishes and started a load of laundry before I stuck my head in on Dee. I saw the flicker of the television hitting the tan and blue twin comforter. I didn't see the head or the body of the little boy I was looking for.

"Dee?" I said quietly, hoping he was playing hide and seek with me. I knew he was too old for that game but I wanted to believe he could still be playing.

I pulled the covers back and was met with rustled bed sheets. It looked like he had been there, but was now gone.

I briskly walked throughout the halls of my house calling Dee's name and as I reached the living room where Pop was, I turned and faced him.

"Have you see Dee?" I said wiping sweat from my brow.

Pop ran his hands over his hair and exhaled.

"Nope. He was here when I fell asleep."

My hands began to shake as I felt for something to hold me up. I had only been Dee's guardian for a day and had "lost" him. I sucked at being a parent. It was almost one in the morning; where in the hell could he be? Pop and I got in my car and drove the streets of Bankhead, trying to think of somewhere that a thirteen year old would go. I was praying that he would show up. I tried to think of a way I was going to explain this to the police.

"Yes, I lost my dead boyfriend's son."

I racked my brain for friends he might have in Bankhead but I kept drawing a blank.

"Where is this boy?" Pop said extending his neck out the window and looking around. The city was far from dead but there weren't many people walking up and down the streets. Some of the dope boys were making their rounds on the corner and as a black Chevy slowed down to make an exchange; I remembered what Ralph told me. There was dampness on the streets and a peaceful silence that accompanied my two party search.

"Pop, I talked to the private detective today about mom's death."

I had to find the appropriate way to introduce the information to Pop; I didn't want to come off like I was already accusing him of something.

"Yeah..." Pop said nonchalantly as he continued looking away from me.

"And, well, he said...something about some domestic abuse reports that were missing," I blurted out. He shook his head from side to side.

"Your mother filed some reports, Lauren, but it wasn't anything."

What did he mean it wasn't "anything"? This was news to me, after eighteen years of wondering, and now Pop was admitting that there had been some abuse in their relationship?

"So...she filed them against you?" I asked for clarification.

Pop shook his head.

"This is something you'll never understand."

I must've looked crazy because even though he was stuttering and looking nervous, Pop continued.

"We weren't perfect but we loved each other," he managed to say as he ran his hand up and down the seatbelt. "We both made a lot of mistakes and don't think I don't regret some of them."

It was the first time I had ever seen fear and guilt on my father's face.

"You...you *beat* mom?" I said struggling to say the words. Growing up I didn't receive beatings like all my other friends, Pop didn't think it was the right way to discipline; so that's why it perplexed me that he could've hurt my mother.

My father's eyes shot towards me and I swore I saw flames spitting from them. Immediately I knew he was hurt by my finger pointing. Before I could apologize he was changing the subject.

"Did you check with Trey to see if he'd seen Dee?" he asked coldly.

I wanted to reach out and touch Pop's face and apologize, but I knew what had been done was already set in stone; I couldn't take it back. I slowed the car down and looked over at Pop.

"Did you have something to do with mom's death?"

Pop didn't reply, he just posed his question again.

"I asked you if checked with Trey about Dee?"

I pulled out my cell phone and Trey's card and called him.

"Hello?" Trey said groggily. I could tell he had been asleep but I pushed on with my questions.

"Hey, Trey. It's Lauren. Have you seen Dee? He's missing," I said blowing through my questions.

Trey sounded like he was trying to catch his breath and scrambling. "Oh damn. What time is it?"

"It's almost two in the morning," I said checking my watch. I was panicking as Trey yawned in my ear.

"I'm sorry, Lauren, he's over here at my house," Trey said "I was going to have him back before you got home but we fell asleep."

I rolled my eyes and blew out air angrily. Who the hell did Trey think he was taking Dee to his house? It was one thing for him to invade my privacy, but now he was crossing the line. After I got directions to Trey's house, I told him I'd be right over there.

"What right does he think he has to just *up* and take him?" I said to myself in the car as Pop stared out of the window, visibly more relaxed.

"Calm yourself down, Lauren; the man was doing you a favor by watching that little boy," Pop reminded me.

It was one of the few times when he called me Lauren, where his tone alone made me realize that he wasn't in the mood for my bitching and complaining.

"I guess so," I said turning the volume up in the car.

When we arrived at Trey's house I couldn't believe what I was seeing. Trey was doing well, I mean really, really well. His traditional, yet contemporary, brick home was two stories and had the cutest wrap around driveway with a three-car garage. His lawn looked like those from a gardening magazine; I was impressed. I knew Kenya told me he was doing it big, but I didn't know it was that big.

When I got to the front door I was fuming. I spent twenty minutes thinking about what I was going to say to Trey but when the door opened and I saw him wearing an undershirt and sweat pants, I lost my train of thought. Before I could yell or scream I saw Dee wiping his eyes sleepily.

"Get in the car, Dee. Pop is in there."

With my arms crossed, I watched as Dee did just as I said.

"See you later, man," Trey said to Dee.

"What the hell were you thinking?" I said irritably. "Do you know how worried we were?"

"I'm sorry. Dee and I were talking about him wanting to be a rapper and I told him I had some old school rap tapes I thought he should listen to," Trey said.

"We were just supposed to run in and out; get the tapes. But we started watching television and we both fell asleep."

"Anything could've happened to him," I countered.

Trey continued to apologize as I looked up and down his sculpted body; I was listening but not closely.

"Come inside for just a second," he pleaded. I wanted to say no but my legs said yes.

"Pop is in the car and I really need to get Dee home."

"It'll just be a second," Trey responded as he grabbed my hand and led me into the foyer.

If I thought the outside of Trey's house was impressive, the inside was a designer's dream. Hardwood floors, glass tables, beautiful elegant carpet, granite countertops and a beautiful spacious layout. Trey-trey had come a long way from Bankhead.

"This is beautiful," I said looking up at the high ceiling.

"Thanks. I hope I can do something like this to your crib," he said softly.

As soon as he blew air in my ear, my entire body got chills; I was putty. I couldn't move, I couldn't speak and I couldn't decipher what was going on. All I knew was that this felt amazing.

"I...I should be going," I said snapping out of my momentary fit of insanity. Jasmine and Brendan's faces popped into my head as I imagined Trey undressing me.

"I'm really sorry, again. Hopefully you'll let me make it up to you?" Trey said slyly.

I grinned at his humor and quickly retreated to the door. As much as I liked the layout and beauty of Trey's home, I knew I didn't belong there. I was a Bankhead girl, with Bankhead tendencies and simple Bankhead desires. I had more but I didn't feel the need to branch out beyond what I knew and was comfortable with.

Trey stood on his doorstep and looked at me. It was strange to me the timing of his return into my life and as I looked in the backseat at Dee sleeping soundly, I exhaled.

I knew Pop was still livid with me but was covering it up well.

"This here is a nice house," he said admiring the house from the car.

"Yeah, Pop, maybe one day you'll let me buy you one like this," I joked, knowing my father didn't want to be anywhere but Bankhead.

"No, not me; this is your life," he joked as he reclined his seat and closed his eyes.

I pondered things on the way homes. I missed Brendan so much I couldn't think or see straight; yet I felt something strong for Trey. I had devoted every waking moment to Brendan and his pleasure; now it was time for me to figure out what *I* liked and needed. It wasn't going to be easy.

CHAPTER 9

Dear Diary-

It's been a couple of days and things still aren't back to normal; at least in my eyes they aren't. I still wake up in the morning waiting for Brendan's call. I still sit at my desk, hoping that flowers will come my way; but they never do. I woke up last night with tears streaming down my face; I didn't even know I had been crying. I've been trying to get in touch with Ms. Pat to find out everything I can about Dee and Tanya. How could she not tell me that he had a son? Better yet how could Brendan, the man I thought loved me, fail to tell me something so major? It makes me want to say forget him and forget everything I ever thought we were but I can't. My heart won't let me forget and my mind has a tendency to hold on to good memories despite the bad.

Ever since I asked Pop about the domestic abuse reports, he's been acting strangely. I've apologized in more ways than one and still nothing. I don't know what to do other than hope he comes around.

Dee is transitioning well, I believe. He has a girlfriend, and from what Trey tells me, she's a nice little girl. I completed one of my hosting gigs last night and it was pretty cool. Big Boi came out to show his support. I love my ATL-iens! Anyway, this morning I'm taking Dee down to the barbershop so we can cut off that wild hair that's been growing! Plus I need to find out from Michael, the assistant manager, if he remembers anything about the week Brendan died. Maybe he has some answers. I sure hope so because all of this is running me ragged.

I've got to jet.

TTYL

Lauren Washington

I've never been a frequenter of "Cutterz" salon, not because it wasn't the best barbershop/salon in Atlanta, but because I'm so picky about the people I let touch my hair. Since we met, Kenya has been the only person that's been my regular hairstylist and I'm more than happy to keep it that way. Brendan prided himself on that salon, too.

"I don't want to cut my hair," Dee whined as we got in the front seat of the car and buckled in. I glanced over at him sternly. Whining wasn't going to get him out of a trip to the barber.

I didn't let Mike know I was coming but I figured he'd be cool with seeing me. It was the first time I had stepped in there since Brendan died. I wasn't looking forward to seeing Brendan's chair, or seeing the front desk where he would take care of business and I definitely wasn't looking forward to the empty parking spot marked "Owner only.".

It had actually been a couple of months since I had been able to make it down to the shop and the visit felt long overdue.

"I want you to see, first-hand, the blood, sweat and tears your father put into this barbershop and salon, okay?" I said not wanting a reply from Dee who rolled his eyes and sat back in the seat with his hands across his chest.

I knew he was sick of me forcing lectures on him but he needed it. He needed to know that deep down, although he had only seen one side, his father was a good man with a good heart.

I had tried to give Tanya a call a couple of times throughout the week, just to let her know that Dee was okay but the phone was cut off, after our last visit I definitely wasn't going anywhere near her house.

As I pulled up to the business, I noticed a big grey Chevy Suburban parked in Brendan's usual spot.

"*That's strange,*" I thought as Dee and I got out of the car and headed towards the door.

When my foot hit the black and white tiled floor of "Cutterz", all eyes were on me. It was like everyone was waiting on me to show up. Some of the girls gathered in a corner and whispered amongst themselves while the guys all gave me their "wassup" nods. It wasn't the welcome I had been hoping for but I hoped after seeing Michael that things would pan out.

"Hey!" I said when Michael came from the back of the shop with two cardboard boxes in his hands. He looked shocked to see me. I could tell something was different about him.

"Hey there," he said finally. He put the boxes down and hugged me.

Everyone else fell in line to share their condolences. I smiled bravely as I pointed out Brendan's son; everyone gasped at the resemblance the two shared.

"I didn't even know he had a son," Michael said rubbing his goatee

"Join the club," I said low enough that Dee couldn't hear.

I could tell by looking at Dee that he was relishing in the attention he was getting from being the "boss man's" son. A grin came over his adorable face that I hadn't seen up until that time.

"What can I do for you today?" Michael said looking Dee and I over again before sitting in his seat.

"We need a haircut," I said sarcastically as I pointed to the pile of mangled hair atop Dee's dome.

"You sure do," Michael joked as he went and checked the stylist's calendars.

"Looks like everyone is booked but my appointment is late so I can cut him," he said pulling out his black cape and showing Dee where to sit.

On Saturdays barber and beauty shops were like a totally different world. While the smell of hot curling irons, "Pump it Up" hairspray and barbeque floated around the shop, the loud sounds of laughter and clippers rang out. There was something about the togetherness amongst the people in the shop that felt so comfortable. I could remember sitting in the beauty salon with my mother as a child and loving the elegant women and their stories that *made* the beauty salon what it was. On any give Saturday you could get finger-licking barbeque delivered to you, while also grabbing the newest bootleg mix CD. It was like a mini-flea market that came to you.

People were moving around the shop with urgency as they tended to their clients and walk-ins. I watched with a grin on my face, slightly proud of the Brendan's legacy.

I took a seat in the lounge and picked up an old copy of Ebony magazine and flipped a couple of pages before getting bored and putting it down. It was amazing all the changes they had made in the two weeks since Brendan's death. Gone were the Coke machines. Complimentary beverages were now served to all clients. The tacky music that used to play loudly was gone and replaced with an overhead system blasting out some of the best old school hip-hop and R&B I'd ever heard.

It seemed like an hour passed before Dee was ready. When he stood in front of me with his fresh low haircut I saw Brendan. My eyes filled with tears and as he rushed to my side, I wiped them away.

"Are you okay?" Dee asked concerned.

"I'm fine, honey," I said catching my breath "I'm fine."

Michael came over and hugged me again before sending me away with a free haircut; but he didn't know I'd come for more than that.

"Mike, can we talk in the back for a second?"

When I got to the back office, where Brendan and I had made love so many times I lost count, it felt strange; like an entirely new place.

"What's going on?" Mike said casually as he cleared the desk of a couple of papers and motioned for me to sit down.

"It's about Brendan," I started as I closed my eyes. "I just don't understand why he ki...why he did it."

Mike watched me with little emotion and blinked a couple of times as I continued.

"Was he acting strange the week of his death?" I inquired hoping I wouldn't have to say anymore.

He seemed deep in thought.

"I couldn't say."

"What do you mean, you *couldn't* say?"

"Just what I said, Lauren, I don't know what state B was in when he did that shit," he said angrily. Mike was a relatively calm guy with an emotionless face, droopy eyes and the business sense that few college graduates had; I understood why Brendan had chosen him as the assistant manager.

I took my time before responding; I looked around the room at the plaques and trophies on the walls.

"The last time you saw him, what did he say; how as he feeling?" I asked

Mike looked at his desk and ran his hands through his bushy, thick afro and moaned loudly. It was like it was paining him to fill me in on the little things I needed to know.

"The last time I saw him was about four months ago," he said inhaling and holding his breath. He was looking at my reaction; trying to gauge how far he'd have to go.

"*Four* months?!" I screamed loudly before catching myself. "What the hell are you talking about? Brendan's only been dead two weeks," I reminded him.

"I don't think I should be the one to break this news to you like this."

"What news? What are you talking about?" I said leaning forward. I could feel it in my veins and in my heart; another secret.

"Look, you need to talk to his mother or something; not me. It's not my place," Mike said firmly. I refused to leave. I was fed up with crying and feeling sorry for myself; someone was going to tell me the truth, even if I had to drag it out of them.

"No, Mike, you're going to tell me *exactly* what the hell is going on!" I said grabbing him by the shoulder.

"How could you have seen Brendan four months ago? This *is* his shop and you *do* work here, right?" I said putting my hands on my hips.

He turned around and looked into my eyes, those same eyes that were pleading for an answer, and shook his head.

"B sold me the shop about five months ago," he said dropping his shoulders.

My mouth dropped open as I continued listening.

"I was letting him cut hair here, though, but he hadn't been here in like four months."

"W-what?" I stuttered.

"He said he wasn't going to tell you because you'd just try to talk him out of it. But then I heard he got involved with Quito and...he stopped coming in."

As I stood motionless in the office, I could feel my breakfast coming up so I ran to the restroom with my hand over my mouth. Luckily, though, nothing came out.

I sat on the cold tiled bathroom floor and I gripped the toilet tightly with my hands. How in the hell could all of this have been happening right underneath my nose?

Brendan had kept his child from me, and the sale of his shop, his most prized possession. And as soon as I heard the name Quito, my skin crawled. Quito, or Marquise Jonsen, was one of Brendan's friends who rubbed me the wrong way. He didn't have a job, had plenty of trashy women around him, lived deep in the hood, yet he sported the latest fashions and the hottest rides. It didn't take a genius to know what Quito did for a living. Knowing that Brendan had been involved with Quito and his low-life thugs made my head and stomach hurt. Who had I loved? Who was Brendan? And most of all where had the man I knew gone?

I hung my head over the toilet bowl and sobbed silently. My heart was thumping uncontrollably and I was sweating. All the times Brendan called me and said he was at the shop, had been a lie. When I'd offer to come by and bring him lunch, he'd quickly rush me off the phone. It had all been a lie. *One big lie.*

I straightened up and flushed the toilet. As I was leaving, I ran into the mystery woman from the club and Brendan's funeral. I knew it was her by the look she gave me when our eyes met. Her hair was still in a short, texturized do, and I could see a little pouch sticking out of the t-shirt she was wearing. She was short, too, really short and had dimples that I could see, even though she wasn't smiling. She spun around after she saw my face.

"What's your name?" I said forcefully with tears staining my cheeks.

"Brandy," she said nervously. She was a cute girl but because of the situation, I hated her. She had come in between me and my man and for that, she was on my bad list.

"I'm sure you already know who I am," I said rolling my eyes.

Brandy shook her head while she dried off her hands and looked at me.

"Look, I'm not looking for trouble," she said reaching for the doorknob of the bathroom.

I blocked her hand and stood with my hands on my hips.

"You're going to tell me everything," I said

Brandy looked like she was about to pee all over herself. I could understand her fear. "How did you know Brendan?"

"We met here. He hired me to work at the shop as a shampooer about two and a half years ago," she revealed. I racked my brain; why hadn't I ever seen this girl before?

"Uh huh," I said signaling with my hands for her to continue. I knew there was more and I knew she was holding out on me.

"And..." she said looking at the ceiling as she tried to keep the tears from falling. I felt bad for the girl but not bad enough to stop the interrogation.

"Were you sleeping with my boyfriend?" I asked bluntly, not expecting an honest reply.

"Yes."

Brandy looked at me defiantly; she wasn't backing down. As I recovered from the blow my heart was dealt I gasped for air.

"We started fooling around about two years ago; I swear I didn't know he was with you, but by the time I found out I was already in love with him," she said

It felt like someone picked me up, pulled my hair and slammed me into a concrete wall. As I listened in I felt everything in front of me spinning. How could Brendan have been cheating on me? What wasn't I giving him that he felt the need to go out and get elsewhere? My eyes filled with more tears as I fought to hold everything in; I bit my bottom lip.

I held up one hand for her to stop and took a deep breath before responding.

"You were...in love with him?"

"*We* were in love," she corrected. "He loved me too."

I felt like I couldn't breathe, like someone was literally knocking the wind out of me. Maybe this little girl had Brendan confused with someone else, I silently prayed.

"I've been with Brendan for eight years. Did you know that?" I asked curiously.

For some odd reason I couldn't cry. I wanted to scream, but I couldn't cry. I was more pissed off than anything.

I felt like I was on an episode of Maury Povich and someone was about to come out and tell me some outrageous, drama-filled secret. It felt that surreal, and as I listened to Brandy talking, my eyes met with an unusual shine on her left hand.

"What's this?" I asked annoyed.

"My engagement ring," she said smiling widely. "Brendan proposed right after he sold the shop."

I stumbled backwards against one of the stall doors and clutched my stomach in my hands.

Brandy reached out, kindly, to help me stand. I smacked her hand away and covered my head in my hands in embarrassment. Now I knew why everyone was so shocked to see me in the place where Brendan and his mistress had decided to call home. I wailed loudly, partially in physical pain and partially because I was emotionally wounded. I stared up at Brandy who had tears in her eyes as well.

"What the hell is going on?" I screamed.

I tried to think back to a time when Brendan and I weren't happy. He always told me he loved me and his moans were always genuine during love-making. I slumped to the ground and ran my hands through my hair. I wrapped my arms around my body and sat on the ground rocking slowly. Brandy joined me and it looked like she wasn't going anywhere. I brought my knees into my chest and laid my head down on them.

"I *loved* that man and he did *this* to me," I said pointing to her. I wasn't trying to be rude but it was definitely a hell of a way to find out that the man I'd been committed to had loved and lived for someone else. My heart ached as Brandy rested her hand on my shoulder.

"I'm sorry. I told Brendan a long time ago that he needed

to straighten things out," she said softly. I wanted to hate her and I wanted to hit her but it wouldn't do anything. She was still sporting the rock I'd dreamed about.

Brendan had obviously loved her a little bit more than me, I thought as the canary yellow diamond shined in my face.

"And I swear I was going to end things but then..." she said trailing off as she dropped her head.

My eyes were filled with tears and as I looked over to her, I could tell that her hand was on her stomach and she was caressing it slowly.

"But then what?" I asked trying to regain some sort of composure.

"I got...*we* got pregnant."

At this point Brandy could've told me anything and I wouldn't have been shocked. Brendan was engaged to and having a baby with another woman and he had a thirteen year old son I was now raising; how much more shocking could things get?

My mouth trembled uncontrollably as I banged my fists against my head. How stupid could I have been to think Brendan, the man with more numbers in his phone than a celebrity, could be with me and only me? Brandy continued talking before I could ask anymore questions.

"But when he found out he flipped on me. He stopped returning my calls, he wouldn't answer his phone and he said he wasn't ready for all of that," she said wincing as she relived the day.

I stood up and splashed water on my face over and over. I had to get out of the bathroom because it was driving me crazy. Brandy followed closely behind me and as I turned around we ran into each other. I hesitantly reached out and rubbed her small bump of a stomach.

"How far along are you?" I asked.

"Three months," she said beaming. "I'm so sorry you had to find out like this,"

she said looking back up at me. I wasn't sure why I was conversing with my boyfriend's mistress but one thing was for sure, I had all the answers I'd come for and I hoped there wouldn't be anymore.

"Mike told me that Brendan had gotten involved with Quito, what was that about?" I asked hoping she could shed some light on the situation.

Brandy rolled her eyes and crossed her arms. I was guessing

that Quito had that type of effect on a lot of people.

"He was making drop offs for Quito so he could stay afloat and keep the condo and the Escalade," she sighed. "I told him he didn't need all of that stuff but..."

"Why did he sell the business?"

"Money; he said he was going broke."

It was sad and almost humorous that another woman knew my man and his secrets better than I did. Brandy looked like she was young, almost too young for Brendan; she was pretty, too. The thought of Brendan cheating on me had crossed my mind a time or two but I never thought he'd actually do it; yet I had a pregnant, in love little girl showing me that it was true, he was cheating.

"Was Brendan acting strange the night he killed himself?" I asked.

"The last time I talked to Brendan was when we came to your birthday party," she said sucking her teeth and continuing.

"He called me out of the blue, told me to get dressed and said it was a surprise. I was so happy because I figured he was coming around about the baby," she smiled before sadness poured over her face.

"But he was only using me to get you jealous," she revealed as the knife in my heart went deeper. I loved this man, why would he want to intentionally hurt me? I'd heard enough and as much as I wanted to continue to hear all the juicy details of the secret affair, I had to leave. I had to get out of there. I was clamoring for breath as Dee jumped up and opened the front door.

"Are you okay?" he said patting my back gently.

"No," I said out of breath. "I'm not."

But I looked up in the sky and prayed that I would be.

I called Trey and asked him if he would mind watching Dee that night, while I hosted my gig at Compound; so after I dropped off Dee, I headed home. My routine of hiding my emotions was starting to wreak havoc on my sanity. As soon as Dee exited my car, I couldn't think or see straight, so I cursed Brendan the entire way home. I was over feeling sorry for him or the situation; although I was pissed, I didn't want Dee to have a negative opinion of the father he never knew. Kind of like the pot calling the kettle black.

I didn't feel like hosting the party that night but it was what I had scheduled and I wasn't about to back out. Being in a club full of people who were dancing and having a good time wasn't the way I wanted to spend my weekend but what choice did I have?

My body was hurting and as I looked at myself in the mirror all I saw was pain; when I tried forcing a smile, I grimaced.

Kenya and Jasmine were on a three-way call with me when I updated them about what I'd found out; like me, the wind was knocked out of them.

"My goodness; this is like one of those damn soap operas," Jasmine said as she sighed heavily.

"I know, right," Kenya chimed.

"So now what?" Jasmine asked curiously. My best friend was always thinking about the next move, even when I was still stuck on the current one.

"I don't know; maybe I'll call her to get more information."

"About what?" Jasmine said with plenty of attitude.

"About Brendan's death."

"Haven't you already found out enough of his skeletons? What else is there to know?"

Kenya exhaled.

"Why *wouldn't* she want to know why her boyfriend killed himself, Jas?"

I was through with going back and forth with the two of them and while I understood Jasmine's hesitance with me continuing with the investigation, I had already made my mind up. I had come this far so I might as well finish the race.

"Hey guys, I'm getting ready to go. I've got to get ready for tonight," I said cutting into their argument.

"Do you want me to come over and help you get ready?" Kenya asked sympathetically.

"No, I got it. Thanks though."

After I hung up, I sat in the tub and took a nice, long, relaxing bath. The suds from the bubble bath surrounded me and soon I felt like I was in heaven. I closed my eyes and wondered what Brendan was thinking when he pulled the gun out, when he put it to his chest and when he pulled the trigger. I wondered if he was nervous and if he was thinking of me or Brandy. I slid lower into the tub, allowing the bubbles to cover my closed mouth; before I could rise up I thought about what it would be like to drown right there in my bathtub. Would I be taken away and not have to deal with anymore drama? Maybe I could sleep forever without any interruptions. Would anyone miss me the way I missed Brendan? I slid lower and lower until the water was at my forehead and I couldn't see anymore. I was over the pain and I was through with the secrets. All I wanted was to die and have it all be over.

But before I knew it I felt hands. Manly, callous-filled, strong hands gripping my backside and gently pulling me up; yet when I looked around the room I was the only one there.

"Hello?" I said as I wiped the bubble residue from my face and looked around the spacious bathroom. I knew I wasn't crazy; I knew what I felt but who was it? I inhaled and quickly got up from the warm water; I cursed myself for even allowing the thought of suicide to enter my mind. The pain I felt from being alone, driving alone and sleeping alone was something I prayed I could deal with one day; I couldn't imagine making Pop, Jasmine and Kenya go through the same thing I was. It wasn't an option.

I had no idea what I was going to wear for the club, but as I rummaged through the closet I started feeling sorry for myself. I didn't have the right to feel sorry for myself. If anything I felt sorry for Brendan. Sorry that he had to be such a wimp that he couldn't end things with me so he could be with the one he loved. The angrier I grew the shorter and tighter the clothes got. When I normally did club events, I would always wear tight jeans and a cute, trendy t-shirt. But tonight, I was stepping out and I was going to show any and everyone that I wasn't mourning, even though I was. Brendan didn't give a damn about me so why should I care about why he'd done all the things he did to me?

I stepped into a skin-tight, metallic blue dress and inhaled as I pulled it over my stomach. It didn't look bad. I turned from side to side and examined my get-up. My butt looked perfect, my legs were freshly shaved and my hips were undeniably thick-just what the dress called for. The top of the dress crisscrossed around my neck and gave my perky breasts the support they needed.

I remembered when Kenya had purchased the dress for herself only to find that "blue wasn't her color." I knew I would never wear the dress so I tossed it in my Goodwill box to give away; but, luckily, it never made it.

As I turned and checked myself out, I smiled. I applied some NARS bronzer on my legs and shoulder blades for a glowing look and made sure I wasn't ashy. Since my hair was wet from my underwater adventure in the bathtub it was perfectly crinkled and curly. I smoothed the edges down and fluffed it up. I normally didn't wear my hair curly but tonight I wasn't going for the ordinary, plain, safe Lauren; I was going for "Wow!"

I applied my deodorant, make-up and perfume perfectly and then grabbed my silver stilettos and matching clutch purse and headed downstairs. My thighs rubbed together as the dress pressed them closer and closer. It wasn't a sluttish dress but rather a seductive one that left something to the imagination.

When I entered the kitchen and found Pop watching television at the bar, I raised my eyebrows, as if to ask how I looked.

Pop's mouth dropped open and the fork he was holding fell from his hand while his eyes grew large.

"Sugar baby?" Pop said looking at me. I spun around in a circle with my hands to my side and threw my leg up in the back, like I'd always seen those sexy models do.

"How do I look?"

"You look...you *look* like a woman," Pop said.

I laughed to myself as Pop stood up beside me and pulled the dress down a little bit.

"I've always been a woman," I said matter-of-factly.

"But you've always been my Sugar baby; now you're *Lauren*," he said tugging at the material again.

I shooed his hands away as I adjusted the top.

"I've got to get out of here," I said as I twisted off towards the front door.

Pop rushed around me and raised his eyebrows like the concerned parent he'd always been.

"Where are you going?"

"I have to host a part tonight, remember?"

"Um...okay. Do you think you'll be home late?"

I cocked my head to the side as I replayed the question in my head. Pop had always trusted me and never questioned my whereabouts. Where was all this coming from? Pop must've seen the confused look on my face as he relaxed and exhaled.

"It's just you're dressed so...*differently*," he said pointing to the dress.

My father knew me, almost too well. He knew when I was in trouble, when I was scared and when I was running from something; that night it was all of the above.

"Lauren, don't change who you are because of what's going on. You are who you are for a reason," Pop reminded me. I tried to ignore his comments. But he was right and I knew it. The only reason I was in disguise that night was to prove something to myself. I didn't need Brendan and I didn't need to be who he wanted me to be.

I kissed Pop on the cheek..

"I'll be back later tonight."

As I got in my car I watched Pop hang his head and finally

retreat into the house. I felt bad, but I couldn't change my course now. There were things that had to be done and I had to do them.

I scoped out Compound from the parking lot across the street. As I strapped my shoes on I bobbed my head to the music that flowed from my speakers. I must've been really into the song because I didn't notice the line getting longer.

I jumped out of my car and headed towards the club as I pulled down my dress. Guys were whistling out of their cars while some girls rolled their eyes at me.

In that moment I wanted to run home, throw on my sweats and t-shirt and curl up on the couch while watching "Living Single". Hell, I thought as I strutted across the street, I still could if I wanted to. The appearances I made paid well but they were minimal in the grand scheme of things. I was different from the other on-air personalities and DJs in the business like DJ Kay Slay, Greg Street and Wendy Williams because as much as I loved my fans, I only did club events once in a blue moon.

As I approached the club entrance, the club promoter, Drew, walked out talking on his cell-phone. One look at me and Drew was obviously impressed with how I cleaned up.

"Damn you look good tonight, L," he said winking.

I hated when people called me L, L.A or even Ren. It takes two syllables to say Lauren, so what's the use in shortening it?

"You ready?" he asked as I stopped to speak to fans.

Drew was a cute guy with newly started dreadlocks. He was high yellow and had a booming deep voice that sent chills down my spine. If it wasn't for his enormous ego I might have thought he was the kind of guy to take home to Pop. I finished my conversations and hustled past Drew and into the club. I headed towards the DJ booth and chilled out there watching the crowd slowly pile in as sounds from Atlanta R&B singer, Johnta Austin blasted from the speakers. Girls in short dresses and fellas in white T's and jeans were making their way to the dance floor.

It wasn't hard to host a party; all I had to do was show my face, say a couple of words and make sure people had a good time.

Drew appeared in the DJ booth and shoved a microphone in my hand and whispered in my ear all the things he wanted me to say. I honestly never saw the sense in hiring someone to host a club night. People didn't pay attention to me for longer than five minutes; but this was what I was paid to do so I was going to make the best of it.

"Hey y'all! It's your girl Mystique from 104.5 The Buzz. The most talked about DJ in all of Atlanta. We got a lot of people stopping through tonight! I heard that Luda was in the building and even Keshia Knight Pulliam! Lil' Rudy is going to be popping bottles with everyone in V.I.P.! Are y'all ready to have a good time?" I screamed into the mic. The crowd screamed back at me with their drinks in the air.

"Then DJ run that joint!" I said pointing to the DJ who winked at me as he started the record.

I stepped off of the stage and headed towards V.I.P., where I was ready to do some live cut-ins and took a seat in one of the plush couches. I had done this club so many times before, that I had the routine down. But this night it seemed like the girls were cautiously eyeing me while the guys' smirks were growing wider and wider as my dress rode up higher and higher.

"Hey there, I'm Rome," a dark skinned guy said as he slid next to me on the couch. I tried not to laugh as his ten gold teeth shined in my face, but the giggles were hard to contain.

"Hey," I said not taking my eye off of the dance floor.

"You know you're looking sexy as hell in here tonight, right?" he asked rubbing his ashy hands together.

I smiled and nodded my head.

"Thanks, sweetie," I said as I started to get up from the couch and make my way somewhere else; anywhere else.

"I'm going to *let* you have my number because, see, girl I can tell that you are *the one* for me," he said winking his eye like he was doing me a favor. I swear I could've choked on my own tongue if I wasn't careful.

What did he mean he was going to *let* me have his number? This guy in dirty pimps clothing had to be kidding. What would give him the idea that I was even remotely interested in dating a man with teeth shinier than the sun? I laughed to myself as I got up and ignored his comment.

"Baby, I paid $100 to get in this V.I.P. to get next to you. You're going to talk to me!" He shouted as he got up to chase me. He grabbed me by the waist and pulled my body into him. I could feel his manhood on my stomach. As much as I wanted to say I wasn't turned on by his force, I was. Hell, it had been weeks since I'd had sex, and frankly, I was horny.

"You like that don't you?" he asked as he whispered in my ear. I backed up as his funky breath hit my nose.

I stepped back and looked at him like he was a loon before turning to walk away. Rome mumbled something to one of his friends before turning to pick up a bottle of liquor and sloshing it around. I rolled my eyes. This is why I should've stayed home, I thought.

I did my cut-ins and kept to myself in the DJ booth as everyone had a good time. As much as I wanted to prove to myself and everybody else that I had moved on and was ready to be happy; I wasn't. I quietly sat with my legs crossed listening to music.

Saturday nights in Compound can go one of two ways; either it will be a festive night with great music, people and dancing or it will end in a huge fight. I prayed that this night it wouldn't be the latter.

But as I eyed Rome from V.I.P. talking to another girl by the bar, I knew that *he* was going to be the reason for any issues we had that night. And, as if on cue, I saw the thick girl push Rome away violently. I could see Rome's eyes, even from the booth, and it wasn't about to end in a good way.

"Do you see that guy? You might want to get him out of here; I think there's some trouble over there," I said to the bouncer standing beside me.

I pointed out Rome just as he looked in my direction. I dropped my hand and hoped he hadn't seen me rat him out.

Teddy the bouncer jumped down within minutes. All I could see were fists, arms and legs swinging. I couldn't tell what was going on; so I decided to make my way out of the club. The DJ tried to calm people down but, after a few minutes, even he was packing his things and leaving. I had stayed around one too many fights turned gun shoot outs. No amount of money Drew was paying me would make me risk my safety.

I grabbed my purse and began the dangerous trip through the club and managed to duck and weave all punches being thrown in my direction.

But as I looked up and saw Teddy kneeling at the bar in pain, I knew I couldn't just leave him there.

"Are you okay?" I asked putting my hand on his back and kneeling down to his face.

A shoe whizzed by my face and I heard the rumbling and arguing getting closer.

"Yeah...you get out of here," he said as he saw other women running towards the exit.

"No, let me help you."

I put my arm around Teddy's shoulder and tried to help him up. But when I lifted my head I saw Rome.

With plenty of malice and anger in his eyes, he walked towards me, smirked and pulled his big, black, ashy fist back.

"Duck, Lauren!" Teddy said as he tried to pull me down.

The last things I remember seeing is Rome's fist colliding with my face. I felt my body hit the ground and I heard a scuffle ensue as I blacked out.

"Mystique, are you okay?" I heard Drew ask pathetically as I opened one eye and stared at him.

"What happened?"

My head was hurting like never before and I could taste a little blood in my mouth.

"That crazy mother punched you," he said sighing.

It was then that I remembered Rome and his sucker punch that had landed me right on my ass.

"Is it bad?" I asked rubbing my slightly swollen cheek.

Drew blew out air while gently stroking my cheek.

"It's not *that* bad but I hope you don't have any photo shoots coming up."

I closed my eyes and exhaled as I stood up. I could see that the club was completely cleared out and myself, Drew, Teddy and two police officers were the only people still there.

"We were hoping you'd wake up so you could give the police your statement," Drew said rubbing my back.

My cheek was throbbing like I'd been fighting Mike Tyson and Muhammad Ali at the same time. From the look on Drew's face, I could tell Rome had done a number on my face.

"Where's my purse?" I asked as I sat on the couch and pulled my dress down.

Teddy scrambled to me and handed me my clutch.

"I'm sorry about all of this," he said sounding like he was feeling guilty.

I knew it was no ones fault that half my face was swollen.

"It's not your fault," I said taking the purse from him and cracking it open.

The police were approaching me and all I was concerned about was how I was going to explain the black and blue swelling to Pop. I pulled out my compact mirror so I could get see the damage.

"Wow," I said running my hands softly over the bruise. It

wasn't as bad as I was thinking but it was enough to upset me.

The swollen area, which was about the size of a small plum, was growing by the minute and I knew I needed to get some ice on it as soon as possible.

"Ms. Washington, do you mind answering a couple of questions about what happened?" the white officer said as I closed the compact and looked up at him.

"Fine."

The officer went through question after question as I answered them all to the best of my ability. I didn't know who Rome was, we weren't having a domestic dispute, and no, I hadn't put my hands on him first.

"Okay, this is good. Let me get you a copy of the police report and I'm sure you'll be hearing from us," the officer said as he scribbled something down on a piece of paper.

I sat back in the chair and exhaled.

"I'm sorry about your night being ruined, Drew,"

Drew blew me off and shook his head.

"Never mind," he said smiling.

None of us could have predicted the night going the way it had.

I placed my hand over the sore spot and took a deep breath.

"Here you go," the policeman said as he ripped a piece of paper off and handed a copy to myself and Teddy.

"Is this all?" I said standing up and yanking on my dress.

What had I been thinking wearing something like this to the club? What kind of attention had I been asking for when I'd advertised myself the way I did? Drew and Teddy both saw me wobbling and ran to catch me before I fell.

"I'm fine," I said agitated.

"You are *not* fine. Let me take you home," Drew said moving Teddy's hands off of my back.

"I'm okay, Drew, really I am," I said as I opened my eyes widely. I wasn't drunk, high or even out of it. I was just a little bruised and a lot embarrassed.

"I'm taking you home," Drew said grabbing my purse from the couch and then putting my hand in his. I looked down at our hands and quickly slipped mine out of his.

"I don't need you to take me home, I'm fine," I said as I took my purse from him.

Drew looked like I'd taken my hands and punched him in his gut; like I'd taken the wind out of his sail and I felt bad, but not bad enough to let him take me home.

"Mystique, are you okay?!" I heard someone yell from the crowd as I slid into the leather seat.

I ducked lower into the seats as I thought I saw a camera flash.

"Tell us your side of the story!" I heard someone scream.

I tried to start my car and quickly noticed that I'd left my interior lights on.

"Dammit!" I said as people stared at me from across the street.

I tried dialing everyone I could think of, with no luck.

Finally, I called the only person I could think of who would be ready, willing and able to get me home; Drew.

"So you changed your mind?" he laughed as I sulked in his seat.

"My car wouldn't start; I didn't have a choice," I sighed. "I can't believe all of those people were there. I hope this shit doesn't get back to The Buzz. That's the last thing I need."

Drew turned up the volume on his stereo. I sat back in the seat and thought about my night.

"Crazy night, huh?" Drew asked as he looked over to me from my legs to my face.

"Right," I replied just wanting to be left alone.

"How's your face feel?" he asked sympathetically as we slowed down at a light.

I smiled as much as I could before cracking a joke.

"It could've been worse; he could've punched you in the face," I said playfully as I thought about how Drew would've reacted to someone messing with ; his pretty boy face.

Drew chuckled as he revved up the car and started driving.

"I would've whooped his ass," Drew said loudly. I could tell he was trying to impress me.

"Right," I said trying to hide my disbelief. I didn't doubt that Drew, who was athletic in his own right, couldn't have handled Rome. But something told me he was all talk.

"Girl you don't know about me!" Drew snickered

I nodded my head. I knew getting in a ride with Drew was going to be a mistake. For as long as I could remember he had been trying to get me in the sack and I had been brushing his flirtations off. I wasn't into Drew and regardless of how cute he was and how much money he flaunted, there was nothing between us. Like with Brendan, the fireworks, butterflies and desire had always been there; I always wanted him. The only thing I wanted from Drew was for him to shut up.

"You know I don't blame him for getting all uptight over you," Drew said lowering his voice as he looked over at me. He looked like he was trying to pucker his lips seductively. But it ended up looking like he'd sucked on a big, fat lemon.

"Why's that?" I said unsure of where this was going.

"If I had your fine ass next to me I would've been fighting anybody I could to keep you near," he said as he started to whistle.

The cat was out of the bag and Drew let it be known that he was feeling me. I was about to be sick. It wasn't that Drew was repulsive, or even ugly, but he wasn't the guy for me. If he wasn't going so fast I would've jumped out of the car as quickly as possible; but as I stared out at the street, I decided one bruise was enough for the night.

"I know you're going through a rough time right now and I want to be here for you. I think I can make you feel better. Trust me," he said grabbing my chin lightly and pulling my face closer to his.

I jerked back and crossed my arms. There was no amount of smooth talking from Drew that was going to convince me that being with him was a good idea.

"Hey, can you get off on this exit?" I asked.

"I thought you lived in Bankhead not Buckhead?" Drew said turning off the interstate.

"My friend lives over here and I'd much rather go there tonight," I said smiling as I rubbed my sore face.

"You could always stay at my crib."

I raised one eyebrow and kept my attention on Drew's face. I was trying to figure out how serious he was.

"I don't think that's a good idea, Drew..."

I gave Drew the directions and he drove in silence, with a salty attitude brewing in the air.

When we pulled up to the house I sat back in the leather seats and put my hand on top of Drew's.

"Thanks for the ride."

"Yeah, sure," he said not looking at me.

I hesitated before getting out of the car but realized if I lingered any longer I would be giving Drew all the ammunition he needed.

I walked up the perfectly manicured grass. I rang the

doorbell. Drew screeched off down the street as the door opened.

"Lauren? W-what are you doing here?" Trey asked rubbing his eyes.

The darkness must have initially covered my bruise because when Trey finally did see it he pulled me into his house.

"Sit down," he demanded as he rushed to the freezer and grabbed some ice. "What the hell happened?"

"I'm okay, just a little fight at the club."

"*You* got into a fight?" he said fishing for answers.

"Something like that."

"Lauren, either you're going to start talking now or we have a problem."

I told him the entire story. It wasn't until we both sat on the living room couch, that he saw my outfit.

"You went to Compound dressed like *that*?" he interrupted.

I nodded, pleased at the reaction Trey was giving me, and continued with the story.

"Are you okay?" he asked. I was sure I looked disfigured, deformed and a mess, but despite all of that Trey wasn't backing up.

"I am," I said softly as I closed my eyes and continued to enjoy his soft hands around my face.

"You're bionic woman, now, huh Skeeter?" Trey joked as he flexed his muscles.

"No, I'm not," I replied rolling my eyes.

It seemed like every time Trey would make an intimate gesture, he would screw it up with some corny joke.

"Remember that time in school when you broke your leg and hopped around all day looking like a one-legged deer?" he laughed as he hopped around the room playfully.

Trey sat down on the couch.

"That's not funny to you?" he asked poking my side.

"No, it's not," I said getting bold. "And, in fact, it's never been funny. You know all throughout elementary school I put up with you making fun of me, even when I was at my lowest; I will not do that now!" I said crossing my arms.

Trey quietly sat back in the chair.

"Wow, that's what you thought I was doing? Making fun of you?" he said turning to face me. I shook my head. What else was I supposed to think he was doing?

"The only reason I ever *joked* with you was because I saw how sad you came to school, day in and day out, and I figured if

I joked I'd make you smile. After your mom died, I made it my mission to see you smile at least once a day; I always met that quota. But I am sorry if you thought I was making fun of you," Trey said dropping his head.

I had never looked at it that way. After all those years I thought Trey didn't even notice me, I now knew his true intention. I remembered that Trey *had* made me laugh everyday in school. I felt bad for coming down on him the way I did.

"Where's your car?"

"It wouldn't start; I left it at the club."

"I see."

"Please take me to get my car. I'll need a jump."

"Go upstairs, the second door on the left is the bathroom. There are plenty of towels and wash rags up there. Go take a shower and I'll bring you something to change into." Trey said forcefully. "You're staying the night and we'll take care of your car in the morning."

Something about the way he took charge turned me on. I didn't fight his orders and as I undressed in the spacious bathroom I looked at myself in the mirror. My hair was a mess, my bruise was a solid dark blue and I still had some remnants of blood below the swelled spot.

"Yuck," I said to myself as I stepped under the warm water and allowed it to cover my body. It felt relaxing as I allowed the jet showerhead to hit all the aching spots. My back, my butt and my neck were killing me, and as I allowed the water to do its job, I thought about Brendan. What would he have done if this happened when he was alive? Would he have been there for me like Trey was?

I grunted as I remembered my pact to forget about Brendan Deondre Lewis for one night; here I was showering, relaxing and still stressing about the man with a million secrets.

I hadn't heard the door open, but when I stepped out of the shower there was a beautiful silky nightgown sitting on the toilet. I'd never seen anything as elegant and beautiful in my life. But what was Trey doing with something this gorgeous and feminine just floating around his house? Maybe I'd misconstrued everything and there *was* a woman in his life.

The nightgown fell to my ankles and hugged my body perfectly.

I walked past the bedroom where Dee was fast asleep and I stuck my head in.

"That boy even sleeps hard like his daddy," I said to myself as I leaned against the wall and watched Dee snore loudly. The more I looked at Brendan's son the more I was starting to love him like he was my own.

"Hey," Trey said eyeing me.

"Hey," I repeated as I spun around to fully see his face.

"You look amazing in that," he replied.

"This is beautiful. Where did you get it?" I asked biting my bottom lip.

"My ex-wife..."

"Wait a minute. I'm *wearing* your ex-wife's nightgown? Trey that's..."

Trey was laughing hysterically as he pulled me away from Dee's bedroom door.

"You've *got* to stop interrupting me," he said as I walked with him back downstairs to the living room.

"I was saying I bought this for my ex-wife the day before she left me."

I could've knocked myself upside the head for jumping to conclusions.

"Oh," I said with my head hung.

"So are you hungry? I can cook something for you," he said eagerly as he walked over to the marbled kitchen and flipped on the light.

Trey's kitchen was, by far, the classiest I'd ever seen; I was impressed. Stainless steel appliances, beautiful dark cabinets and a rack full of expensive wine.

"I'm not hungry."

I felt stunning in the gown. I watched Trey closely.

His body was amazing and his swagger was undeniable. He walked like he had all the confidence in the world. This man was beyond fine. My body began to throb as I watched him bend over and pick things up in the kitchen. I could feel myself getting damp from his presence alone.

As Trey threw something in the microwave I watched with satisfaction as his muscles bulged from underneath his white wife beater. I wondered what his manhood looked like. It made me horny.

After the food was cooked, he plopped next to me and began eating a hot dog slowly. I leaned into him and inhaled, taking in his manly fragrance. I could feel myself going to a place I'd promised I wouldn't; I had to stop.

"What room can I sleep in?" I asked standing up. I turned to find Trey staring at me; finally our eyes met.

"I'm sorry," he said blinking nervously. "It's the first room on the right."

I smiled and thanked him for taking me in and headed toward the steps.

"Are you sure you're ready for bed?"

"Yeah. I'm a little worn out," I lied. I was wide awake and the only thing that kept me from pouncing on him was Jasmine's voice in my head. I wanted him and my body was begging for me to make the move. I wanted to know what his hands felt like as they rubbed up and down my thighs, what his breath felt like as he breathed heavily over every inch of my body. Did his lips tasted like cinnamon? I wanted to know it all.

As I tucked myself into the cute little guest bedroom with boat sails hung all around the room, I sighed. "Dammit," I said as I thought about Trey naked.

I tried to think of something, anything, to keep my mind off of the fact that my body was pleading for pleasure. A couple of thoughts of Brendan popped in my head but I quickly dismissed them and tried to fall asleep.

I closed my eyes and pictured myself in Trey's bed, laid out wearing the fabulous gown he'd given me. I wondered what it would feel like to have him inside of me, kissing me, holding me and making me feel loved; my body began to quiver.

I tossed a pillow between my legs and clamped down tightly.

"No!" I said to myself as I thought about walking back to the living room.

"Good night!" Trey said as he stuck his head in the dark room and looked around for any sign of movement. Even though I was awake, I feigned sleep and listened as he walked down the hallway towards the master suite.

I heard his bedroom door close and soon the house was as still and silent as it was before I'd banged on the door earlier that night. I started breathing heavily and thought about what Kenya would tell me to do. Sure this was her cousin, but what piece of advice would she give if it wasn't?

"Do it girl!" I heard her say to me. I could visualize Jasmine telling me not to do anything, but I was already heading to his bedroom door. I waited outside for minutes until I saw the light go out. He was alone, it was dark, and I hoped I wasn't about to embarrass myself. I turned the door knob and entered. It was huge; bigger than any bedroom I'd ever seen. My feet hit the cold hardwood floors and I moved slowly towards the bed. Since the door didn't squeak, Trey didn't hear me coming and as I tip-toed I looked around the room at all the fancy things he had. There were paintings, statues and beautiful plants everywhere. It looked like one of those bedrooms you see on "Cribs". The King sized bed sat in the middle of the floor. I reached halfway before I thought, was I ready for this? What would people say? I decided there was no way to know if my body would be satisfied by another man other than to do it. The moon was shining into his huge bedroom window and hit his beautiful toffee colored skin perfectly.

I crept up behind him and glided underneath the covers and onto the foam mattress that swallowed my body comfortably. I slid close to him and within seconds my hands were around his waist.

"What the..."

I put my finger to his mouth and I slid my hands up and down his leg until I got to the spot I had dreamed about for weeks. For once I wasn't feeling guilty. I wanted Trey and I wanted all of him.

My hands met with his manhood and as I looked in his eyes I could tell he was confused; but that didn't stop me. I stroked him gently and felt him getting bigger by the moment. I grabbed him and began to jerk him seductively. He leaned in and kissed me roughly; it was all the validation I needed that he wanted this.

His hands crept up and down my nightgown and before I knew it, it was over my head and on the ground. I lay on my back and covered my breasts with my arms. He removed them slowly.

"Let me see them," he said.

I moved my arms away from my breasts and allowed them to peek out. My caramel skin and dark brown nipples stared back at him. Trey stared at my breasts with adoration in his eyes and began to slowly lick and suck each mound while he caressed the other. My body tingled everywhere as his warm tongue went around my clean body; although no words were spoken, he knew I was satisfied. I grabbed his neck tightly and pulled him from my stomach to my face and looked at him for direction.

"Are you sure?" he asked as he watched a single tear fall. I *was* ready and I was sure. I leaned in and kissed him. Our tongues collided and I tried to keep myself off him but I couldn't. I felt irresistible as he grabbed my hips and pushed my legs open.

Without hesitation he dove into me with his tongue. I shivered at the perfect ways he dibbled and dabbled. With every lick and suck, my body was closer and closer to being his. I lifted my hips higher and watched as he continued devouring me.

"Oh my gosh!" I screamed as I neared a climax. I had never cum so quickly. I was shaking and felt sensations throughout my body.

Trey looked at me with a sly grin, like he'd conquered something, and licked his lips.

"Delicious, girl."

I laughed loudly as I pulled his boxers down and took off his wife beater.

"Do you have protection?" I asked.

"Yeah," he said reaching into his nightstand and pulling out a box of condoms. He slipped one on and looked at me closely.

I watched as he guided himself into me. We exhaled out of satisfaction. I knew Brendan fit me like a glove but the fit between Trey and I was on another level. It was like every groove in me was being perfectly filled. He slowly pumped in and out of me and after building momentum, we got our rhythm down. Our wet bodies clapped together as we held onto one another. I couldn't keep quiet as we connected.

"Oh my damn!" I said trying to muffle my cries of excitement.

He opened my legs up wider so he could see himself going in and out and see the grip I was having on his manhood. I clinched tighter as he whimpered in satisfaction. He rubbed his hands delicately over my clit as he continued making love to me. I wanted to scream, but didn't want to wake Dee.

He then flipped me onto my stomach and entered me from the back and smacked my butt powerfully and grabbed my waist for a better grip.

Trey was grabbing some of my hair and pulling it back, which made me go wild. It was like he knew everything I liked, disliked and even had thought about trying.

In a frog-like position Trey continued thrusting until I could feel his legs unsteadily shaking; he was about to cum. I placed his hands on my breasts and leaned into him until he couldn't say anything but "Damn."

As his thrusts got deeper and harder, I knew the time as coming and my body was gearing up to cum with him. He leaned down into my ear and began flicking it around until I couldn't take it anymore.

"Oh my gosh, I'm cumming!" I screamed loudly as Trey continued pounding me. Within seconds of me climaxing Trey was reaching his own peak. His body shook ferociously.

We lay still for a moment trying to catch our breaths. Trey then made his way to the bathroom.

"Damn!" he said loudly from the bathroom as I giggled in the bed. I got underneath the covers and rolled around in the moist sheets, still not believing I'd slept with Trey.

When he returned to the bed I wanted to go for round two but as he yawned I could tell I had worn him out.

"I can't believe that just happened," Trey said scooting closer to me underneath the covers. I felt his penis rub against my arm as he pulled me into him. I looked up at him and I smiled widely.

"Me either," I said grinning.

We kissed. I couldn't keep my hands off of his perfectly chiseled chest as I swirled my tongue in and out of his mouth.

I lay my head on his chest and exhaled. I finally felt close to someone again and I had Trey to thank for that.

"Thank you," I said smiling.

"For..."

I looked up, and for a second, saw Brendan. Shaking myself I crawled on top of him and kissed his lips softly.

"For just being *you* and being there," I said softly as I lay my head on his chest.

Trey didn't say anything.

I didn't know it but I'd complicated my life more than I could have ever imagined.

But for that moment, I wasn't concerned about complications. As I curled up against Trey, I finally felt normal returning. Or did I?

CHAPTER 10

Dear Diary-

Okay. I'll admit it; it's been a week since I last wrote. I've been out of commission. I got in a fight and got my ass whooped at Compound the other night by some dude named Rome. Crazy! But it's okay, the police told me this was his third strike and homeboy is going to be spending A LOT of time trying to not drop the soap. I can't say I'm glad he's going to jail for so long but if you do the crime you do the time!

After that night, I went to Trey's house to unwind and relax. Well, relax I did. Trey and I had THE best sex I've ever had. But then, the only other man was Brendan! I've seen him everyday since and it's been something I look forward to. Our conversations are getting deeper. It's like Trey's my drug and he's filling those cravings I get at night. But I don't know how far I want to go with him. He's a good guy and, he's established, successful and handsome but my heart is still with Brendan (I know it shouldn't be, right?). Maybe this is just some sort of rebound? I've been trying to block out all the thoughts I'm having about Brendan and his deceit and as much as I try I can't. I think about him when I wake up, when I go to sleep and while making love to Trey. I don't know what I'm doing, really.

Lenny has been out of town for a week on business and he returns today. Great! So I have to make sure I'm there on time because he's called some sort of staff meeting. We'll see what that's about.

I'm supposed to meet with Ralph in a week or two; hopefully he has some new information. Ms. Pat called yesterday to ask if I would help her clean out Brendan's condo this weekend; I said yes. I'll be sure to take Dee with me!

I've got to get up from here; I think I hear Trey bumping around downstairs.

TTYL

Lauren Washington

"Hey there," I said pulling my hair into a ponytail and smiling as I leaned up against the oven and looked over at Trey. He nodded his head and finished what he was doing before turning to face me.

"Hey, yourself!" he smiled as he wiped his hands on his jeans and moved in for a hug.

I fell into Trey's familiar body with eagerness, and quickly inhaled his scent. I wasn't sure what was going on but I gripped his back tightly. I knew exactly what Terry McMillian was writing about when she penned "Waiting to Exhale". My body relaxed and my breathing became softer as our bodies collided.

Pulling away slowly, Trey backed up and put his hands in his back pocket.

"So what's new?" he said slowly as I regained my composure.

I shook my head, still a little gone from our hug and exhaled.

"You were going somewhere?" Trey inquired as he picked up some tools and started placing them neatly in a toolbox.

I grabbed a plum from the refrigerator and returned to my spot so I could watch him closely.

"I have a meeting at work this afternoon."

"Cool," he replied.

I watched as he moved and worked in the kitchen. I wasn't sure what I was looking at, but my eyes wouldn't leave his body, his eyes or him.

"Wanna get something to eat later on?" I said taking a deep bite into the plum.

"I...I can't," he stuttered sounding a lot like Brendan and Dee wrapped into one.

"Okay," I said embarrassed.

Up until then our conversations had occurred while watching television or over dinner, with Pop and Dee sitting close by.

Trey wiped his hands and walked towards me. "I've got another big client that I've got to take care of tonight," he said placing his hand on top of mine gently.

Something changed. It was as if the spark, the fireworks and the interest was gone.

I nodded my head as I continued biting into the plum; stuffing all of it into my mouth so I wouldn't have to respond.

"I'm actually going to be pulling an all nighter, which is why I showed up so early today."

"It's fine. I understand," I said trying to force a smile.

Trey silently watched me as I brushed past him and retrieved some items from the kitchen before heading for the front door.

"I'll see you later," I said nonchalantly as I turned to face him in the kitchen.

I was so glad that Dee had opted to stay home that day instead of hanging out on the corner.

Dee was starting to grow on me. He did what he was told, he was always respectful, and most of all, he loved Pop and Trey, which I was thankful for. Since I was off that day I'd planned on catching up with Jasmine and Kenya before heading back to the house to get Dee and then heading to Brendan's condo to help Ms. Pat. Every time I mention Brendan's condo I get this weird feeling in the pit of my stomach. I was hesitant about setting foot in Brendan's home. Was I ready for this? According to Ms. Pat she had the majority of the things packed and shipped to Terrence, but she wanted me to go through some things as well. I wanted to tell her how devious I'd found out Brendan had been to me, but I knew she was grieving like I was and didn't need the additional stress.

I checked my watch and gasped at the time. I hadn't realized I was running five minutes late for the staff meeting. In Lenny's e-mail he asked that everyone "Be prompt and on time."

"Dammit," I said as I weaved in and out of traffic towards the exit.

When I reached the station I was ten minutes late.

When I entered the conference room, everyone turned and looked at me silently.

"I'm sorry I'm late,"

Everyone turned back to Lenny, as though waiting to hear his response.

"Do you know how many people would've been fired because they were late today, Lauren?" Lenny shot at me with fire in his eyes.

"A lot I'm sure."

"You better be glad these sponsors are paying for you to..." Lenny started. I sat next to Gina "GiGi" Teesly, the station's promotions director who looked at me with sympathy.

My face got hot as Lenny turned back to the dry erase board where he'd written a message about team work in purple marker.

"Did I miss anything?" I whispered to GiGi who shook her head while keeping her eyes on Lenny.

After Lenny had given us an update on the ratings, listener feedback and upcoming promotions, he pulled a paper off his clipboard and smiled widely. Lenny's smiling was such a rarity that everyone in the room had to catch their breath as the yellowish teeth became exposed.

"And speaking of promotions, we've got one of the biggest names in radio, Steve Harvey, stopping by *exclusively* with The Buzz this coming Monday. He's promoting his movie *"Steve Harvey Exposed"* and he's going to be doing one of the biggest giveaways in 104.5's history," Lenny said excitedly.

I leaned forward and placed my hands close together.

"104.5 and Steve Harvey are teaming up to give away a 2008, fully loaded Range Rover courtesy of his new movie!" Lenny said looking around the room at the stunned faces.

We'd given away vacations, Ford Escorts and even cash prizes but a fully loaded Range Rover *was* a big deal.

As all of us whispered amongst ourselves, Lenny's serious face returned and he raised his hands high, exposing his pit stains and hushed everyone.

"But this is a quick promotion. We're going to start running spots today and the winner will be picked *live* on Monday during Lauren's show, right after the interview," Lenny said.

I was excited as I thought about the questions I'd ask my favorite comedian. I'd ask about the movie, his syndicated radio show (which we carried), and of course, his divorces and marriages.

As I snapped out of my daydream I smiled at the possibilities. People in Atlanta loved Steve Harvey and this promotion would, no doubt, be the talk of the weekend.

After everyone cleared out of the conference room I stayed so I could talk to Lenny about my tardiness. After Lenny and GiGi finished up their conversation I leapt from my chair and walked towards him.

"Lenny, look I'm really sorry about being late; that's completely my bad," I said as he gathered some of his papers together without acknowledging me.

"And I really appreciate you choosing my show for the Steve Harvey promotion. I think..."

He quickly looked at me, and within seconds he tossed his papers onto the desk as he glared at me. I couldn't be sure if he was joking or if he was seriously upset about me being late.

"You should be *glad* corporate told me I *had* to put him on your show. You think I would've recommended him to be on *your* show?" Lenny shouted.

I backed up from Lenny and listened in confusion. What was he talking about? My show was the highest rated show on the station and I was one of the most recognized faces in all of Atlanta.

"What are you talking about?"

"The way you've been parading around here...you're lucky you even have a damn job," Lenny said turning his back to me and digging in a pile of papers.

"Wait a minute, you're going to need to slow down and explain to me what the hell you're talking about!" I shouted.

"This!" he shouted as he tossed a picture at me. I bent down to pick it up and before I could place my hands on it, I knew what it was. I saw my blue club dress before I saw anything and then there was the huge, black and blue shiner on my face. There I was laid out on Compound floor with my dress hiked up and my hair mangled.

I slowly picked up the picture and gripped it tightly in my hands.

"Where did you get...?" I said looking down at the piece of paper. Without finishing my sentence I knew who'd planted the picture. I recalled that Drew had shown the police officers pictures of me from his camera phone.

"Damn, Drew," I said as I rolled my eyes.

Lenny shook his head as we both stood silent, breathing like angry bulls, looking at each other. "This is the second time in two months you've been in the news about stuff like this?"

I couldn't say anything as flashbacks of me arguing with Brendan surfaced.

"Yeah. You're speechless now, right?" Lenny said sounding as if he had some sort of power over me.

I cleared my throat and allowed him to finish his rant.

"First off, I was assaulted that night by a club patron. I can bring the police report in for you, if that's necessary," I said as my blood started boiling. "Secondly, you act as though I wanted to be photographed after I got my ass kicked by a fucking man!" I screamed while people stuck their head in the conference room. But Lenny and I were nowhere near letting up. Lenny started laughing as I carried on with my explanation.

"And lastly, what kind of man are you to automatically

worry about your precious reputation and not the safety and well-being of your staff?" I said turning my back to march out of the conference room.

Lenny quickly grabbed his things and chased behind me.

"I don't give a damn about your safety. What I do care about is the way people view this station," he finally admitted as everyone gasped. It stung, but I kept it moving towards the exit.

"I've been at this station for more years than you've been living little girl, and I'll be damned if you just come in here and throw away the reputation we've built! If it was up to me you'd be out on your ass!" Lenny said as I impatiently waited on the elevator. I was tapping my foot nervously as he stood close behind me. It was taking everything in me to not call Lenny a racist name or hit him; but I knew that's what he wanted so he could fire me. Just as I was turning to say something, the elevator opened and I hopped in quickly.

"Bastard!" I said as I stared directly in Lenny's eyes. I wanted him to know how much I hated him.

"You need to have your ass here on time and ready to work on Monday, okay?!" Lenny said ignoring my comment.

When I got in my car I put my hands in my head and screamed. I wasn't sad about my behavior and I wasn't nervous about losing my job; but I was frustrated. It was going to take a miracle to lift my spirits.

Dee seemed like he was in a shitty mood. I watched him sulk all the way to the car. I had decided to reschedule my lunch with the girls so I could get the condo cleaning over and done with.

"What's wrong with you?" I said, irritated. I thought that maybe the two of us should've been relaxing versus spending an hour helping Ms. Pat go through the belongings of my ex and his father.

"Nothing," Dee said looking out the window.

I wasn't in the mood to prod Dee for any information; I was dealing with my own stress.

The two of us rode in silence to the condo and the closer we got the more upset Dee was getting. He threw his arms across his chest and huffed loudly. I wasn't in the mood for his attitude. He suddenly kicked my dashboard.

"What is your problem, Dee?"

He took a second before responding. He seemed to be thinking over what he wanted to say.

"I don't see why the hells...excuse me...why I have to help *her* out with cleaning *his* condo. He killed himself and that's *her* son. Shouldn't *she* be the one to do it?" Dee said angrily.

I looked over at him and all I could see was anger. I was mad at Brendan for all the lies he'd told and the years he'd taken, but I still loved him; I felt an obligation to him. In some crazy way, I felt in debt to Brendan for what he had provided me with: security. Regardless of the pain I was feeling, the deception I knew he'd taken part in or how upset I was over things, my heart wouldn't allow me to be anything but loyal.

"*She* is your grandmother and *he* was your father."

"She's the mother of my daddy, big difference," Dee shot back.

"He ain't never done a damn thing for me other than send those small ass child support checks. He never taught me nothing; he never came to see me...hell he never even sent a damn birthday card. Why should I care what happens to his shit...excuse me...his stuff?"

I completely understood and agreed with Dee's argument but we were still going and he was going to meet his grandmother.

"Listen, your father was a great man and I just want you to see sides of him that you probably never would've known about," I said keeping my eyes on the road as we exited the interstate. My stomach began to do nervous flops as I got closer and closer to the spot Brendan had called home.

"If he was such a great man then why do you cry every night about him?"

I looked over at Dee and tried to figure out the best answer. Our rooms were so close I knew he'd probably hear the moans, cries and shrieks that emitted from my room almost every night. I didn't respond to his question. Instead, I turned on my blinker and drove into the community of Buckhead Grand.

Buckhead Grand was one of the most elite condo communities in all of Atlanta. The luxurious thirty-six floor building looked like something out of the pages of an upscale magazine. With its funky glass designed ledges and trendy tenants, Brendan always fit in perfectly. I parked my car and played with my keys as Dee slowly got out of the car.

We didn't say anything to each other as we boarded the elevator in the lobby.

"This is nice," Dee said under his breath as he played with the stainless steel railing in the elevator. I had to admit that every time I had been to Brendan's place I was always impressed at how upscale the place was. The building had a wine cellar and tasting room, massage services and even a full-service juice bar and lounge. It was nice but I'd always felt completely out of place.

As we got off of the elevator my mind wandered everywhere as I thought about the many times I'd come to Brendan's place ready to see his face, hold his hand and kiss his lips. If I closed my eyes and breathed in slowly enough, I could almost smell his cologne. This was almost more permanent and real than the funeral. I prepared to part with all his possessions. Was I ready?

I took a deep breath as I rang the doorbell and waited for someone to answer.

Dee stood behind me with his hands crossed and a defiant look.

"Hey there," Ms. Pat said as she wiped her nose with a wrinkled tissue. Her nose was red and her eyes looked as though she'd smeared her mascara crying.

I leaned in to hug Ms. Pat lightly, exposing Dee who was standing wide-eyed at his grandmother.

"Hey Ms. Pat," I said letting myself in. Dee trailed behind me and looked around in awe.

There were tons and tons of boxes packed against a wall while all of Brendan's sports memorabilia lay on his red leather couch. I looked around the almost bare room.

Dee headed straight to the kitchen and ran his fingers over the cold dark brown and black granite countertops. I watched him loosen up as he opened the huge, stainless steel refrigerator.

Ms. Pat stood back looking like she wanted to scream or cry at the curious child. I couldn't tell if she knew who Dee was.

"Can I see you in the bedroom?" she said coldly as she wiped her nose.

I looked over at Dee who was going through one of the boxes and looking at the football jerseys that were strewn over them.

"Dee, I'll be right back I need to help Ms. Pat with something," I said without giving him a chance to respond. He shooed me away.

I stepped into the empty bedroom and almost lost my balance. Everything that had once filled the room was gone. My heart dropped as I looked at the pale white walls. I swallowed to keep from screaming.

"Who is that?" Ms. Pat said as she crossed her arms and stared at me for an answer.

"That's DeAndre; *your* grandson. You know? The son that Brendan had but everyone mysteriously forget to tell me about?" I said putting my hands on my hips and jerking my neck.

If I couldn't take things out on Brendan, Ms. Pat was the next best thing. She nervously began wiping her forehead and pacing.

"I don't have any grandchildren, chile," she said sweetly as she spun around to see if I believed her.

I rolled my eyes and started to lay the evidence out when Ms. Pat cut me off.

"I *said* I don't have no grandchildren. That boy aint Brendan's. I've never even seen him."

I couldn't believe that after everything Ms. Pat was lying to me.

"This is your son's son; your grandson. I have the birth certificate and your child support payments to prove it."

Ms. Pat looked as though she wanted to reach across the room and slap the living daylights out of me. I, however, wasn't backing down. I needed answers and I needed her to start cranking them out.

"You can take the three boxes by the door; all of those seem to be things I'm sure you'd like to see," Ms. Pat said as she ignored my comments and pushed past me to get back to the living room and kitchen.

I followed closely behind her and watched as she started at Dee. The mini-Brendan was sitting on the red couch reading a school yearbook.

"Give this back to me!" Ms. Pat said as she rushed up to her grandson and snatched the book away from him.

Dee looked shocked and a little hurt by the cruel tone coming from Ms. Pat's voice. It was as if he'd spit in her face, killed her best friend or even stomped on her prized flower bed..

Ms. Pat held the yearbook tightly to her chest and inhaled and exhaled loudly.

"I think you need to leave," she said looking at me as tears formed.

"This is *your* grandson, the last link to your son and you're just going to send him off?" Who did she think she was to treat her own flesh and blood that way?

"I told you I don't have no grandchildren!" Ms. Pat said screaming.

"Get out of here, now!"

Dee stood up from the couch and walked slowly towards

me; we both watched as Ms. Pat flew into hysterics. Her body was shaking, tears flowed down her plump cheeks and her hands were trembling. I became worried when I saw Ms. Pat wobble towards the couch and fall flat on her face. She was still shaking and trembling.

"Ms. Pat?!" I said trying my best to turn her over. Dee stood back with his hands crossed and watched as I struggled to turn her over.

With Ms. Pat's history of diabetes and high blood pressure, I was scared that I had just killed my dead boyfriend's mother. *"Great,"* I thought, *"isn't this exactly what I need today?"*

Dee took a second but eventually came around and helped me roll her over.

"Get me a glass of water,"

I heard him fumbling around in the kitchen and quickly he returned with water. I lifted Ms. Pat's head and put it in my lap and slowly poured the water into her mouth. She wasn't swallowing and the water poured over the sides of her mouth.

"You've got to swallow this water, Ms. Pat. Please swallow it," I plead as I stroked her hair. We'd had our problems but now I just wanted her to get up and get better. Sure enough she started swallowing the water.

"Is she okay?" Dee said. I knew that every time I gave Dee a chance to prove he was a good kid, he'd impress me. He might have seemed wise beyond his years but as I looked into those big brown eyes I knew he was nothing more than a scared child.

"Yeah, she'll be fine," I said as I lay my head back on the couch and took deep breaths.

We sat on the beautiful hardwood floors, for half an hour watching Ms. Pat slowly improve. She was eventually hoisting herself up from the ground.

"I'm...I'm really sorry about all of this," she said smoothing out her wrinkled shirt. Her salt and pepper hair was matted to her head and her eyes were bloodshot.

Dee and I hopped up from our seats and looked at Ms. Pat as she tried to resume the things she'd be doing before her breakdown.

"Like I said, you can take these three boxes," she said trying to avoid eye contact with Dee and me.

"Ms. Pat we need to talk..."

She looked up at me and pursed her lips, like she was trying to hold a whimper from coming out and quickly dropped her head;

I took that as my cue to continue with the questions.

"This is your grandson, DeAndre. I think you already know about him," I said as I continued.

"DeAndre, this is your grandmother Ms. Pat," I smiled looking over at Dee who was staring at her.

"I told you I don't have any..." Ms. Pat started as her voice began to quiver.

"Lauren, can I go to the car?" Dee asked.

I had to rectify the situation. I had taken Dee from a mother that didn't want him only to bring him to meet someone else whowasn't claiming or acting like she wanted any parts of him.

"Ms. Pat, look at me!" I said sternly "Look at me!"

Slowly Ms. Pat brought her eyes to mine and I marched up to her.

"This *is* your grandson and regardless of what you want to say, Brendan fathered a son. I know you paid the child support. I can send Dee away and you'll never have to worry about seeing him or me again," I said confidently as I took a deep breath.

"But do you know the young man that you are passing up on getting to know? He's smart, he's funny and he is *exactly* like his father. I wanted to expose him to the people who knew his dad best; so he could see that Brendan wasn't a low-life, non-supportive, dead-beat father."

Ms. Pat's eyes lit up as she turned to Dee.

"Brendan wasn't a dead-beat," she said softly.

Dee crossed his arms and looked up at me.

"Dee's never known the man you and I have known. All he knows is he has a father who sends a little bit of money each month but wants nothing to do with him," I said

"Is that the man you want Dee, and even me, to remember?"

Ms. Pat took a deep breath and began talking; this time her voice was clear.

"When Brendan came to me and told me he'd gotten that girl pregnant, I was devastated. I've had Brendan and Terrence's lives planned out from the day I came home from the hospital with them," Ms. Pat said with a reminiscent smile on her face. "Brendan was going to be an engineer and Terrence, well, he'd made it clear that he wanted to be a doctor. My boys' were going to be the saviors of my life. So when Brendan told me he was going to be a father to some heifer's baby, I did the best thing I knew how to do," she said looking away from Dee and instead looking at a picture of Brendan.

"I took care of the situation for him. I paid child support for his...*son* until he was financially able to do so. When he got some money he *did* pay a huge lump sum of it to the child's mother and he heard that she squandered it on some foolishness; so he just sent a little money every month."

My mouth dropped as Dee shook his head, not in disbelief, but in shame.

"My son was fourteen when he got that girl pregnant and I thought it'd be best if she just took the money and lived her life with that baby. I didn't want my son involved with that mess," she said. "Brendan had his entire life in front of him and everything I'd planned for his was flushed down the toilet the moment that girl came home pregnant."

"She didn't get pregnant on her own. Brendan played his part too," I said reminding her of how babies are made.

"It was my decision to keep that child away from my son and our family. So if you're going to hate anyone hate me," she said pointing to her chest as she stared in Dee's eyes.

I looked over at Dee and nodded my head at him to speak.

"I don't hate either one of y'all," he said, like the words were coming to him as he spoke.

"I just feel sorry for you."

"Lauren can I sit in the car?" he asked as I nodded my head.

"Yeah, here, take these two boxes down with you," I said tossing him the keys and pointing at the boxes.

I watched as Dee left the apartment with his head high. As soon as the door slammed, Ms. Pat was on me like white on rice.

"Why'd you do that? Why'd you bring that child here? My son didn't want anything to do with him when he was alive and now that he's dead you want him to be father of the year?" Ms. Pat rambled on.

I put my hand in her face to block her from getting any closer.

"You don't see the idiotic way of thinking you created in Brendan, do you?" I asked with a sad laugh.

"What are you talking about?"

"Your son learned how to skip out on responsibilities and do what *he* wanted, not what he was supposed to, and he missed out on being the father that he never had."

Ms. Pat's eyes got watery as she looked at me.

"That littlescrambled save your life.Thank God ignorance

and irresponsibility doesn't trickle down throughout generations. Truth be told, Dee's life will probably turn out better than the ones you had planned for your sons," I said picking up the box and heading towards the exit.

Ms. Pat scrambled behind me shouting. "Get out!" she said over and over as I smirked.

"When you realize how wrong you were about the decisions you've made and lives you've screwed with, let's hope it's not too late," I said before leaving.

"I'm fine with my decisions little girl! You remember that!"

When the elevator doors closed I closed I thought about Dee. The afternoon hadn't exactly panned out the way I was hoping but after dinner and drinks with my girls, I hoped for some sort of light at the end of the tunnel. The truth was, however, I'd just entered the tunnel and light seemed extremely distant.

"I'm looking for a party of two, Kenya Green and Jasmine Wilkes," I said peering over the hostesses' podium to see if I could locate my girls.

"Right this way madam," the white male hostess said as he picked up a menu and led me towards the booth.

I exhaled when I sat down with them and quickly ordered a drink.

"What's wrong with you?" Kenya said smiling as she looked over the menu.

"Stressful, stressful day!" I said as I massaged my temples.

I'd somehow managed to calm Dee when we got back to the house and left him in Pop's care. I understood his frustrations and I echoed them but I couldn't imagine what he was feeling. A child's biggest fear is rejection and Dee had been rejected twice, both by people who should have been protecting him.

"We've already ordered. Do you know what you want?" Jasmine asked tapping my menu.

The waiter appeared with my Apple martini. I gave him my order before taking a sip of my Martini.

"What happened with the condo cleanup?" Jasmine asked as she crossed her legs and picked up her glass of water.

I tried to explain everything; capturing every heartbreaking, shocking and cold moment I experienced.

"Damn!" Jasmine said sitting the glass down.

"She's at least admitting that Dee is her grandson, right?" Kenya said jumping in.

"She's admitting Brendan had a son and Dee is him; but she doesn't consider him her grandson or herself a grandmother," I said.

"I think you're putting way too much stress on yourself when *you* should be the one grieving; not taking care of everyone else's grief," Jasmine said.

Kenya looked over at Jasmine and nodded her head in agreement.

"Listen Lauren, you just lost the love of your life..."

Jasmine interjected and put one finger in the air. "The man she *thought* was the love of her life."

I picked up my drink and took another swig before looking at Kenya.

"It's just...we don't think you're allowing yourself the time it takes to properly grieve."

I was listening to them but all I could think about was Brendan and Trey standing side by side. On one hand I had Brendan, the man who made every part of my body quiver with excitement, the man who held every piece of my heart in the palm of his hands. Then, on the other hand, I had Trey who made me laugh beyond words and was one of the most handsome and successful men I'd ever met. I knew I didn't have a choice at this point because obviously Brendan was out of the running, but comparing the pros and cons was becoming a daily escape for me.

"I really do appreciate the two of you thinking of me. I guess I could do a better job of taking care of me, huh?" I said smiling sheepishly.

My girls sat back in the chairs smirking and then started laughing.

"Girl you would take care of the devil before you took care of yourself!" Jasmine joked while Kenya covered her mouth and laughed.

We laughed, talked and drank until our meals arrived. I wanted to share with them my situation at work.

"So I heard on the news that the guy who hit you in the club, Rome something-or-another, was being charged with aggravated assault. Have the police made contact with you for anything?" Kenya said digging into her chicken salad.

I shook my head as I cut into my steak, "They told me he admitted guilt for everything and it wasn't going to trial; he plead guilty."

"Well, thank the Lord because I was going to have to go down there and show them that they'd messed with the wrong chick!" Jasmine said smiling widely.

I'd ordered my fourth Apple martini, and somehow, convinced Jasmine and Kenya to have a drink. I knew Kenya had a barbeque to attend with one of her clients and Jasmine had to get home to her babies; I wasn't trying to get them drunk, just trying to loosen them up.

"Oh yeah, I forgot to tell the both of you..." Kenya said finishing off her third Cosmopolitan.

"Oh boy, what now?" Jasmine asked as she dabbed her mouth.

"It's nothing bad, calm down," Kenya joked as she continued with her news.

"Lorenzo has asked me to move in with him and I said yes!" Kenya said enthusiastically. I set my fork and my napkin down on the plate and watched as Kenya called the waiter over for another drink.

"One more round! It's a celebration!" she said after she placed the orders and shooed the guy away.

"Wait, are you kidding? Kenya you've known Lorenzo for all of...what, a month or two?"

She'd always been the sensible one, but I was sure Kenya could see that her decision wasn't a smart one.

"No I'm not kidding, girl; aren't y'all happy for me?"

"Happy? About what? You moving in with somebody you barely even know? What's the rush, anyway?" Jasmine said with attitude.

Kenya rolled her eyes and looked in my direction, like my words were going to be much different.

"I'm with Jas, honey. Why are you in such a rush to move in with Lorenzo? I know you said you like him a lot but...moving in? That's kind of a big step," I said rubbing her hand on top of the table.

"It's not like I'm marrying the guy y'all, damn. I just spend all of my time over his house and he does the same over mine. So we thought it would save time and money."

Jasmine turned to me.

"There have been plenty of times I've accepted news y'all have shared with a smile. I voice my opinion and if you still want to make *your* decision I respect that and have your back. Why is it so different now that I want to take a chance at something?" she shot back while looking at the both of us.

The way she'd laid it out I had to totally agree with her. We always expected her to be the safe friend; the one who never made bad decisions, always helped us with ours and never moved too fast with a guy. But Kenya was her own woman and I respected her for standing up for what she believed in and wanted; obviously Lorenzo was just that.

Jasmine and I sat silently staring back at Kenya who, upon seeing the drinks, snatched hers off.

"I love that man, okay?" she said after she slammed the glass down.

Love? Wait, I thought, when had it escalated from moving in, to love? But I didn't bat an eye as I watched my friend move uncomfortably in her seat.

"Kenya, if you decide to move in with Lorenzo, I've got your back. Hell, you've had mine through everything," I said hoping she wasn't too mad at me.

"Thanks," Kenya said staring into her pink drink.

Jasmine wasn't budging, though, and I knew she wasn't about to give Kenya her blessings; although they weren't officially needed. I glanced over at Jasmine and slightly kicked her underneath the table until she spoke.

"I think it's a bad idea, honestly I do; but if it's what you want then it is what it is."

Kenya cracked a smile and nodded her head.

"I appreciate that," she said winking at Jasmine.

I sat back and finished my meal and my last drink and I was, officially, feeling right. I wasn't stressing, I wasn't thinking about Trey, Brendan, Dee, Pops or even my job being in jeopardy.

"When do you move in?" I said breaking the silence.

"Probably next weekend, girl," she said with excitement. It felt great knowing that my best friend was happy and in love. And, yet, I was a tad bit envious. I wanted a man to sweep me off of my feet, offer to let me move in with him and change my life around. But the more I thought about it the more impossible it seemed.

"Damn," I heard Jasmine say as she sipped her drink through a straw.

Kenya ignored the comment.

"Do the two of you want to go to this Barbeque with me tonight? It should be fun!" Kenya said nudging me. "And we know who could use a little fun."

I rolled my eyes playfully, "I'm game."

Jasmine chimed in and said she was down for crashing the

party as well. "Y'all know I'm going wherever the party, people and drinks are!"

"Where is it?" I asked as I checked my make-up in my compact mirror.

"I think it's somewhere in midtown."

"Damn, are you putting it on him or what?" Jasmine asked as we left the restaurant and stood face to face with Lorenzo's silver, fully loaded Mercedes Benz 745i.

Kenya laughed while she clicked the alarm and slid into the leather seats. I had to admit, this car was beyond perfect, it was *the* car of the moment and my best friend looked fabulous. I got in the passenger seat and Jasmine climbed in the back.

"Lorenzo has a nice car!" I said letting the window down and sticking my arm out as the wind whipped it.

"It's mine, actually," Kenya said not taking her eyes off the road.

Jasmine and I sat up quickly and looked over at Kenya who was cracking a smile.

"Yours?!" We both screamed in disbelief.

In seconds Kenya was giggling like a school child and was giving us all the juicy details we were dying to hear.

"He surprised me with this last night and then asked me to move in with him!" she said grinning.

"Wow!" I said running my hands up and down the black leather seats. This was impressive and as much as I knew about Lorenzo I couldn't have predicted this by a long shot.

"I know, right?" Kenya said looking at Jasmine and I as we exchanged glances.

"What about your car?" Jasmine asked curiously as she settled into the seat and the idea that Kenya was smitten.

"Lorenzo said I really didn't need that old thing anymore so he's going to give it to his nephew for his birthday."

"That *old thing*?" I said confused "Kenya, you drove a 2005 Acura SUV- - and it was in perfect condition."

"Yeah," Jasmine agreed.

"Just trust me," she begged pathetically.

I sat back in the seat and thought about Kenya's situation. Why was she allowing Lorenzo to walk into her life and completely turn it upside down? Who was she becoming? I considered various scenarios for the outcome and immediately settled on the calmest one. Kenya and Lorenzo, matched up with Jasmine and Lance, along with myself and Trey could become the new "it" couples. I imagined us taking trips to beaches, exotic islands and faraway countries. Trey and I would get married in a quiet little ceremony with only the couples and Pop invited; then we'd all celebrate over fabulous dinners. I smiled as I thought about the possibilities.

"Hand me those directions, girl," Kenya said pointing to her Louis Vuitton purse.

I reached in and pulled out the MapQuest directions and handed them to her.

Jasmine seemed restless in her seat as she wiggled and moved and sighed.

"What is wrong with you back there?" I said turning around to find her with a frown on her face.

"I keep sliding out of this damn seat! Tell your man he needs some seat covers or something," Jasmine said playfully as she sat up.

Kenya gripped the directions and quickly turned left at the light. "So what about you and Mr. Trey?" Kenya said smiling slyly towards me.

I sunk lower into my seat as I felt Jasmine's eyes burning the back of my head.

"What do you mean? We're friends," I said not making eye contact with either of them.

"Um hmm...I'm sure," Kenya said slapping my leg.

If I could have given Kenya the signal to shut her mouth, I would have. The only problem? I hadn't been prepared for her sudden interest in her cousin and me. Had Trey opened his mouth? Did he tell her about our night out? Embarrassed, I looked out the window while biting my bottom lip.

"Seriously, we're only friends."

"Friends with *benefits*," Kenya snickered. She didn't realize how red my face was getting from the mention of our "special" relationship. I had opted not to tell them about the night because I was sure they'd both jump down my throat; I didn't need it.

"Whatever," I managed to say as I crossed my legs and looked out the window.

"Let's say hypothetically you were kicking it with Trey, would you tell us?" Jasmine said.

I took my time answering this question and thought about it long and hard.

"Probably not."

"Why not?!" Kenya screamed with a smile on her face. I could see out of the corner of my eye that Jasmine wasn't smiling.

"Because...hypothetically it would be *my* business and I know how judgmental *some* of us can be.".

"You're talking about me, right?" Jasmine asked as she slid closer. "Just say it."

"So what if I was?"

Jasmine was quiet for a while.

"So now you're mad?" I quizzed playfully.

"No, I'm not mad," she said softly. "But it's funny when you mistake judgmental for caring about someone. I'm sorry if during our friendship I've looked out for you when you couldn't do it for yourself," Jasmine said.

"Jasmine..." I started.

"No, hear me out, L," she cut in. I could see Kenya focusing on us.

"Go ahead," I replied.

"I see you looking at Trey and I see you thinking that you can automatically jump back into this fairytale relationship; it can't happen like that. You've got to give your heart time to heal. You were with one man for a long time," she said passionately. "You need to know that not all men are good guys. Look at all the secrets Brendan was keeping," she said.

I took a deep breath and silently nodded. "Thank you."

It wasn't that I wasn't appreciative of the things Jasmine was saying, I was. But I also knew that I had to trust my heart. If I felt like I wanted to jump into another relationship why couldn't I? Brendan had lied, hurt and screwed me up and if another man was willing to come along and heal my heart, I was ready for him. We pulled up to this marvelous mansion that looked like it had been on the Sopranos. It had huge ceramic statues of nude men in front and there were lantern lights strung around all the perfectly maintained hedges. The driveway, which was in the shape of a horseshoe, had tons of cars packed in and Kenya's new ride, surprisingly, didn't come close to the rest.

"Damn!" Jasmine said as she climbed out and stared in amazement at the beautiful blue water that was spraying from the fountain.

I had to admit that while Jasmine and I were extremely well-off, we still reverted back to our childhood days when we lived in Bankhead and would flip through the pages of Ebony and Jet and stare at the beautiful homes that graced the pages. When we stepped into the party, it didn't look like any kind of barbeque I'd ever been to. There were naked women and men prancing around the house, music blasting and people, who I assumed were drunk, dancing to their own beat.

The house was beautiful. Tiled floors ran throughout the house with ketchup and mustard splattered all over it. I could smell the scent of burnt coals in the air as Jasmine and I looked around the room in astonishment.

"Y'all go outside, I need to find my client," Kenya said as she continued looking around the house.

Jasmine and I clung to each other, amidst the cat calls and aggressive grabs, and headed out towards the pool. It was a little bit calmer outside so Jasmine and I took a seat at a table and watched the fireworks unfolding. Women were kissing on women and men were watching close by, egging them on. I wanted Kenya to bring her narrow ass back outside and take me back to my car so I could go home.

Jasmine laughed loudly as one girl got thrown into the pool.

"You know I'm not judging you, girl," she said. "I'm just looking out for you. I love you."

"I know."

"I just want you to take it slow with this guy, if you two are *actually* kicking it like that," she said raising an eyebrow.

I didn't have the courage to tell Jasmine that I'd slept with Trey.

"We've been talking and getting to know each other better, that's all."

Jasmine nodded, like she understood what I was saying but was still searching for something.

"And you like him?"

"I do."

"Just be careful," Jasmine said.

"I will."

The two of us continued watching as a drunk older man came towards our table. His stench, a mixture of black & milds, beer and weed was too much for us. We went back into the house looking for Kenya.

As soon as I stepped foot inside, instead of finding Kenya, I saw Trey.

My mouth dropped wide as I replayed the conversation the two of us had the morning before, when he told me he couldn't go out because he had an all night project to finish.

I looked around the room. I didn't see any projects that

needed to be finished. Jasmine, sensing my anger boiling and seeing Trey approaching with a pitiful look on his face, tugged on my arm.

"Come on, let's go this way," she said before I could yank my arm from her.

Trey walked right in front of me and stood silent for a couple of seconds.

"So *this* is your project, huh?" I said getting an attitude.

"Wait..."

"So next I suppose you're going to tell me that she's your assistant and the two of you just happened to come by this party," I said pointing to the woman who had tagged along as he walked towards me. She wasn't cute at all; that pissed me off even more.

What was it with all of the men in my life picking other women?

"Lauren..." Trey said trying to get some control. Jasmine had her arms crossed and was staring the woman up and down, daring her to make a move.

"Shut up, Trey! I thought you were different!" I said trying to fight back the tears that were on the brink of falling. "But then you *lie* about this?"

Trey's head was in his hands and he was breathing heavily.

"Let me explain; come with me," Trey said pulling my hand. Before I knew it Jasmine was intervening and stepped in between us.

"She's going home...now!" she said as she pulled me away. I was moving towards the door but my eyes never left Trey's.

When we got outside Kenya was sitting on the front steps with her cell phone glued to her ear and in a, seemingly, deep conversation.

"Kenya we need to go!" I said pulling her by the arm.

"Baby, I'll call you back," Kenya said quickly as she looked over at Jasmine and I concerned.

"I've been trying to call you two; I didn't know where you were," she said pulling out the car keys. "My client must've gone home early; I can't find her anywhere."

Jasmine and I walked to the car and I was trying not to fall apart but I couldn't help it. I felt like I was reliving the night of my birthday party all over again. How could Trey, the person I'd grown to trust and care about, do this to me?

"What's wrong?" Kenya said when she climbed in the car and glanced over at me. I had my head on the window and tears were slowly rolling down my face. I thought I was over being hurt, lied to and jerked around but Trey had proven me wrong.

"I hate him!" I screamed as I looked out of the front windshield and saw Trey sprinting down the steps towards the car. I wanted Kenya to speed out of there, but my body took over; before I knew it I was swinging the door open and rushing towards him.

"Listen to me!" he screamed.

"You know what? You don't even deserve me listening to you? After all that we've been through and you do *this* to me? You lie to me about this stupid stuff?" I wailed as my girls sat glued in their seats.

"I can't believe you would do something like this to hurt me. Why? Why would you do this? Why?" I screamed as I stared into Trey's confused eyes. "I loved you! Did you know that? I loved you!"

My eyes were closed and I was having the conversation I'd been dreaming about having for weeks, but it was with the wrong man.

"Lauren..."

"I hate you! I hate you! I'm glad you're dead..." I said.

I covered my mouth. My anger towards Trey had, somehow, boiled into the on-going anger and frustrations I had towards Brendan. I was unconsciously using Trey to say all the things I would never be able to tell Brendan. I thought I was ready for a relationship with Trey, but apparently, I wasn't.

"I'm not him," Trey said. "I'm sorry I lied, but I'm not him."

Jasmine hopped out of the car as Kenya sat dumbfounded in the front seat. I was a broke-down, snotty nosed fool and I couldn't stop myself.

"Come on, girl," Jasmine said placing her arms around my shoulders and pulling me into her chest. I sobbed like a baby as all the different emotions hit me. First it was shame, then embarrassment and finally shock. Who was I fooling? Why did I think I was ready to move on from Brendan? I was still angry about his lies.

Trey walked up to me and wiped one of my tears. "I got off early from one of my projects and called you at the house but Dee said you were out with your girls; I decided to go out with my cousin," he said pointing to the girl.

I felt like an idiot and I just knew Trey saw me as one.

"I'm sorry," I said looking up at him. "I can't do this anymore with you."

Trey looked like I'd sucker punched him as he backed up and looked me over. I wasn't making sense and I didn't know where the words were coming from but I knew it was what I needed to say.

"But I said I was..."

"I'm a mess and I need to get *myself* straight, first," I said.

I laid my head on the car window and watched as Trey stuffed his hands in his pocket and glanced over at me. I couldn't tell if he was pissed or if he was just stunned by my revelation. I watched him closely as the car pulled out of the driveway; it was as if we were moving in slow motion. Before we'd pulled completely out, Trey was taking a seat on the steps watching our every movement.

"Lauren..." Kenya said after a few minutes of riding in silence.

"I really don't want to hear either of you have saying "I told you so"" I said trying to catch my breath between words.

Jasmine reached forward and massaged my shoulder, "We wouldn't do that!"

I sighed deeply and wanted the pain to go away.

"I just thought...I thought...I could just walk away from the pain," I said inhaling as tears continued to fall.

Jasmine leaned forward in the seat and wrapped her arms around the back of the seat all the way to the front of my chest.

"Honey, you did what's best for you," she said sympathetically.

"Your boyfriend died a month ago, and already, you're trying to find someone else to distract you from that pain? That's not fair and it's not right, Lauren."

"But..." I started. I wanted to let Jasmine know I hadn't set out to find Trey; rather he'd surprisingly come to me.

"Think about it Lauren. All your life you've had one distraction after another. When your mom died, your dad bought you every toy imaginable and gave you whatever you wanted whenever you wanted. Then when you met Brendan, he took over. Then when Brendan passed you jumped on Trey, hoping he'd keep you from experiencing the one thing you can never *truly* escape, pain," she said tenderly. "But a man can't help you get over something like this; this is up to you. Only you can forgive Brendan--if you choose--and move on. Only you can find peace and only you can choose to be happy without someone distracting you."

My eyes filled with tears as the truthful words stung me deeply. I had never realized how many people I relied on to "distract" me from the obvious things I didn't want to deal with.

"I think it's time for *you* to see what life is like by your terms. Cry, scream, yell and let things out, honey."

Kenya nodded her head as she slowed the car down at a yellow light.

"You can't make someone else happy if you aren't happy. I think for so long you told yourself you were happy and content with Brendan when you weren't. You were dependent on him for your happiness and it shouldn't be like that," Kenya said as the light turned green.

I wanted to be happy. But it was going to be a journey only I could take.

CHAPTER 11

Dear Diary-

I've been asleep all day and when I woke up this afternoon my house is was silent. Pop left a note saying he and Dee had gone to church. I know I need to be in there with them, but I needed to rest and collect my thoughts while plotting my next move. Tomorrow is the Steve Harvey interview and Lenny has already called twice, today, telling me that I need to get up to the station today to cut some promos for the promotion and the interview. I don't feel like it, but it's part of the j-o-b. Last night was such an eye opener that I'm not sure I'll ever be able to look at Trey the same again. I'm ashamed of myself for letting my emotions and the situation get the best of me. I woke up this afternoon and found three messages from Trey asking if we could talk; I can't, though. I've officially decided to drop out of the race. I've got to stop running from my problems and after my three-hour long conversation with Jasmine and Kenya; I realized that my life has been one big distraction. But if I continue down this road I'm going to self-destruct. And as much as I think I've done an okay job, things have to change. I'm going down to the station so I can prep for the show.

TTYL

Lauren Washington

When I got to the station no one else was there. I was able to crank out all the promos and spots that Lenny had left on my desk. I jotted down all my questions and placed them in my chair. I was prepared in every way possible and I prayed that tomorrow went off without a hitch. After I was finished with the preparation for the interview I headed down to Centennial Park for a jog. This was the first time that I'd jogged without being angry about something; it felt good. I slipped my headphones over my ears and my iPod around my arm and began stretching. With each bend and extension of my arms, my muscles began to slowly loosen up. I watched as couples ran by me and I smiled. I was still envious, but I was more focused on figuring out my own way to happiness rather than standing back and hoping it would find me. When I completed my workout, I was sweaty and content. Kanye West was blasting in my ears as I did my post-workout stretching beside my car. A dark blue Mustang pulled up beside me.

"Excuse me," I heard a lady say as I looked up and removed my headphones.

"Yes," I said kindly.

"Are you Mystique? You look so much like her," the girl said.

"Yeah, I am."

"Well, I'm sorry for interrupting your workout but I had to come over and thank you for telling the story of your boyfriend's suicide on-air."

"Uh...okay...you're welcome?" I said as I wiped the sweat my forehead.

Of all the things, Brendan's death didn't register as one of the things I thought people would be appreciative for.

"I'm sorry, my name is Lina," she said extending her arm.

She was wearing a pair of jogging shorts and a sports bra and I could tell she was definitely one of those chicks who could run five or ten miles without missing a beat.

"I'm a faithful listener," she commented as I shook her hand.

"And I'm a crisis counselor for the Georgia Suicide & Crisis hotline."

"Oh okay," I said nodding my head. Now it made sense. I listened as the woman continued.

"When you told your story, and then I read about it in the paper, my heart went out to you and your boyfriend's family," she said dropping head to the ground.

"Thank you."

"There are a lot of brothers and sisters who are losing their battle to suicide and...well, for someone like Brendan to have committed suicide; I think it opened a lot of people's eyes to the reality of it. It doesn't just hit white communities; African-Americans are prone to it as well."

"Yeah, that's true."

"If we had more suicide awareness in *our* community I was

thinking we could save so many more lives," Lina smiled. "So I was wondering if maybe we could do something with you. You know, like shoot a commercial or do a radio spot or something?" she said cautiously.

My eyebrows raised and while it was something I was definitely interested in, I didn't know if I was ready to be an advocate for suicide. After all, I was still mad at the term and could barely even speak the word. How would I look standing in front of a crowd speaking *out* on one of my daily struggles?

"Well..."

She turned and went to her car and pulled out a brochure and a business card.

"Just think about it. Here's my information. Please think about it and the lives you could save," she said handing the documents over.

I took the colorful brochure and looked it over.

"I've got to get to my personal training session, girl," she said looking over her shoulder at the buff guy who stood with his arms crossed; I assumed he was the reason she looked so damned fit.

"Yeah, okay."

I looked the information over and wondered if *I* could really do this. There were a lot of helpful things inside, including tips for coping with the loss of a loved. I flipped the pamphlet open to the tab and read.

"Step 1: Allow yourself to go through your feelings about the death."

I, obviously, had skipped this step.

"Step 2: Let go of any self-blame." My entire mantra after Brendan died was that *I* could have single-handily saved him. As I sat in the car, I knew that wasn't true.

"Step 3: Join a support group."

"Step 4: Nurture yourself."

"Step 5: Take any pressures or expectations off of yourself to "get over it" quickly."

"Step 6: Talk to a doctor if you start having trouble with sleeping or eating."

I stared at the words over and over and comprehended the fact that I had skipped over each and every one of the steps listed. I had my own plan and it evidently hadn't worked out very well.

I headed towards the house in silence. I thought about advocating suicide awareness, and told myself I wasn't ready. I was taking baby steps at handling all of this, and while I knew it was a good cause, I needed to do it on my own terms.

As I pulled up to the house I saw Trey and Dee standing in the driveway. Trey had his hands on his hips and Dee's shoulders were hunched over and his eyes on the ground.

I took my time getting out of the car but when I did, Dee scurried off into the house.

"Hey," Trey said as the anger on his face disappeared and was replaced with worry.

"What was that about?"

"Nothing, I handled it."

"What do you mean *you* handled it? He's my responsibility, Trey. What was that about?" I said firmly, this time letting him know I was serious.

"When I got here to finish up some things with the backyard, your father was on his way out the door for a meeting at his job. So he asked if I'd watch Dee; of course I said yes. When I finished I went up to Dee's room to see if he wanted to grab a bite to eat. I opened the door and him and little girlfriend were on the bed; in an...uh...compromising position."

My eyes shot open just as mouth dropped.

"Are you sure?" I asked as Trey clenched his jaw and nodded his head.

"It wasn't sex, but it was definitely getting there."

I couldn't believe what I was hearing and before I knew it, I was pushing past Trey and rushing into the house. Everything I'd done for Dee, and he had the nerve to come in *my* house and blatantly disrespect it? I was twenty-seven years old and I'd hesitated about bringing Brendan to my house for a little action. As I got to the stairs, skipping every other one, I thought about how I was going to handle Dee. I knew his hormones were getting the best of him but I'll be damned if I started raising my ex-boyfriends, secret son's child. It wasn't happening.

"What the hell were you thinking?" I said as I flung his door open. He didn't respond.

"I *said* what the hell were you thinking? You brought a little girl up in my house so you could sleep with her? Do you know how disrespectful that is?" I said as Dee zoned me out.

Realizing I wasn't getting the attention I needed or deserved, I grabbed him by the shirt and pulled him up.

"Do you hear me talking to you? What were you thinking?" I said as Dee looked up at me with his lips pursed.

"I wasn't."

"Exactly, boy," I said pushing him away. Dee looked at me like he wanted to push me back and cry, all in the same breath.

"Talk to me, tell me something," I said frustrated. Dee paced his room and finally plopped back on his messy bed.

"I just brought her up here so we could *talk* but then one thing led to another and..."

"First, you don't just invite anyone in my *damn* house without permission and secondly, y'all could've talked outside."

Dee looked away from me, crossed his arms and acted like he wasn't listening to me. I knew he was, though.

"So you don't care about my rules?"

Dee stared at me quietly.

"If I would've known you were going to deliberately disobey me and the rules I'd laid out, I wouldn't have taken you in, Dee.".

He looked down at the ground, and then, as if the words finally registered, he snapped his head up towards me.

"I knew you didn't want me here to begin with. You didn't have to take me in just because of that nigga," he said standing up to face me.

For a split second I thought he was going to hit me. I watched him closely. He then went back to the bed and dropped his shoulders.

"I didn't only take you in because of your *father*," I said. "I did it because I see a lot of potential in you and what you can do."

Dee seemed to be shocked by this answer and looked up at me skeptically.

"But if you can't follow my simple ass rules then I don't know."

"I'm sorry," he said reluctantly.

"Do you want to end up a father at a young age?"

"Well, they do say like father like son, right?" Dee joked.

I leaned against a wall and put my head back. What had I gotten myself into by taking on Brendan's son? This was stuff his father needed to be taking care of, not me.

"Did you have sex with her?"

Dee looked at me seemingly embarrassed.

"Did you or didn't you?"

"No. Today was going to be our first time."

I exhaled and thanked God Trey walked in when he did. There was no telling what I would have done had it been me who opened the door.

"If you want to stay here you'll keep your hormones in check and respect my rules. If not..."

"Fine," Dee said quickly before falling onto the bed with his hands behind his head.

I left his room and headed downstairs. Trey was sitting on the loveseat with his hands clasped together.

"He's going to hate me tomorrow," Trey laughed as he stood up and smoothed out his pants.

I tried not to look into his eyes and I instead headed to the kitchen; he followed me.

"He'll be *okay*," I said opening the fridge. "By tomorrow, all that anger will be gone."

"What about you?" Trey said draping his smooth arm over the open refrigerator door and looking down at me as I looked up at him.

I was speechless. I had a response figured. I closed the door and took a seat at the kitchen table. Trey looked at me and waited for a response.

"I think we should keep it strictly platonic. You can finish the house and when it's done I'll pay you and that will be that," I said not making eye contact. I was afraid that if I looked into his eyes he'd be able to see how much I didn't want my words to come true.

"What? Why? I thought we had a connection and..."

"It's just not going to work out, Trey. I've got too much baggage I need to work out and if I'm with you I can't," I said confidently. I knew what I was saying was true but it hurt like a bitch.

"I'll deal with your baggage," he said sounding as if he had no choice but to beg.

"It's not about you it's about me..."

"I can help you deal with the issues; don't shut me out."

"I don't have a choice."

"Yes you do, Lauren. You have a choice and it's standing right here," he said pointing to himself.

When I looked up at him I could see his stress. I wanted to take him into my arms, like I'd done Brendan so many times before, and make everything right. But my issue would still be there. By being with Trey I was denying myself the full right to properly grieve. I deserved that, at least.

"I can't."

Trey stood motionless for a minute before reaching into his

pocket for his car keys. He hesitated before turning and heading to the door without a word. I heard the door slam and my heart felt heavy. Everything was telling me to chase him and beg him to help me with this pain, but I knew this was something I had to do alone.

That night I tossed and turned in my bed and heard when Pop returned. Although I was wide awake, I stayed in my bed staring at the ceiling. When thoughts of Brendan entered my mind I didn't fight them, and instead, allowed them to flow in and out. During some points I cried and others I laughed; the memories are what put me to sleep. Gripping the empty pillow beside me I smiled and thought about where my life was headed.

The next morning I was refreshed and ready for the day. Announcing the winner for the promotion with Steve Harvey was said to be one of the biggest events in The Buzz history. As I prepared breafast I silently hoped that Dee wasn't salty over our conversation; either way, I needed him to hurry up and eat so I could drop him off at school.

"Dee! Let's go! Breakfast is ready!" I screamed loudly as I stirred the pot of grits.

Pop emerged from his bedroom and grabbed a plate and sat at the table.

"Trey told me what happened with Dee and that little girl," he said yawning into his food.

"Yeah..."

"What'd you do, other than scream?"

"I told him he needed to follow my rules if he wants to stay here because I didn't take him in so he could continue to be disobedient. If he can't follow my rules then maybe he needs to go back to his mom..."

Pop looked up at me and shook his head.

"You didn't say that last part to him, did you?"

"Yeah, why?"

"Nothing; it's just...that boy has been rejected repeatedly and told that no one wants him. So the first time he messes up , he probably thinks you don't want him either," Pop commented as he sipped on a cup of coffee

"He knows I want him here but he has to understand that he's a child," I said as I went to the entrance of the kitchen.

"Dee! Let's go!"

After five or ten minutes of no response, I headed to his

room to yell at him for ignoring me.

"Don't you think you need to come on, boy?" I said opening the door to find it empty.

I glanced around the room and realized that it was exactly how I'd left it before he had moved in. Gone were the stacks of Fubu and Enyce clothes, PlayStation 2 and countless hip-hop CD's that had been strewn across the room.

"Dee?!" I said wondering if he was hiding in the closet trying to scare me. But as I opened the closet door, I grasped the reality that Dee wasn't there. I checked underneath the bed where we kept his bags and saw that they were also gone.

As I rushed down the steps to Pop I kept thinking about what I'd said to him the night before. Had he confused my disappointment to mean I didn't want him around?

"Pop, he's gone!" I said out of breath "He's gone! All of his stuff is gone!" I repeated as Pop sprung up from the table.

While Pop searched the rest of the house and outside, I scrambled to the phone and called Trey, who answered on the first ring.

"Trey, have you seen Dee? He's missing," I said hoping he had run to his mentor.

"No. I haven't seen him since yesterday," he said sounding frightened.

This time it wasn't a joke or a misunderstanding, Dee was gone.

It was four in the afternoon and my show was starting in three hours. Pop had no choice but to go into work. Trey and I sat in his car trying to decide where else we could look. We'd gone to his mother's house, his girlfriend's house, his school, his friends' houses and even the malls; all with no luck. I was becoming desperate and running out of places he could be.

"Do you think we should check the bus stations?" Trey said sounding exhausted.

I nodded and sat back in the seat. "I did this to him. I made him think he wasn't wanted," I said.

"No it's not, Lauren; stop blaming yourself. Dee is confused about his place in the world; with everything he's dealt with I can't blame him. But it's not your fault."

I cringed as it got closer to show time. But I had more than enough time to find Dee and make it to the station in time for my show.

"Have you all seen this young man?" Trey said holding up a picture of Dee to the attendant at a bus station.

"Naw, try the other bus station," the young girl told us as she slid the picture back.

Bus station after bus station that we visited, had the same answer for us; none of them had seen Deehim.

"Don't you have that big interview today?" Trey asked as he checked the time and realized my show had started 45 forty-five minutes earlier. I checked my phone, which had been on silent, and saw that I'd missed 20 twenty phone calls, all from the station. I contemplated calling into the station after I noticed how late it was but I knew, by that time, the damage had been done. I was better off facing the music on the following day. I knew I was in trouble but it didn't matter one bit;. Dee did.

"I did..."

"Where could this boy be?" Trey said hitting the steering wheel. For the first time, I could see that Trey wasn't doing this for me. He actually cared about Dee's well-being. I glanced down at my phone and saw that yet another call had been missed. I didn't recognize the number and listened closely to the message.

"Lauren...this is...uh...Ms. Pat and I need you to come by my house. My grand...DeAndre is over here and I don't know why."

I dropped the phone and quickly directed Trey on how to get there. What the hell was Dee doing at Ms. Pat's house? I imagined Dee had completely lost his mind and was trying to hurt his grandmother. I prayed that wasn't the case though.

"Ms. Pat! It's Lauren, open the door!" I said as I banged on the screen door.

Trey stood behind me rubbing his hands together. We had been running all over Atlanta looking for Dee. It was nearing 8:30 pm.

Ms. Pat slowly opened up the door and had a horrified look on her face.

"What have I done?" she said falling into my arms and hugging me tightly. I looked over her shoulder and saw Dee sitting at the kitchen table.

Trey let himself in and stood over Dee. I pulled away from Ms. Pat and rushed into the house towards Dee. I pulled him up by his shirt and held him close to me. "I'm sorry," he said hugging me back.

I felt the tears falling down my cheeks.

"I'm so glad you're okay," I said as relief set in.

Ms. Pat came into the kitchen and clutched a picture of Brendan close to her stomach. She was swaying back and forth and humming a song.

"What is going on here?" I said looking at an ashamed looking Dee and a mellow Ms. Pat.

Neither of them spoke so I sat down. I wanted some type of response as to why Dee was there.

"He just showed up on my doorstep," Ms. Pat said as she slowed her rocking.

I looked over to Dee who was staring at me and Trey; finally he spoke up.

"I just wanted to find out what it was about me that made her not want anything to do with me. I just had to know," he said breaking down. Dee's shoulders shook uncontrollably as he cried into his hands.

"As much as I like staying with you, Lauren, I want to be accepted by people who are supposed to be my family," he said between gasps for air.

Ms. Pat stood back and wiped a few tears from her face.

"I didn't know the situation. I didn't know he was living with you. I had no idea a relationship with me meant so much to him."

I lowered my head; I hadn't either.

"So I wanted to tell her everything about me; everything I've been through, every dream I've ever wanted and tell her why she would like me; that's when she called you."

I looked over to Ms. Pat, who was back to rocking from side to side and humming a song.

"So what does this mean?" I asked slowly.

"I don't know..." Dee replied looking at his grandmother.

"I want him to stay here with me, if that's okay with you," she said nodding her head at Dee and then to me.

Dee's eye lit up with excitement, the same way they did when I told him I wanted him to move in with me, and he looked over to me with wide eyes.

"Really?" he said looking at a grinning Ms. Pat.

"Really. Lauren is it okay with you?"

"Of course it is...this is wonderful!" I said trying to hide the twinge of sadness in my voice.

I was glad that Ms. Pat had come to her senses and realized that this little boy *was* partially her responsibility now that Brendan was dead. Trey and I got up from the table and looked over at Dee and Ms. Pat, who were in a tight embrace.

"I'm sorry, baby," she said as she cried. "I'm so sorry."

"Well, I guess we'll be going, now," I said softly as I headed towards the door.

Ms. Pat and Dee hurried to the door before we could and stared at us.

I wanted to cry. How was I letting Dee go so easily? I wanted him to come back and continue living with me.

"Dee, I guess I'll see you around?" I said leaning in for a hug.

"I'll still come around."

"Do that, please."

I don't know why we were acting like the distance between my house and Ms. Pat's house was thousands of miles when in fact, Dee could easily walk.

"Actually, I'd appreciate it if Dee spent a couple of hours a day at your house. We wouldn't be here if it wasn't for you," she said putting her arm around Dee's shoulders.

Dee smiled at his grandmother and looked back at me. It was then I knew that just as quickly as I'd assumed the responsibility for Dee, I had to let go. This made more sense, anyway.

"Are you okay?" Trey asked as we drove back to my house.

"I'm getting there."

CHAPTER 12

Dear Diary-

I woke up early this morning and for no reason at all. I don't have Dee here to take to school and I don't have to be to work until this evening. Pop was really sad when he found out Dee wasn't returning, but he understood. Since I'm up I think I'll go into the station early and try to do damage control. I know I messed up by not showing up, especially when we had a huge promotion. Ralph called me late last night saying he needed to see me as soon as possible. I'm going to tell him to meet me at home. Pop still hasn't given me anymore answers about the domestic abuse reports other than "I'll never understand." Hopefully Ralph will be able to shed some light on this. Just like I'm no closer to finding out what happened to mom, I'm not closer to solving the "Why did Brendan kill himself?" case, either. But, on the good side I am doing much better with taking care of myself. I don't have any distractions and I can really see the difference. Jasmine and Kenya were supposed to come over last night so we could watch "Girlfriends" on Tivo— but Kenya never showed up. Jasmine came and we called her and she said she'd have to bail because she had "stuff to do" I wonder what that's about. I've got to make a mental note to give her call today. I just got back from working out and now I'm going to jump in the shower and get ready for an early day at the office.

Hopefully the day will continue in the direction it's headed.
TTYL
Lauren Washington

"What are you doing, girl?" I said as Kenya answered the phone groggily.

"Nothing," she said quietly and quickly.

"What happened to you last night?"

"I told you I had some things to take care of, Lauren," she snapped.

I looked at the phone for a second.

"*Excuse* me for being concerned."

"I'm sorry, girl. I just...hold on, okay?" she said.

She returned obviously more relaxed.

"I'm back."

"Okay...what was that about?"

"Lorenzo and I had a fight last night and..."

"You at home?"

"Yeah, why?"

"I'm on my way," I said hanging up before she could object.

The truth was I was less than five minutes from her house and had every intention of stopping by anyway. As I pulled into the driveway I saw Lorenzo's SUV parked in the driveway behind Kenya's brand new one.

"Hey," I said as Kenya opened the door before I could ring the doorbell.

Kenya looked disheveled, like she'd been making love all night and possibly all morning. She was wrapped in a tight silk robe.

My best friend couldn't hide much from me. But I still couldn't put my finger on why she was acting so withdrawn.

"What's going on?" I said lifting her chin, exposing her red eyes.

She seemed to be thinking about whether or not she was going to share things with me. She then quickly pulled me towards my car. We both jumped in and Kenya played with a couple of the window buttons before looking over at me.

"I did something yesterday that I'm not sure I thought through."

My mind immediately thought about Kenya and her strong feelings for Lorenzo; had she gotten married? I sat back in my seat waiting on the revelation.

"I...got an abortion."

I felt like my heart was being ripped out, piece by piece. She was pregnant and had an abortion without telling me. I knew she didn't need to ask my permission, but I thought she would have at least told me.

"You were...pregnant?"

"We found out Sunday."

"Why'd you get an abortion? You've always talked about wanting a child."

Kenya bit her bottom lip and covered her face with her

hands. It was as if my words were the reality check.

"I know; I did...I mean I do."

"But..."

"Lorenzo says he's not ready for that kind of commitment."

I dropped my head and thought about Brendan telling Brandy that exact same thing. Yet she was still madly in love with him. Was Kenya still holding onto hope that Lorenzo could be the "man of her dreams"?

"It's *your* body, though."

"We'll have kids someday when his career is a little more stable; you know he got let go from the Tyler Perry film because of contract problems."

I had heard that rumor but I'd heard it was because of a sexual harassment suit pending from one of the films lead actresses. I knew Kenya was holding back but I let her continue.

"Don't turn into me, girl," I said respectfully. She looked at me as though looking for clarity.

"My life was Brendan and anything he wanted, he got. Whatever he said was final and that's not the way it should be in a relationship. Now look at me...I'm trying to figure out how to find *Lauren* at twenty-seven years old!" I said trying to smile.

"But it's different..."

"It's exactly the same. The only difference is that you have a chance to get out before it consumes you."

After we were done talking and I'd told Kenya I had her back, she headed back towards the house.

"I love you!" I said with the window down as I tried to tell myself that everyone was going to have to handle their *own* problems. I wanted to trust that Kenya would make the right decision.

When I got to the station I noticed that someone else, other than Lenny, was parked in my assigned space. When I went to swipe my badge it wasn't working.

"What the hell?" I said trying to swipe it repeatedly.

Luckily the secretary, Abigail, was walking to the front door just as I was having my difficulties.

"Hey girl, my badge isn't working," I said holding it up to her.

She nervously swiped hers and opened the door for me.

"What's going on?" I said as we got in the elevator.

"You need to talk to Lenny; he should be up there," she said. Abigail and I had always been pretty cordial so it was a surprise that she was treating me like an outcast.

"Lenny, why the hell is my badge not working and who's parked in my spot?" I said rushing towards his desk.

Lenny slowly raised his head from the computer and looked at me for a second before returning his attention to the computer screen.

"You need to get your things and be out of here before I call the police." ," He he said with little emotion.

"What? Where am I taking my stuff?"

"You're fired."

"Fired? Yeah, right...look, I'm sorry about yesterday but I had a family emergency." ," I said playfully slapping Lenny's desk.

"And you couldn't call? Do you know what we had riding on yesterday?" Lenny said finally raising his voice.

"I didn't have access to a phone, Lenny ," I lied as I got nervous. If I was reading him right, this *wasn't* a joke.

"Bullshit."

"Look, I'll do some extra commercials or something, anything...I know I messed up but..."

"There are no more buts, no more excuses and no more "Mystique.". Now, get your stuff and get the hell out of here."

I stood motionless in the middle of the office and looked around at people as they slowly trickled in. As embarrassed as I'm sure I should have felt, I was more pissed than anything.

"What do you mean I'm fired? Huh? Talk to me!" I screamed as I knocked over a coffee mug on Lenny's desk and got his attention.

When he didn't say anything, I continued my rant.

"Do you know how much money I've made for this damned radio station? How much time I've done all the shit no one else wanted to do? And now you're telling me, because I messed up one time, that I'm *fired*?" I screamed in disbelief.

Lenny looked up at me and smirked "It's actually been three times and corporate has officially given me the green light to let you go; but don't worry we'll buy out your contract."

The money was the last thing I was worried about and as I turned to start screaming, I saw Crystal Bright, the intern I'd praised and encouraged to apply for full-time positions, sitting at my desk.

"What are *you* doing?" I said turning my attention to her.

"Crystal is your replacement," Lenny said, seeming satisfied at the egg on my face.

"Crystal?" I said looking at her, not understanding how she could have betrayed me.

"I'm sorry," she said.

I looked beside my desk and there was a brown box filled to the brim with all of my things. I understood, as I looked at that box, that my time at The Buzz was over; no amount of yelling or screaming was going to get my job back.

"Fine," I said snatching the box off of the ground as I headed towards the elevator. "You'll be sorry!"

I felt heat on my face as I passed all the sales reps and other on-air personalities as they eyed my box. They all knew what it meant and without a "goodbye" or "see-you-later," I pulled out of the radio station parking lot. Mystique was dead.

I laid on the couch and tried to figure out a couple of safety nets I had lined up. I had enough money saved for a year, so I wasn't that stressed about losing my job.

I could call V104, but I didn't want to go crawling so early; I could call a couple of promoter friends and try to host parties, but that seemed desperate too. While I kept running down my list of ideas, the doorbell rang. Anxiously I answered and saw Ralph.

caughtwent to"I'm sorry I'm running so late," he said as he rushed into the door and towards the living room table.

When I got to the table, Ralph had already laid out the documents and was standing with his hands on top of his head.

"I found some things out, Lauren; you may want to sit down for this."

I doubted anything that he was going to tell me could shock me at this point.

"I was able to get my hands on the *official* police report from your mother's murder; there seems to be a suspect that was never interviewed, although I'm not sure why."

"Do they live in Atlanta?"

"Not anymore. From what I've found out, he lives up north. Here's his work address." He handed me a piece of paper. "I don't know why the police didn't follow up. They had enough probable cause; enough to create a file on him."

"Why did they think he did it?"

"I'm still checking into that. I was going to catch a flight to New York later this week and see if I could ask around his neighborhood for anything."

I went through the paperwork and tried to grasp it all. I

possibly had my mother's killer in front of me; the last question was why. I hoped with all the work Ralph did that he could handle my concerns.

"What's his name?" I said looking up from the papers. I felt like I needed to know his name.

"Taariq Mohammad."

"And you think this is our guy?"

"I'm 95% sure it is."

I took a deep breath and decided now was the time to stop living life from the passenger side. I was taking the steering wheel into my hands.

"I'm going to New York; I want to see him."

"Lauren...this isn't ethically right nor is it completely safe."

"I don't care. I'm going," I said.

"I can't let you go by yourself, let me go with you."

I thought about it and realized I needed to do this by myself. Ralph had gotten me this far and was sure this was the guy who murdered my mother. I knew that as soon as I laid eyes on him, I would know. I felt like my mom would give me an indication, a signal or a sign that *this* was the man. I didn't want to approach the person or even get them to confess to the crime. My eyes just needed to see the person responsible for my pain. I needed to know who and maybe then I could understand the why in my equation.

"I'm going Ralph," I said closing the folder and looking up at him.

I glanced down at the address and the name Ralph had scribbled down and said the name aloud. "Taariq Mohammad, here I come."

Now that the words were spoken, I had no choice but to book my flight and sit back and wait for my time to come.

CHAPTER 13

Dear Diary-

I t's amazing how flying at thirty something thousand feet in the air can make you feel like you're escaping everything. I can't believe I'm heading to New York to find out if this guy Taariq Mohammad is mom's killer. Ralph keeps stressing that I need to be careful, because if he is in fact the murderer then we know his capabilities. It's like God works things out in ways we don't think he will. If I were employed with The Buzz, I wouldn't have been able to make this trip. I don't know what this guy looks like or anything; all I have is an address. I've booked a hotel for four days; I hope that's enough time. Pop freaked out when he found out I was going by myself and Jasmine and Kenya well, they agreed with Pop that I was crazy. I'm not sure if I'm crazy but I know this is very much out of my character. I realized that this *could* actually be my mom's killer. I wondered if he would be proud of me and how I'm taking this by the horns! Ooh! We're having a little turbulence so I'm going to take a nap.

TTYL
Lauren Washington

I arrived at my hotel, suitcase in hand. I'd been to New York before but it had only been business and it had rarely been longer than one night. By the time I'd checked in and headed to my room I was exhausted. But no matter how tired I was, it couldn't hold me back from making a pit stop at the work address. New York was loud, way too loud. People hustled and bustled around me. I stood on the corner and hailed a cab. I handed the cab driver the address and sat back quietly in the seat.

"You don't look like you from around here," he said in a thick New York accent. I smiled.

"No, I'm not."

"You visiting someone special?" he asked.

I pretended I didn't hear him. When the cab stopped I paid the driver, grabbed the address and stood in front of the 50's like diner. As the cars whizzed by and the horns beeped loudly, I darted in and out of traffic and made my way inside of the eatery.

"Is it just you?" the hostess asked as she picked up a menu and held it to her chest.

"Yes, just me," I said looking around. "Are there any tables close to this window?" I asked pointing to a window that faced the sidewalk.

"Sure."

I ordered my food and sat with a notebook in front of me. I watched the comings and goings of the neighborhood. It seemed to be a pretty upscale and diverse community. I wondered where Taariq was and what he would do when I finally showed my face and announced who I was.

"Here you go," The waitress said sitting my BLT and orange soda down in front of me. She handed me a straw and napkin and smiled sweetly before asking, "Anything else I can get you?"

"No I'm good....but wait," I said remembering I needed to ask questions.

"Do you know a Taariq Mohammad?"

"*Know* him? he's the manager here," she said raising an eyebrow suspiciously.

"Oh."

"Why? Do you need me to call him down for you?"

I shook my head and started stuffing my mouth with food.

"No, I'll catch up with him later," I managed to say.

I swallowed the huge lump of food and watched the woman saunter away to a

co-worker and point me out. They were gathered in a close circle, which broke apart when a customer entered the shop. My cell phone rang and startled me, causing me to spill my soda.

"I'm sorry," I said attempting to blot the orange liquid up with the thin napkin that was sitting in my lap.

"It's okay, girl! What do you think all these napkins are for?" the waitress said smiling widely.

"Hello?" I said.

"Hey there..." the familiar male voice said over the phone.

"Trey?"

"The one and only."

"Is everything okay?" I said as visions of my house in flames ran through my mind. I mean, why else was Trey calling me?

"Everything's fine, relax," he said laughing a little bit. "I just wanted to call and check on you and I know you said to give you space but…"

"No, it's cool," I said relieved he had called.

"So, have you met the guy yet? I mean is this going to be like a sit down interview where you ask him if he *did* it? Or…"

I laughed at Trey's silliness. Even in the most intense moments, he made me smile.

"No not yet; no I'm not interviewing him," I said laughing. "I'm just going to ask him if he lived in Atlanta around the time mom was killed."

Trey listened in as I rambled about nothing in particular.

"How will you know it's him?"

"I think I'll just *know*."

"Okay. I saw Dee today; he came by to see you."

"How was he?"

"Good…really good. I think him moving in with his grandmother was a great idea."

I played with the lettuce and pickle that had come off of the sandwich.

"Me too."

"So, do you know when you'll be back or is this just a play it by ear kind of trip?"

I was touched that despite me trying to push him away he was still being a good friend. I loved that.

"I think I'll be back on Monday."

"Cool."

"You know it's so loud up here I couldn't hear myself…" I said stopping mid-sentence as I saw a man enter the restaurant.

"Trey, let me call you right back," I said hanging up before I had a chance to hear his response.

I knew this face; it was familiar. I stood up from my table, and without hesitation walked towards him. It was as if my legs were guiding and my body. He was standing by a coat rack at the entrance fooling with something in his pocket.

"Excuse me…" I said as I tapped him on the shoulder.

"Yes," he said turning abruptly.

As soon as our eyes met my heart melted, my skin crawled and my body reacted. This wasn't the killer but it was a familiar face to another mystery.

"Terrence?" I said remembering all the pictures I'd seen and studied of Brendan's older brother.

"Do I know you?"

I stumbled over my words as I giddily extended my hand to him "I'm Lauren...Lauren Washington, your brother Brendan's girl...ex-girlfriend," I said grabbing his hand.

I knew it was him by the way he was dressed. He looked just like his pictures.

"W-what are you doing up here?" he asked smiling.

"I..." I started as my mind studied the characteristics of the "other" brother. But before I could continue, my waitress appeared with her hands on her hips and cut in.

"I see you found Taariq, huh?"

"What?" I said looking at her with confusion.

"You said you were looking for Taariq Mohammad, right? Here he is," she said pointing to an edgy looking Terrence.

"*You're* Taariq?" I asked.

"My name is Taariq Mohammad now. I changed it a couple of years ago when I converted to Islam."

My heart stopped as I stared at Taariq for an answer. While I'd come to find answers on one mystery, it looked like I was killing two birds with one stone. Taariq or Terrence, whatever he was calling himself, sat across from me as I fidgeted with my fork and spoon. He didn't seem to know why I was there or why I was acting so strange. I couldn't get Ralph's voice out of my head that he was "95% sure" Taariq Mohammad was my mom's killer. I looked into his eyes and quickly dropped my head. As much as I told myself I was ready to confront someone, this, I wasn't ready for.

"What are you doing here, Lauren?" Taariq asked.

"Huh?" I stumbled before swallowing and forcing myself to look into Taariq's eyes.

"Is everything okay?" he inquired as he clasped his hands together.

"Everything's fine. I was just in town visiting a...uh... friend,"

Taariq nodded his head and looked me over. I looked deep into his eyes and stared at his features. If I hadn't buried Brendan almost two months earlier, I might have thought this was him sitting in front of me. Aside from the thick beard growing on his face and the course hair on his head, Brendan and Taariq were almost identical. I must've been gawking because when Taariq cleared his throat I saw a strange look on his face.

"What?" he asked rubbing his face.

"You just look so much like...*him*," I said unable to think about my reason for the trip or the questions I was going to eventually ask him. I looked at his hands in amazement. They looked just like Brendan's.

"We used to get that a lot when we lived in..." he said trailing off as he stared into the distance.

"Bankhead?" I quizzed.

"Yeah."

"Why'd you move, anyway? Brendan always said you just needed a change of scenery but you've never even back, right?"

Taariq squirmed a little in his seat and eventually nodded his head.

"Atlanta isn't for me sister. I'm a totally different person."

"Aren't we all?" I smiled apprehensively.

"So how long are you in town?"

"Until Monday."

"Well, we'll have to catch up for lunch or something. Are you staying near?"

"I'm at the Four Seasons."

"Okay...well, I wish I could sit and chat all day but there is work to be done and people to manage," he said respectfully as he bowed his head and stood up from the table.

I knew if I didn't do it now, it wouldn't get done. I had to ask Taariq what he knew about mom's death.

"Terrence...I mean Taariq, can I ask you a question?" I said motioning for him to take a seat.

"Go ahead," he said.

I had rehearsed the way I would ask the person all of the questions Ralph had equipped me with. But I suddenly couldn't get it out. My hands were shaking as I played with the napkin and finally looked into his eyes.

"What do you know about my mother's death?" I blurted out.

Taariq didn't bat an eye and he didn't look shaken by the inquiry. It was as if the question didn't phase him. He leaned back and crossed his arms over his chest.

"Nothing," he said finally. "I don't know nothing about that."

He sat still in the chair for a minute, maybe to see if I was going to challenge his statement. When I didn't he exhaled.

"Why?" he asked.

"I *know* that you know something."

"I just told you I didn't know anything about that sister."

I had been nervous about asking the questions but the more Taariq denied knowing anything, the angrier I felt.

"Your name is all over the police report as being a suspect; you mean to tell me you don't want to tell me *anything*?" I asked again, this time leaning forward in my chair.

"I've got to get to work, Lauren. Like I said we can get together for lunch or something before you leave," he said uneasily. This time I knew he didn't mean it.

He wasn't going to have lunch, dinner or anything in between with me. Either I was onto his past or he was extremely insulted that I'd accused him.

"One more question," I said holding my finger up. "Brendan left a note at the scene and I was wondering if you knew anything about why he did what he did?"

I still couldn't speak the words suicide.

"You mean why did he kill himself, sister?" Taariq asked.

"I'm not sure what my brother was going through then," he said pushing his chair back from the table and standing up.

"Now if you'll excuse me," he said. He walked towards the "Employees Only" sign at the back of the restaurant.

I stayed at the restaurant for another hour, hoping I would see Taariq and ask him more questions, but to my surprise, he never came back out.

As I hailed a cab, I could feel myself getting stronger. I didn't know what was going on or why people were intent on keeping secrets, but I was about to do the unthinkable and *find* the secrets myself.

My next two days in New York were pretty boring. I went to the diner everyday, ordered the same meal and sat in the same chair. The same waitress, who was so helpful to me when I'd been there earlier, was tight lipped about when and if Taariq would be returning.

I wasn't ready to go to his house. I wanted that to be my final destination and last resort.

"Your name is Christa, right?" I said wiping my mouth as I pulled out a twenty from my purse.

"Yes," she said as she started picking up the plates. Obviously Taariq had told her not to talk to me or tell me anything; but I knew what color would always have people talking: green.

"Would you know where Taariq is *today*?" I said waving the twenty around so only she could see.

Christa thought about it and shook her head, no.

"I haven't seen or heard from him in a few days," she said biting her lip.

Reaching into my purse I pulled out two more twenties and placed them on the table.

"Still don't know?"

Christa looked at me and quickly snatched up the sixty dollars.

"Look, he's only been coming in really late at night, like eleven or twelve, around closing time. Other than that, you can find him either at his apartment in Harlem," she said as she pretended to wipe the table down as she continued talking.

"Here's the address," she said as she scribbled something down on a paper.

Just as quickly as our conversation began, it was over and I was out of cab fare.

I left the diner and headed to a Rite-Aid and waited in line for the ATM. I looked behind me and saw that the line was only getting longer. Finally the guy in front of me got his stuff together and got out of line with his money.

My transaction was smooth and quick and I pulled two hundred dollars out of the machine and stuffed it into my jeans. I turned to walk away and ran smack dab into a gentleman who was talking on his cell phone.

"I'm sorry," I said picking myself up from the ground.

The guy looked at me for a second then ended his phone. He then started pointing at me.

"Your name is Lauren, right?"

I was used to attention like that in Atlanta, but I was miles away from anything and anyone familiar. How did this guy know me?

He was in his forties, sported a bald head and had dark moles all over his face. I could tell he was someone in high authority because of the Prada coat and shoes he was wearing.

"And you are..."

"Sorry, the name's Troy Gaines," he said chuckling as he stuck his hand out.

"Nice to meet you, Troy Gaines; do I know you?"

"Not really but I'm a huge fan. I'm the new general manager of Hot 99."

I had heard of Troy. He was a Georgia boy, which might have explained why he recognized my face.

"Oh okay, it's really nice to meet you," I smiled.

"You know, I used to listen to you when I was home on vacation; you're really good. Ever thought about leaving The Buzz behind and relocating to New York?" he inquired seriously.

I actually hadn't thought about making the jump. The on-air personalities in New York were deep and heavy into the game and some of them had waited ten years, sometimes interning at a station before being considered as a DJ.

"I actually am no longer with The Buzz but I'm only here on vacation."

"Wow. Well, then I guess it's a good thing that we ran into each other, huh?"

"I guess so."

"Why don't you take my card and give me a call before you leave. We should do lunch and discuss some possible opportunities for you up here. I think you're just what we're looking for."

I grabbed the card and watched as Troy walked away. I couldn't believe the way things were shaping up. New York *really* wasn't my cup of tea and the thought of leaving Pop, Jasmine, Kenya, Dee, and even Trey kind of frightened me. But maybe it was just what I needed in order to break free, I thought. I had plenty of time to think about what I wanted.

"Please God don't let anything go wrong in here and please let Taariq tell me something," I prayed as I crossed the street to the apartment.

I flung the door open and headed to the elevator. When I got to the thirteenth floor I slowly stepped off and looked to my left and right. The apartment building was nice, really nice. Almost too nice for a diner manager to afford. Apartment 1312 was on my right. I placed my finger over the peep hole and knocked on the door heavily.

"Who is it?" I heard Taariq say. I could tell he was placing his face to the door and trying to see who it was, but I wasn't moving my hand and I wasn't saying who it was.

"If you don't move your hand I'm not letting you in," he said.

Slowly I pulled my hand away and I heard Taariq say something under his breath before moving the chain and opening the door.

"Lauren? Why are you here?"

"I needed to see you. We needed to talk."

"About what?"

"You know about what…"

"I'm afraid I don't sister."

I wanted to smack the smug smile off of his face, but he held the key to the answers I so desperately needed.

Glancing around the apartment I noticed that he was either still unpacking or packing.

"Going somewhere?"

He spun around and saw the evidence that were the boxes and turned back to me with sweat on his brow.

"I'm actually just redecorating, that's all."

"Taariq, don't you think you at least *owe* me a discussion? I was with your brother for years. Don't you think we should sit down and talk; even about him?"

Taariq waited for a minute before opening the door so I could enter.

"Would you like some water?" he said calmly.

"Actually, I'm okay," I replied as I ran my fingers over a picture of Brendan, Taariq and Ms. Pat from the early 80s.

We sat on the couch and looked at each other until I broke the silence.

"Taariq, I just need to know what happened—that's all. I'm not looking to put you in jail if you had something to do with this. I just need to know for my sake."

"Sister, I can't tell you something I don't know."

"*Please,*" I begged looking into his eyes. "Anything you can tell me."

Taariq dropped his head and then looked away from me.

"You seem like a good man and it *was* eighteen years ago and if it wasn't your fault, I'll understand,"

I did have every intention of turning the killer's name into the police, regardless of what I promised Taariq.

"I'm sorry," he started. "I'm going to have to ask you to leave."

I couldn't believe my ears. I had gotten *this* close to getting some answers, and I could see Taariq breaking down. Now he was kicking me out. I needed to work some magic and I needed to work it *now.*

"When I was nine years old, I was awakened from my sleep by a phone call from the Atlanta Police Department telling my father that life as we knew it was over; my mother was dead. And ever since, my heart has stopped when the phone rings at night.

Then, eighteen years later, I get a phone call from the same police department telling me my boyfriend, the man I loved more than anything, was dead. Do you have any idea what that feels like? I just want some answers. I want to live my life Taariq," I said allowing a tear to fall.

He looked almost emotionless.

"I didn't ask for *any* of this, yet I'm the one that has to deal with it all. I'm trying to move on but until I have answers I feel like I'm stuck in the same place, the same nine year old with the same insecurities and worries. I want to live!" I screamed. "I just want to live!"

Taariq reached out and rubbed my back lightly as I continued with my impromptu speech.

"I had to bury my boyfriend in the same cemetery as my mother, Taariq. I'm not asking for you to understand where I'm coming from, because you can't, but I'm asking for you to see that I'm only trying to find out the truth about everything."

"But if you need me to leave, I will..." I said as I smoothed my jeans and wiped my tears.

Taariq pulled on my jean leg. I stumbled to the couch and looked at him.

"We just wanted our father, that's all!" Taariq screamed with his head toward the ceiling. I sat back and watched as he poured his story out to me.

"When we left Jersey for Atlanta, mom and dad had separated and were taking a break; then some years later, after we were settled in our new life, they decided to give their marriage another try. You don't understand how much that meant to Brendan and I. All we wanted was to have the "Cosby Show" family. You know the mom, the dad and the well-behaved kids," he smiled, not paying attention to me as I pressed record on the tape recorder I had in my purse.

"So, everything was going great! Mom and dad were finally back on track and it looked like he was going to be permanently moving his things to Atlanta to live with us! But then *she* came along. For a second time a woman with big hips, a pretty face and long hair took our father away from our mom. He was sneaking out to bars with her, taking her on dates and Brendan and I were listening every night when mom would go to bed and cry herself to sleep. We hated *her*," he said with anger in his voice. His eyes were fixed on something, but I couldn't tell what.

"I mean it was like she had some sort of hold on him,

mentally; he would do anything for her but nothing for us. And it started to eat away at us. So one night we randomly hit the streets looking for her. We had a plan to kill her and hoped that dad would find his way back into mom's bed and arms," Taariq said dropping his head.

"We stole my dad's car and headed out into Bankhead looking for the home wrecker. When we found her there was no turning back; *she* had to go."

I was trying to follow but I didn't know who "*she*" was, so I interrupted.

"Who is *she*?" I said knowing I'd need all the questions answered before I could understand.

"Your mother," he said looking at me.

"Excuse me? My mother was *not* having an affair with your father."

"Yeah...she was."

I shook my head and looked around the room. "This can't be true."

Ignoring my comments, Taariq continued.

"So when she pulled us over for the stolen car she told us to get home and she wouldn't file a police report. But the more we argued with her the more she realized we weren't going anywhere and so she started calling my dad. I knew that if my dad knew we were with her, and that we killed her, he'd put the puzzle together and *definitely* leave."

I listened with my eyes closed, trying to envision it all as it was happening.

"And it was you and your friend or..."

"It was me and Brendan. Brendan and I were the only ones in the car."

I felt like I couldn't breathe and like little pins were sticking me all over my body. Tears slowly fell as I realized what Taariq was telling me. But before I could sort it all out, Taariq continued.

"I pulled out my dad's gun and told her I was going to shoot her. But then I got scared. I couldn't do it. I couldn't just *kill* her like that. So, Brendan picked up the gun and fired. She lay on the ground shaking while we argued about what to do. We wanted her dead but I never actually thought it would happen," Taariq said as tears stung his eyes. He wiped them away and continued with his story.

I couldn't keep tears out of my eyes and air in my lungs. If what he was telling me was true, Brendan had killed my mother.

"I knew she wasn't dead when we shot her because she was still moaning and crying so I did the only thing I knew how to do. I ran her over with the car. I'm sorry! I'm sorry sister!" he screamed as he came to terms with what he'd done.

I stared at a stain on the carpet and tried to remember all the times Brendan had told me that hiring a P.I. was a bad idea or that he thought I should leave it alone. Now I knew why. I couldn't think or see straight. All I heard was Taariq screaming. *My boyfriend killed my mother.*

"And your dad...did he know anything?"

"He suspected things, which was why he left us and never came back. He said he couldn't stand the sight of us knowing that we'd done something horrible," Taariq wailed.

"I didn't *really* think I'd kill her, you know? But the next day when I woke up, it was all over the news and I knew this was bigger than what either one of us could imagine."

"Did you know she had a husband and daughter to go home to? Did you know that you took that away from me and my father?" I screamed.

"With all due respect sister, I was fifteen years old when this happened. Brendan was eleven. We were only thinking about our family. Your mother complicated our happiness."

I walked to the window and placed my hands on the cool glass. I wanted to pinch myself and say this had all been one big, bad dream; but it wasn't. How was this happening? Why was this happening?

"Why me? Why'd Brendan date me, love me all this time if he'd done this awful thing?" I cried, hoping Taariq would tell me it had been a cruel joke.

"He loved you, sister. He did. But he always told me he wanted to right the wrong of killing your mother. So he loved, protected and showered you with affection. But everyday he looked at you and saw you falling deeper in love, he realized he was seeing your mother; he had to pull away..."

"Is *that* why he killed himself? Because of all of this?" I said waving my hands in the air.

What was Taariq telling me? That he and Brendan had killed my mom and Brendan had begun dating me out of pity turned to love?

"I *really* don't know what was going on with Brendan when he took his life; that's the truth. He was supporting me for a while but when he sold the shop, the money stopped coming; eventually he stopped calling, writing and sending anything. I found out about everything from mom and I couldn't bring myself to come home for the funeral."

I could feel myself getting lightheaded so I turned and grabbed my purse and clutched it tightly to my chest.

"Please, don't leave," Taariq said lightly blocking the door. But I couldn't breathe and I needed to get out immediately.

"Please forgive me," Taariq said dropping to his knees and wrapping his arms around me. I could feel his sobs getting heavier and heavier and soon, we were both crying loudly. I howled at the thought of all the years I'd invested in a man that had committed the ultimate betrayal, killing my mother.

"I've got to go," I said pushing Taariq off me and opening the door. I darted down the hallway, turning only when I reached the elevator. Taariq dropped his head as I stepped onto the elevator and I listened as he screamed, "I'm sorry!"

I cried a refreshing, and confusing, cry. Had I been so blinded by someone, *anyone* helping me get over my pain, that I allowed this *man* who I didn't know anymore, into my life?

I closed my eyes and tried to force myself to forget about Brendan and everything good he'd ever done for me. Because in my mind he had taken away my childhood and had created the person I now hated.

I closed my eyes and waited for sleep to take over and take me to a place where I could sort out the things that had turned my world upside down.

When I woke up the next morning, I felt energized. I hadn't figured everything out but I knew there was nothing I could do to reverse everything I'd heard. It was over. My plane didn't leave until four so I called Troy Gaines and set up a mid afternoon brunch. Although I was still shaken up from my encounter with Taariq, I couldn't let it dictate my life.

I looked outside my hotel window. I wanted change, I wanted clarity and most of all I wanted a new start; I knew exactly what my first step was going to be.

"Something short like Halle Berry or something," I said.

"Are you sure?" the lady asked.   I wanted to get rid of baggage.

"Positive," I said closing my eyes. I was ready to say goodbye to a lot of things, and I knew my hair was the first thing I needed to shed in order to start over.

By the time it was finished I already felt like a huge ton had been lifted off my shoulders. It was just like Halle's was earlier in her career. I ran my hands down the back of my freshly shaved head and turned from side to side, trying to decide if I *really* liked it.

"It looks fabulous on you!" the hairdresser said as she stood next to me fixing a couple of stray pieces.

I met Troy over lunch. He walked past me a couple of times without recognizing me.

"I'm over here!" I smiled sweetly.

"Wow! New look, huh?" he said looking over my new cut. "That really fits you!"

"Thanks."

"This lunch is going to be quick but I just wanted to let you know that we really want to work something out to get you to Hot 99; if you're interested I can fly you back out in a few weeks for a meeting."

"Do you need an air check tape or anything?"

"The big guys are taking my word on you. They know you sound great and have that 'umph' factor."

"I never really thought about moving to New York."

"Well, start thinking about it now because, if I can help it, we'd like to have you on-air in less than two months."

Everything was happening faster than I expected.

"Do you have a card?" he asked me.

I took one out of my purse and passed it over to him.

"We'll be in touch," he said embracing me and then racing out of the restaurant.

My eyes widened as I screamed. I couldn't contain it. Was I really about to be on-air at the hottest radio station in the United States? I ate my food and relaxed my legs and watched as people walked around. It amazed me how wonderful it felt not to worry about things. I thought about Trey and the places I'd told myself I wasn't going with him and then I thought about Pop and the news I was going to have to break to him. I wondered if Kenya had handled her situation with Lorenzo and whether or not Dee was happy with his new living arrangement. My mind wandered about Lina, the suicide counselor I'd met in Piedmont Park; I questioned why I'd been so scared to record the PSA or commercial she'd told me about.

I walked back to the hotel and studied faces and a couple of times I could've sworn I was seeing Brendan. I would look at someone only to be disappointed when he got closer. I don't know why I was allowing my mind to play tricks on me, to think that he was actually going to be alive and walking towards me on a New York street. I hurried and got my things together and got ready to check out.

"This was dropped off for you," the hotel clerk said as she checked me out and swiped my credit card. She'd slid an envelope, which was addressed to me, right in front of me.

"From who?"

"I'm not sure madam. He was a thin guy with a thick black beard."

Taariq, I thought to myself.

I jumped in a cab and got myself settled before opening this unexpected letter. It was from Brendan.

"Lauren,

I'm sorry. Let me just say this. If you are receiving this then I know you've figured out my secret. I'm sorry. I don't think I can say that shit enough. I'm writing this letter and listening to you on the radio at the same time; your voice is so beautiful, baby. Tonight I'm going to do something that I know you'll never forgive me for; but I can't take this anymore. I'm mailing this letter to my brother Terrence; I hope it finds its way to you. I was eleven years old when the incident with your mom happened. I was young, I was stupid and I really just wanted my life back; instead I took your mother's. I'm sorry. Damn, I'm sorry. If I could take it back, I would. But I can't. I've struggled with telling you the truth, but every time I saw you drop a tear because you missed your mom I knew I couldn't do it.

In a perfect world, though, you would've been my wife. But then I met Brandy, the girl I brought to the club at your birthday party, and she was a safe outlet. I never loved her the way I loved you...but I did love her. I didn't realize how in over my head I was until she told me she was pregnant. I wasn't ready for that. I have a son. His name is DeAndre Lewis and he should be about forteen now. I never meant to be a bad father but I didn't know anything about being a father at such a young age...and so I just left it to his mother, which was a mistake. I would've made a great dad. It's too late now, though. Also, I sold my shop to Mike. I'm sorry I didn't tell you. I needed to know that when I left this earth my shop would be taken care of.

Lauren, you have been there for me and I appreciate it and I love you. I'm sorry for the pain that you'll endure because of my action but know I never meant you any harm. The moment I laid eyes on you I knew I was through, but I had to remind myself that I was the reason for your pain; I couldn't live with myself knowing that. Please try to look out for my son and my mother if you can. I hope that one day you can forgive me and move on. Life is too short not to be happy...I promise I won't be mad. I really, really do love you baby but I can't do this thing called life anymore...it's much too painful and I want out.

Until we meet again...

Brendan Deondre Lewis

I held his letter tightly. The only thing I had to do was face reality back home.

CHAPTER 14

Dear Diary-

I got on an earlier flight and am due back in Atlanta two hours early. This will be perfect. No one will see it coming when I come home with my new hairdo! I feel like a weight has been lifted off me. I have the tape to hand over to Ralph, and I've decided I *do* want to press charges for the murder of my mother. I don't know what I'm going to do with all of the information I have but I hope it answers some questions for Pop. The plane's just landed so I'm going to get off and catch a cab to the house!
TTYL
Lauren Washington

"Hello?" I yelled throughout the house. I knew people were there because I saw Jasmine, Kenya and Trey's cars in the driveway. "Is anybody here?"

I set my bags down by the front door and headed toward the music. I watched as Trey, Pop, Jasmine, Kenya and Dee all played Monopoly. Laughter rang throughout my house; I hadn't heard that in years.

"What time does Lauren's plane get in?" I heard Trey ask as Jasmine rolled the dice.

"I think it's at 6:30 or something," Pop said clearing his throat.

I sprung around the corner and threw my hands in the air.

"I leave for a couple of days and y'all forget all about me!" I said loudly.

"Lauren!" Pop said getting up and rushing towards me.

Kenya and Jasmine sat dumbfounded at the table at my new look. I wasn't sure if that meant they didn't like it or that they liked it so much they were in shock. Trey and Dee were next to get up and hug me.

"I missed you,L-llllauren," Dee said wrapping his arms around me. I smiled; it felt good to be missed.

"I missed you too you little knucklehead."

Trey and I looked at each other, trying to decide how to handle our embrace; finally I stepped forward and wrapped my arms around his neck tightly.

"Thank you for my daisies."

"You look stunning," he said whispering in my ear.

"Thank you."

"Honey, that hairstyle is you!" Jasmine said pushing Trey out of the way so she could get her hug in.

I held my best friend tightly and didn't want to let go. I wanted to grab her hand and tell her everything I'd discovered, but I couldn't. Kenya walked towards me with a huge grin.

"I *told* you that hairstyles like that would be cute on you," she said running her hands through my short hair.

I felt rejuvenated and if I needed any type of booster, seeing my family and loved ones was all I desired.

"Pop, when you have a moment we need to talk," I said as he passed by me.

I headed to my room and crashed on the bed. All around the room were reminders of my life with Brendan.

Some people might have thought I was crazy and irrational, but if I was going to start with a clean slate I needed it completely cleared. I stood up and began tossing everything that reminded me of Brendan into a box. I didn't stop until my room looked like I'd just moved in.

"Perfect," I said out loud.

After searching and researching, I was able to find Lina's number and I placed a call to her telling her that I would be more than glad to record a PSA or commercial for her, free of charge. She was ecstatic. I was moving myself out of my own way and it felt great. I then called Ralph and told him I had a taped confession from Taariq. Just as I hung the phone up and sat back on the bed, my door opened and Pop was standing there like a deer in headlights.

"Hey Sugar Baby..." Pop said cautiously.

"Pop, I found out some things I think you should," I said patting my bed.

My father sat with his shoulders.

"I found out who killed mom."

Pop's eyes grew large as he squeezed my hand tightly. "You *did*?" he said astonished.

"Yes."

"Who was it? Was it anyone from around here?"

"Pop...it was Brendan and his brother Terrence."

I could see the disbelief wash over his face quicker than a forest fire and still, Pop was squeezing my hand tightly.

"W-what?"

"Terrence admitted it all to me yesterday," I said delicately while I stroked Pop's hand.

"W-why?" he said as a tear hit his cheek.

This was the part I had been dreading and I hoped that Pop didn't flip out when he heard the news of mom's affair.

"He claims that mom was having an...affair with their dad."

I didn't get the reaction I'd hoped for as Pop asked me, "What was his name?"

"Darrin....Darrin Lewis," I said as I tried to recall his name.

"That was *Brendan's* father?!" Pop yelled jumping up from the bed as if a thought popped into his mind.

"You *knew* about this, Pop? You knew mom was cheating on you?"

"Sugar Baby, your mom and I had our ups and downs but we were young; I did a lot of stupid things that pushed her to have an affair with Darrin. I had no idea that Darrin was Brendan's father," Pop said rubbing his moustache as he paced my room.

"So the domestic abuse reports..." I said trailing off.

"Were from her relationship with Darrin; they had this passionate, abusive relationship that sometimes got out of hand."

"And you were *okay* with your wife being with another man who beat her?"

"Of course not, Sugar Baby; but it was only so much that I could do to make your mother see that enough was enough. I also knew that neither one of us was going to say goodbye to each other. We were each other's everything. We were just young and confused and thought life would be here for us forever," Pop said stopping to shake his head. "I had your mothers' partner pull the domestic abuse reports because I didn't want any of this to ever get back to you and make you think differently about your mother. She was a *good* woman but we were young and dumb...Did he say *why*?"

"They wanted their mother and father back together and killing mom seemed to be the only way to do that," I said.

Pop shook his head. "Umph! I just can't believe this. How are you?" he said.

"I'm fine. Well, I'm surprised and hurt, of course; but my mind is clear and I'm ready to live life," I smiled. This time, though, I wasn't forcing it.

Pop and I joined hands and walked down the stairs towards the rest of the party. Someone had ordered pizzas and the Monopoly game was getting intense.

"I bought Boardwalk, pay up!" I heard Dee laugh as Jasmine forked over her play money.

I took a seat and watched them. When the game ended everyone broke for something to eat.

"Do you want me to fix you something?" Trey asked pointing to the paper plate.

"I'm okay," I smiled.

Kenya plopped next to me and laid her head on my shoulder. Without a word from her, I could sense she'd made the right decision for herself.

"I decided to stay with Lorenzo," she said wincing as she tried to gauge my response.

"Okay," I said waiting to hear more.

"After I explained my side of things, he understood where I was coming from and we're going to work on things," she said smiling widely.

"Well, as long as you take it slow. Isn't that what y'all told me?"

Kenya giggled and covered her mouth.

"I'm not moving in with him and I gave the car back. I don't want to become that chick; you know the one who is so dependent on a man that she can't function or deal without him?" she said quickly.

Of course I knew that chick; she used to be deeply embedded in my soul.

"You're my girl so whatever you do...I've got your back," I said reaching over and hugging her tightly.

I was sure Kenya had expected me to blow up about her decision, but this was *her* life and like Brendan said, "Life's too short *not* to be happy." If Kenya thought her relationship with Lorenzo was worth working out, I backed her 110%. Everyone joined around the glass dining room table and stuffed their faces with pepperoni and cheese pizza. If anyone would have told me that two months earlier I could be this happy, this content and this free, I would have laughed at them and then called them a psycho. But here I was.

Trey took a seat next to me on the couch and smiled.

"What?"

"Nothing, I just really like that cut on you."

"Well, I'm glad you do."

"I was thinking...I know you said that we're only friends but I'd like to ask you out on a date *strictly* as friends," he said winking his eye.

I'd had the time to think over the Trey situation and I knew, already, the moves I was going to make with it.

"Yeah okay, but only if you let me pick the place."

"Cool, you name it," he grinned.

"Jamaica."

Trey scooted closer and draped his arm over my shoulder.

"Then Jamaica it is, Mon!"

I stared into his eyes and allowed myself, for once, to acknowledge how I truly felt about him. He was everything that I was looking for. I appreciated that. I'd allowed myself to think that there was some sort of flaw in my personality because I'd thought about Trey in *that* way; but in hindsight, there wasn't. Life was moving on and I had no choice but to move with it. I just wondered if Trey was game for the changes.

"How do you feel about NewYork?"

EPILOGUE

I grabbed my headphones and headed into the studio.

"Georgia Peach, we're on in twenty," the producer said as I passed by him.

I've been at Hot 99, the #1 radio station in the U.S. for about a year now and I'm adjusting pretty well. I can't say it's at all like The Buzz but it's been a great transition.

"Okay, cool," I said adjusting my levels and then taking my headphones off.

I wasn't sure how an ATL-ien like me had been able to secure a spot on Hot 99. But I was making a name for myself pretty well. I'd decided to change my on-air name from Mystique, the woman with no real understanding of who she was, to Georgia Peach. When I started, I missed my family, Trey most of all, and jetted home to Atlanta as much as I could to check on everyone.

I had no idea that Mr. Gaines had been in contact with the corporate big wigs over at The Buzz. Turns out, I *wasn't* fired. Lenny fabricated it all. They did ask that I be suspended for missing my show but they never even thought to fire me. So when Mr. Gaines called to verify my status with the corporate heads they were shocked to find out that their golden girl was going, going, gone! By the time I heard the news about Lenny lying, I was already signed on to Hot 99 and my mind was made up. No amount of money could get me to stay in Atlanta. I told Lenny he'd be sorry and look what happened. The corporate guys ended up firing *him*.

It was hard for me to leave behind everything I'd grown accustomed to and everyone that had always been within arms reach, but I needed to branch out. Pop pushed me harder than anyone to leave the nest. I made sure the house was completed and to his liking, and I got him to agree to retire.

My girls are still here for me and they've been to the city two or three times since I've been here. Kenya is happily engaged to

Lorenzo and they're planning the wedding of the decade in Atlanta. I'm so glad I'm not there to get caught up in all the hoopla! I must say I'm proud of Kenya and the way she handled her relationship with her fiancé. Turns out all the rumors I'd heard had been just that, rumors. There was no sexual harassment, no player ways and no egos when it came to Lorenzo. I'm happy for my girl for not allowing us to guide her heart in the wrong direction.

Jasmine and Lance are expecting a baby in about 5 months or so; it's a little girl and she says she's naming her Kori. The two of them decided to seek professional help to soothe out everything in their past that was holding their relationship down.

"Georgia Peach, phone call." The producer said as he interrupted my train of thought.

"I'll get it in here!" I screamed as I picked up the red studio phone, which was reserved for emergencies only. "Hello?"

"Hey beautiful, I was wondering if you wanted spaghetti or linguine for dinner tonight." Trey said playfully.

I blushed and pushed my growing hair behind my ears.

"Whatever Shawntae wants." I replied as I sat back in the chair and stretched my arms, with the phone cradled in my shoulder.

My relationship with Trey, after I returned from New York, was a strange one. I was stuck between trying to figure out *how* to evolve from his friend to his woman and, of course, drama surrounded that. Jasmine still didn't agree, Kenya told me to go for it; Pop was thrilled that I was moving on.

We did take that trip to Jamaica and, let's just say, that erased all of my worries. I'd felt Trey's warm hands all over my body and it felt great; but I knew it was more to us than that. When I cried, the first person I called was Trey; when I was confused I called Trey. I'd slowed myself down enough to where I knew relationships were more than giving and more giving. There had to be some sort of reciprocation in order for everyone to feel appreciated; with Trey I always did.

So 4 months after I moved here, and bought a pretty little brownstone, Trey and Shawntae moved up here. It never, once, crossed my mind that I was moving too fast because I was following my heart, this time, and not my fears.

I walk the streets of New York sometimes, staring at faces- - in hopes that I'll see someone who resembles Brendan. But in a split second, I'll remember that "backwards never" is my motto.

In a lot of ways, I'm grateful to Brendan for what he did.

I went on a gut-wrenching, eye-opening, and, at times hurtful experience but I made it out; with the best prize of all: a renewed sense of my self-worth. I never thought I'd get to a place, in my life, that I felt comfortable enough to appreciate anyone else like I had Brendan; but it's true what they say: You never forget, but you grow to adapt. I'll never forget Brendan, or the great times we shared together, but my past is behind me; I can't change it. The future, however, is still within arms reach.

Ralph had taken the tape to the police and by the time they'd surrounded Taariq's building and job, he was long gone. I figured that he would skip town, so it was no surprise to me.

Dee is doing great and about to start the 9th grade and I can't believe it.

Boy how time flies when you're living life, huh?

Just as I started thinking about the bright future Dee had ahead of him, my producer knocked on the window to tell me it was air time.

"Hey what it do y'all? It's yah girl Georgia Peach and I'm going to be holding you down all the way until 4:00 with the best in Hip-Hop and R&B."

I took a couple of requests and phone calls and then went back on-air.

"So my question of the day is this: "What do you do when an ex-just won't leave you alone?" I'm going to open up my HOT lines right now!" I said pointing to the producer who pressed a button and cued me to speak.

"Caller, wassup. What's your name?" I said leaning back.

"This is Lorraine and I say if a cat won't leave me alone I'll just change my number!"

I laughed into the microphone with Lorraine "Man, that's ruthless!"

After a couple of callers, my producer signaled that this was the last call for the segment.

"Aiight, caller what's your name?"

"My name is Travon and I know you guys are asking about exes and whatnot, but I want to take this time to ask *you* a question Georgia Peach."

I swallowed a heavy lump as I wondered what the hell Trey was doing on my airwaves.

"Go ahead, boo."

"Right now, there should be about 7 dozen daisies being ushered into the studio," He said as I turned and looked at some of the interns carrying the bundles and placing them on a table next to me.

"Okay...." I said getting excited.

"I've never really met anyone like you, Lauren...I mean Georgia Peach; I wanted to know if you would do me the honor of being my wife." He said as his voice cracked.

By this time, everyone in the station was in the control room waiting on my answer.

I couldn't speak, though and my mind- - briefly- - flashed back to Brendan and the expectations I had for that relationship. I was in a totally different place and, in less than one year, I was fully ready to move on.

"Yes! Yes!" I squealed as one of the interns, Josh, walked up with a black velvet box and opened it up.

It was the ring that I'd dreamed of and it was all mine.

"It's Hot 99; we got to go to a break!" I said rushing to pick up the phone as the producer went to break.

"Are you serious?" I said admiring the ring on my finger.

"As a heart attack."

I had never felt so fully accepted and wanted by anyone, other than my father and mother, like Trey. Although we both knew a wedding was far away, our commitment to each other was sign enough for me that happiness was back in my life; and in my case it's only getting better. Neither my pain nor my story will ever be over, but for now I'm content with moving on.

I guess this is what happens after the three dots in the statement "Life goes on..."

Ebonee Monique is a proud alumnus of Florida A&M University. The Tampa, Florida native started writing early in life. A hardcore entertainment and music enthusiast, Ebonee Monique has dubbed herself "The 80's baby authoress." Ebonee Monique is the Entertainment Mistress for Touch 106.1 FM in Boston! In her role as Entertainment Mistress, Author Ebonee Monique delivers listeners with the juiciest gossip and entertainment news while providing hilarious commentary along the way. Inspired by many authors, including the late BeBe Moore Campbell, mentor Sheneska Jackson and her late grandmother poet Margaret Naomi Curle, Ebonee Monique definitely has the passion and drive to succeed in doing what she loves: writing. Ebonee Monique currently lives in Tallahassee, FL with her dog, Sophie. Visit Ebonee Monique online at www.myspace.com/eboneemonique.

Titles from Peace In The Storm Publishing

Serving Justice by Jacqueline Moore
The Ministry of Motherhood by Cheryl Donovan
Mistress Memoirs by Lorraine Elzia
A Whisper to a Scream by Elissa Gabrielle
Hiding in the Shadows by Claudia Brown Mosley
Suicide Diaries by Ebonee Monique
The Baker's Dozen by S.D. Denny
Holy Seduction by Jessica A. Robinson
Good to the Last Drop by Elissa Gabrielle
Point of No Return by Elissa Gabrielle
Do You Still Do? What Happens Happily Ever After by Cheryl Lacey Donovan
THE TRIUMPH SERIES
The Triumph of My Soul by Elissa Gabrielle
The Soul of a Man: A Triumph of My Soul Anthology by Elissa Gabrielle
The Breakthrough: A Triumph of My Soul Anthology by Elissa Gabrielle

Suicide Diaries
Ordering Information

Yes! Please send me _____ copies of
Ebonee Monique's, *Suicide Diaries*
ISBN: 978-0-9790222-8-9

Please include $15.00 plus $2.00 shipping/handling for the
first book, and $1.00 for each additional book.

<u>Send my book(s) to:</u>

Name:_____
Address:_____
City, State, Zip:_____
lephone:_____
Email:_____

Would you like to receive emails from
Peace In The Storm Publishing?
_____Yes   _____No

Peace In The Storm Publishing, LLC.
Attn: Book Orders
P.O. Box 1152
Pocono Summit, PA 18346

Visit us on the Web
www.PeaceInTheStormPublishing.com

LaVergne, TN USA
30 April 2010
181138LV00003B/93/P